Gillian Hanscombe grew up in Melbourne. Despite leaving for England in 1969, where she has been based ever since, she has maintained strong links with family, friends, and feminists in Australia. She has worked in higher education, commerce, and journalism, and has been an activist in various arts projects and feminist campaigns. She has one son; and since 1986 has lived with fellow poet and writer Suniti Namjoshi in rural Devon, where, between time spent teaching, talking, touring, and writing, they have produced collaborative texts in various modes, ranging from poetry, short fiction and drama to academic prose. Gillian Hanscombe has read, lectured, and workshopped in Britain, Australia, Canada and the US. She is currently working on a new novel, a new lyric sequence, and, with Suniti Namjoshi, a light satire.

D1501069

OTHER BOOKS BY GILLIAN HANSCOMBE

Poetry

Hecate's Charms
Flesh and Paper (with Suniti Namjoshi)
Sybil: The Glide of Her Tongue

Fiction

Between Friends

Non-fiction

Rocking the Cradle: Lesbian Mothers, A Challenge in Family Living (with Jackie Forster)
Title Fight: The Battle for Gay News (with Andrew Lumsden)
The Art of Life: Dorothy Richardson and the Development of Feminist Consciousness
Writing for Their Lives: The Modernist Women 1910–1940 (with Virginia Smyers)

Figments of a Murder

Gillian Hanscombe

SPINIFEX

Spinifex Press Pty Ltd
504 Queensberry Street
North Melbourne, Vic. 3051
Australia
spinifex@peg.apc.org

First published by Spinifex Press, 1995

Typeset in Garamond Light by
    Claire Warren, Melbourne
Printed in Australia by Australian Print Group
Cover design by Liz Nicholson, Design Bite

National Library of Australia
Cataloguing-in-Publication entry

Hanscombe, Gillian E. (Gillian Eve), 1945–
    Figments of a murder.

    ISBN 1 875559 43 4.

    I. Title

A823.3

This publication is assisted by the Australia
Council, the Australian Government's arts
funding and advisory body.

Author's Note

Resemblances to actual people, living or dead, are accidental, coincidental, and unintentional. This is a work of fiction.

I have found the following sources variously informative, stimulating, revealing, or astonishing: Reports in: the *Guardian* (London) [5, 6, 9, 12, 16 Aug. 86]; the *Independent* (London) [14 Aug. 86; 17 Nov. 88; 16 Feb. 93; 28 Feb. 93; 2 Mar. 93; 27 Apr. 94]; *City Limits* (London) [8 Mar. 90]; the *Observer* (London) [22 May 88; 20 Jun. 93]; the *Independent on Sunday* (London) [5 Aug. 90; 13 Dec. 92; 4 Apr. 93]; the *Straits Times* (Singapore) [8, 9 Oct. 93]; the *Bulletin* (Sydney) [21 Sept. 93]; *London Review of Books,* [24 Feb. 94]. Material in: Serita Deborah Stevens with Anne Klarner, *Deadly Doses: A Writer's Guide to Poisons* (Cincinnati, Ohio: Writer's Digest Books, 1990); Stephen Trombley, *The Execution Protocol* (London: Century, 1993); Dr Bohumil Slavik, *A Colour Guide to Familiar Wild Flowers Ferns and Grasses,* illus. Vlastimil Choc (London: Octopus, [1983] 1985); Richard Fitter and Alastair Fitter, *The Complete Guide to British Wildlife,* illus. Norman Arlott (London: Collins, 1981); Frantisek Stary, *The Natural Guide to Medicinal Herbs and Plants,* illus. Hana Storchova (London: Treasure Press, 1991); Duncan Campbell, *That Was Business, This Is Personal: The Changing Faces of Professional Crime* (London: Mandarin, 1990); Ann Jones, *Women Who Kill,* Foreword by Beatrix Campbell (London: Victor Gollantz, 1991).

Thanks are due to the women of the English Department at Macquarie University, where a semester as writer-in-residence made possible the final drafting of *Figments of a Murder.*

For Suniti
without whom

Pre/meditations

I don't make any particular claims for myself. Ask any-one. I fit in more or less, depending on the fashion. And to start with, I wasn't much different at all from the others. That was before I had Sybil. In those days, all of us admired Babes. We even venerated her. Babes knew what was what and could say so on tele-vision. She had almost invented the whole idea single-handed, though there were a few others here and there. They'd talked very hard, worked very hard, written pamphlets, set up groups, run projects. Soon they'd created a movement. No one knew then about the cash Babes siphoned off, or the lies she told, or the way she tormented her partners. We wanted a hero and Babes was it: free and fearless, sympathetic, full of fight. And she had a genius for organisation. Without that, no one would have known what anyone else what up to. Babes knew everything about every-body and was generous with her time. In her private life (I found out slowly, from casual questioning, scrupulous snooping, arduous and obsessive research) she stole a hefty amount of feminist money. She did this by sleight of paper involving business documents and bank accounts. In her public life she broke up households by various means, but always for love of feminist principle: male children should be farmed out, for example. One mother committed suicide, which was regrettable, but Babes arranged a feminist funeral and wrote an oration about sacrifice and progress. On another occasion she signed commital papers when an old friend developed lassitude and became introspective. Women's energies (said Babes) must not be spread unevenly or too thin. Professional nurture is our right, after all: we all pay taxes.

It wasn't perfect, of course, even back then. There were squabbles about this and that; there was power-mongering; there was toeing the invisible line. But Babes could somehow smooth things out, make things work, get women back into harness. It was only one-to-one that any of us ever found out how deadly her solicitude could be. In my case, she took all I had, though she did it so slowly I almost didn't notice. My cash dribbled away (all for the cause); my painting dried up (there are more important things); my partner went off with Babes (we have to be brave and honest enough to live out our real feelings); my family saw less and less of me (there's so much work to be done); my friends were alienated (we must challenge the enemy); my confidences were written up for the newsletter (we all need to learn from each other's experiences).

Sybil helped me to see how things really were. Without Sybil, I might have faded away altogether, or just drifted somewhere out of sight. Sybil showed me the bottomless Babes. But what could I do? What is the answer if the object of one's rage and pain is another sister? Is she nevertheless to be embraced? And if so, isn't that a reversion, a retraction, a retrogression to the old rise-above, forgive-and-forget, turn-the-other, which we'd all repudiated along with the rest of the patriarchal ploys we'd analysed?

I tried having it out with the sisters. I asked them (owning my experience, claiming my pain): what can be done about Babes? They were worried and thoughtful. They hid their faces. They murmured murmurings. They advised restraint (we must stick together). They advised secrecy (we mustn't expose the movement to ridicule or contempt). If a sister does wrong, it's regrettable, but then . . . If a sister behaves badly, well . . . If a sister stumbles, it's very sad . . . But we're all weakened, one way or another —we're all damaged, at some point, by the patriarchy. We shouldn't blame her. It's not her fault. The sisterhood must show solidarity.

"What (I persisted) if she isn't a sister?"

But they were adamant about that. All women are sisters. We must all belong. We cast no one out. (And we have no courts, no forum, no appeal, no laws, because we don't believe in judgements and punishments. We've all been punished enough. That's what brought us together in the first place.) And when I countered (owning my experience, claiming my pain), "So is there no justice under feminism?" they bowed their heads, hid their faces, murmured their murmurings. They counselled patience. They said I would heal, in time. I fastened on that. "So you admit (I demanded) that she's nearly destroyed me. (And not only me.) You admit that she's evil."

O shock. O dismay. Not *evil*. An outmoded concept. A dangerous error. We're none of us perfect. We've all been damaged. Yes, you've been hurt, no question. Many of us have been hurt. We're wiser now. But it wasn't *intentional*.

"How do you know? And are you saying no faults or failings are worse than any other? All wrongs are equivalent? No vices exist?"

We're under enormous pressure. We've all made mistakes. *Vice*, dear Tessa, is a patriarchal word. You must learn to be patient. There are (eventually, sadly, calmly) more important things. There's the work we have to do. There's the future to think of.

Now, practising, rehearsing, Sybil's properly dressed in her long black flared trousers, bronze jacket snug at the waist, red silk cravat over pale yellow tailored shirt—purest cotton, cool under most forms of lighting. I'm kitted out likewise: though I'm lifesize, we're two of a kind, and they think, when the spell of the show has been broken, that she's merely a puppet.

I earn my money as a ventriloquist on the women's entertainment circuit, and given the way things are, and the facts of convention, I never protest when I'm unjustly admired. I don't argue when they praise my dialogues and treat me as sole originator. I take the fee, I smile graciously, I put Sybil away in her box and let them take me to dinner. Some lies and deceits are necessary in any human exchange; even Sybil will lie to me sometimes, though she knows her own mind better than anyone, better than I know my own.

Entertainment, as it's evolved within women's walls, is not these days just a series of jokes. The frames for exchange are extremely wide, extremely fluid and flexible. Women want everything they can get: argument, meditation, humour, wisdom, strategies —at the moment they even want ethics. They want things exposed, anyway; they want different possibilities.

Sybil's been on their wavelength all along. She's never had any trouble keeping up with me. Sometimes she's even way ahead. In any case, women are our subject-matter, as well as audience, creditor, agent and banker. They want their money's worth, and Sybil says we should give them just that.

The circuit recently moves closer to the eye of the hurricane. That's why it's wise to take such pains over this rehearsal. When the show goes up, they'll all be there: Sal and Annie, adorable Ria, Gloriana Hardy in her public role as super-nova, the women's centre sisters, Jewell, Susie, Padma and Lakshmi, and that film-maker whose name I always forget. And of course the detestable Babes, with Portland Jo in tow, and the inevitable gaggle of groupies. Babes is a black hole; from falling into Babes, no woman has ever returned alive.

Only Sybil understands the extent of my dilemma: how, though I bury my grievances over and over, my garden is ruined from digging and replanting. She knows how I loathe both fire and ice, how I crave the comfort of a clement climate. She knows that I go on loving Ria because she never notices the weather.

Dear Sybil (I begin): I am engulfed in a swarm of women, overwhelmed by their getting and fretting, and consumed by their gab-gabbing and hob-nobbing. I feel unsisterly. But what is the alternative?

Tessa (says Sybil): are you going to start that all over again? Remember your position. There's a time and place and it isn't here. Women are your *friends!* (She turns to the audience): All you women out there (she shouts) all you women are her *friends,* aren't you? (And the women roar "Yes. Yes".) All you women are her *sisters!* aren't you? ("Yes", they roar) All you women are her *strength and support,* her *pride and joy,* aren't you? ("Yes, yes, yes" they cry, fervently, delightedly.)

And so the atmosphere is established. We're all in this together. Sybil can be a real leader when she lets herself go. And women love a battlecry when there's no war to follow.

Later, when we're undressed, I let Sybil sit up for a while, before I put her in her box. I need the company. Ria's away in Leeds for a couple of days because of some problem in the Rape Crisis Support Group. Anyway, I'm always slightly anxious before an important show and, although Sybil is no substitute for a sympathetic shoulder, she's got a good ear, never gets tired, and is hardly ever shocked.

The appalling Babes (I tell Sybil): *let her sicken and die.*

Sybil says nothing. She watches me put away the clothes, tidy up the table, brush my hair, make tea. She listens intently. She likes to know what I think. She remembers nearly every word. I put her on my knee, in the end. I tell her exactly how I feel.

Babes is the worst of women (I pronounce out loud, practising the pitch and tremor of purest rage): *Babes is a brute, a bitch, an abomination. Let her fall into hell. Let her vanish utterly, between one instant and the next. Let her achieve oblivion.*

As I work myself up, Sybil's eyes grow wider and wider till her eyebrows nearly touch her hair. I move my voice higher, then lower, then higher again. But low is best.

> *Let snakes embrace her; let vultures pick her bones*
> *   bare;*
> *Let her be cursed; let her feel the everlasting fire;*
> *Let the night come, when none can work;*
> *Let the storms rage, when no ship is safe;*
> *Let whirlpools spin her out of sight;*
> *Let the beast of the great sea bed devour her.*

And then let the pitiless smile, and the ungrateful
    be glad;
And the highborn clap, and the lowborn sneer;
And the greedy break open all she owns;
And let the beautiful scoff, and the ugly dance for
    joy;
And the wicked rest from their torments;
And the calumnists have their way.

But let me have the sounds of her sorrow;
Let me have the swell of her drowning;
Let me have the heat of her burning;
Let me have the fright of her falling;
Let me have the feel of her helpless hands;
Let me have the sight of her blinded eyes.

"Feel better?" Sybil inquires. Her eyebrows come down slowly. "Much," I tell her. It's always good to get it all out. Sybil understands better than anyone. She knows it isn't therapy. She knows I mean what I say. She knows as well what happens in the undertow when faith is lost, or when faith is moving and changing. She sees me suspended between one faith and the next. Can murder sometimes be justified? I would only be guilty after the fact, according to all rational measures. If I hate with a good hate, shouldn't I follow through to the kill? When is a passion a grand passion? Which fight to the death is glamorous and glorious?

I don't ask Sybil these questions. She'd only smile and say, "What do you think yourself?"

· · ·

Once I've put Sybil away in her box, I go back to ordinary life without a qualm. A woman's life. A feminist life. A life imbued and embellished with sisters of every kind: rich, poor, famous, obscure, fanatical, easy-going, confident, insecure. It's a pattern, a network, a tableau, an experiment. There's room for everyone and everything. No one is out of place, except Babes, whose evil ways, whose extraordinary malice, whose tremendous vanity, will do for us all if she isn't stopped. She'll destroy everything if she's allowed to go on.

Despite what the sisters murmur, I know I'm not alone; I'm just alone *here*. I've been reading about the Hindu Amazons, for example: Uma Bharati, Sadhvi Rithambara, Rajmata Gwalior. Uma Bharati says, "If Kali were to manifest herself today, she would offer forgiveness to some—but others need punishment. Like Durga, we must take the sword in our hands." (Durga is listed in my *Guide to World Mythology*: Durga is "the manifestation of Kali as the demon-slayer".) And as well as such activists, there are also theorists—though again, they're not *here*. I read about a collection of essays by Annette Baier. The reviewer comments, "Baier says that if a moral theory is 'a fairly tightly systematic account of a large area of morality, with a keystone supporting all the rest', then 'women moral philosophers have not yet, to my knowledge, produced moral theories or claimed they have.' For women, the important moral questions have always been 'Whom or what may I assault or kill and when and how may I kill it?' not 'May I assault or kill?'"

.   .   .

I roll in the cold surf, weightless and abandoned, hearing the suck and rasp of water against sand. I think of survival; of how I must risk everything and become despised. I think of the consequences. When the accused is convicted, what determines the sentence? Is it meant to measure the odium attached to the act? Or to measure the vengeance which erupts from the accusers? How does Our Lady of Perpetual Balance reconcile these incompatibles? Does she consult consensus? Or invoke absolute certainties?

Once beached, I shiver in the wind and long for Sybil's hidden codes, astonished eyes, suppressed sentences. I know there's no woman alive who hasn't worshipped the moon with her own blood. And every woman has salted the earth with all she must lay aside as waste, has challenged the rule of men with aching arms and wizened womb and thin grey hair. Who am I to contend? By what authority?

Tomorrow Ria should be back. Ria. Maria. "The English way," she tells everyone. "Ria with an 'eye' like Einstein—not Ree-a with an 'ee' like Eeyore." I remember when we met. "Rhymes with liar," I said cheekily. "From the Greek?" she countered easily, meaning, the instrument of angels. Ria balances things. She'll gossip and busy herself with chores. It will calm my fever.

. . .

One day can be much like another, give or take the hassle factor arising from any particular incident, though even that depends on whether the women are more or less interesting than the issue. Take the other day, for example. Ria and I are just sitting, relatively quietly, but stoked up ready for the revolution after reading the papers and drinking the second pot of coffee. Gloriana Hardy is serving her sacred muse somewhere in the bowels of the earth. Jane, or Jenny —I didn't catch her name properly—who's Gloriana Hardy's leftover from last night, goes to answer the doorbell.

"It's happened, it's happened," cries AllyPally, leaping up the stairs, full of glee, malice, happiness. Her given names are Alice Pauline Louisa for her mother and grandmothers, but she's long since accepted the London version. "What's happened?" says Ria, languid after a morning of arguing. "Gloriana Hardy," says AllyPally. "Found out in a forest of clichés. Finally!"

"What are you talking about?" I ask.

AllyPally waves newsprint at us, pants with pleasure and exertion. "Her masterpiece. Into the shredder along with all the other rubbish people write PhDs about."

AllyPally's on the side of the workers and doesn't waste sympathy on élitist bloodsuckers. AllyPally believes in success. Unique among us, she's not only a sister, but the daughter of a sister. Her mother was just eighteen when she gave birth; just nineteen when they all started wearing boiler-suits in restaurants. Her mother had actually met Kate Millett *before* she was famous. AllyPally teaches English to motor technicians in a further education college, so she has her reasons for being angry with literature.

Ria reads out one of the reviews. "She can sing a song well," it states loftily, "the first time round. But we've heard it before; and there are other songs. A burst of talent may legitimately be mistaken for a stroke of genius, but it takes more than one book to achieve immortality." It makes Ria irritable. "Who is this dodo?"

"But they're *all* bad," declares AllyPally breathlessly. "Every single one. I read them in the stationer's."

"So what?" Ria's unimpressed. "What do these jumped-up little pricks know about anything?"

"But they're not all men," trumpets AllyPally. "Most of them are women."

"So?" jousts Ria. "They're jealous. They never wrote a book in their lives."

"The point is (AllyPally can't help herself) it will ruin the promotion. Reading's believing, after all. Maybe now she'll stop poncing about. Maybe for a whole week."

"Don't be spiteful," Ria admonishes. "You shouldn't kick a woman when she's down."

"Gloriana Hardy is no woman, Ria. She's a devil. Even you must know that. And *she* kicks who she likes, whoever they are, whenever she feels like it." Ria's starting to look bored, so AllyPally plays her best trump, says, "Anyway, it isn't just the mainstream. Our little friend Babes has called a meeting at the Tram Factory to discuss the whole thing. Look (producing a leaflet from her pocket) it says here: Gloriana Hardy's writing is discrediting the whole movement. Our struggle is being brought into disrepute. Somewhere a line must be drawn—"

Ria snatches at the leaflet. "Give it here. Read it all through. What a turd! What a sanctimonious, two-faced little turd!"

Ria's caught off-guard. I know she'll sulk, or tear up letters, or make avocado dips that no one wants to eat. AllyPally's never restful at the best of times, but armed with this she's capable of creating real trouble. I start calculating. Gloriana Hardy will have to be flattered or soothed. Ria will have to be on call. I should disappear for a day or two. I'm mean enough to enjoy the thought that Gloriana Hardy might have to suffer for five minutes before the great gift of her unfettered egotism reasserts its invincibility. Though somehow she'll probably turn the situation to her advantage. There have been others, after all, who've written awful books or made dreadful films or lived bad lives who've been asked to tell their all on television. Gloriana Hardy talks naturally in sound bites, smiles a lot, and has good teeth. She says pithier things about God, marriage, high-heeled shoes, fitted kitchens, and so on, than most people could if you gave them a fortnight. AllyPally's joy is premature, I decide. It'll take more than a bit of bad press to wing Gloriana Hardy. And as for Babes, she's probably working some hidden strategy underneath all this, as usual.

Then Gloriana Hardy arrives, sees the newsprint and leaflet in Ria's hands, senses the triumph in Ally-Pally's stare, says, "You've seen it all then?"

"I wouldn't take any notice . . ."

"Oh but I have," says Gloriana Hardy. "I've been on the phone to Polly and cooked up a deal already."

"What deal?" I'm intrigued, forgetting my dignity.

"I'm going to do a process book, using all these cretinous reviews. Is there any coffee left?" She reaches for the pot, takes Ria's empty mug, pours herself what's left, sits down comfortably.

"What's a process book?" asks Ria.

"We extract all the extravagances—Polly's doing that—and I add my rejoinders and reactions, and stitch it all up with bits and pieces of work-in-progress. A sort of diary-cum-biographia literaria."

AllyPally snorts. She can't find words.

Gloriana Hardy goes on, "I haven't done a non-fiction yet, you see. It's a perfect opportunity. It'll be a new form. It'll be a near-fiction: half in the world and half my own. They'll use it on writing courses all over the place. I can see it already. It'll be a prototype and sell and sell. It'll be full of guts—some of mine, for sincerity, but mostly theirs."

Ria's unconvinced. "What does Polly think?"

"Polly (Gloriana Hardy pours the last of the cream into her coffee) is already selling it. I left her to it. She's quite as good at deals as I am, so long as I cue her properly."

"Nobody on earth," I say fervently, "could be as good at deals as you are." I'm not sure, even as I say it, whether I'm overcome by admiration or despair.

"But you don't know what our little friend's been up to," says AllyPally maliciously, taking the leaflet from Ria's pile and flapping it at Gloriana Hardy.

"Of course I do." (The contempt is instant.) "You don't think I haven't got friends out there who tell me absolutely everything. Babes is a non-event. Every so often she tries this sort of thing, to get attention. Poor little women like Babes have to grab someone's coat-tails to hang on to so they can fly for a few minutes above the seething masses." She sips her coffee, smiles coquettishly at Jane (or Jenny?) who all this time has sat quietly, patiently, waiting for just such a smile and who now, in response, beams and shines with helpless, hopeless adoration.

That night I'm alone with Sybil, having excused myself from both sides of the plotting about how to pack the meeting Babes has called. What do I care whether women do or don't boycott Gloriana Hardy's books? There's a mainstream out there who won't even notice, one way or the other. Ria's opted out as well. She says everyone knows where she stands and she wants to get on with some notes for the Rape Crisis Centre forum.

. . .

I call her Monster in my dreams. I know about libel laws, slander laws, incitement to hatred laws. We didn't, in the sisterhood, invent them, but we live under them. I know about laws against the person and laws against property. I know about inadmissables in mitigation. But in another country, inside my head, I can call her what I like.

Other people, both friends and detractors, call her Mother-of-the-Movement. She affects ignorance of this soubriquet, but I know she knows. I've seen her hug herself on the quiet when it's casually assigned to some other woman. She's smug about having been round since the beginning and has no doubt convinced herself that she *was* the beginning. I use it myself when I'm working on analysis or innerlogue or viscera or introversion. It's important to reiterate, even to myself, that with such a leader running things, it's no wonder we can't get anywhere.

Mother-Monster is a head first lesbian: one of those heterosexualised women who got persuaded by hubris or Adrienne Rich or peer group possibilities or housewife syndrome or consciousness-raising group intimacies or women-only night life or husband-hating or patriarchal oppression or in-law problems or career problems or any number of things, to become a lesbian. (In those days it was called becoming a lesbianfeminist.) There are hundreds of reasons for becoming a lesbian. I've never seen them all listed, given the time it would take and that no one pays for that kind of research. In Monster's case, she was always rather boastful about it being quite a hard choice, having nothing to do with sexual maladaptation of any kind. Meaning, I assume, that as Adrienne Rich had proved heterosexuality to be compulsory, Babes would be the last woman on earth to be duped and manipulated by that. How could anyone dare to accuse her of mere submission to convention, or mindless collusion with indoctrination? Did they think she had no pride? Did they think she had no will of her own? That she was incapable of free choice? Hadn't she carried banners and joined marches ever since the sixties to show her resistance to compulsory *anything*?

I have no such pedigree. I never took account of my head. I was always a body first lesbian, a falling in love type. Au naturel. If they proved to me right now that becoming a heterosexual was necessary to the progress of feminism, I doubt that I could do it. There's a sense, anyway, in which I don't fully trust the head firsts. If it's so simple, couldn't they easily turn back again? If it's all just a willed intellectual decision, where does that leave the rest of us? Back among the pathogens, where we came from, probably, though the sisters never say so.

Babes developed a technique for flattering aux "naturelles". She praised us for having toughed it out all the way along. (Flattery was one of her most polished skills, learned, I suppose, as part of her heterosexual repertoire, given that the smart ones never fight to get what they want, because they'd lose. They soothe and flatter it out of the men.) She told us we'd always been strong, resourceful, independent, self-motivated—whereas she had had to learn all that. She told us we were the backbone of the movement: wonderfully reliable, superbly dedicated. We loved the acceptance, recognition, solidarity. We weren't used to it, after all.

After our confrontation, Babes ignored me. Not pointedly or angrily: she was sweet-tempered and civil, didn't drop me from mailing lists, didn't exclude me from meetings. Why should she? Obviously I'd never meant anything to her in the first place. What mattered was setting up projects, appearing in public, keeping the movement on the boil, maintaining her profile. There were issues at stake.

She continues to star at meetings and conferences, stretching out her small arms to embrace the multitude. She never shouts. That would risk rejection. Instead, she half-whispers, half-ogles, tosses her hair (she's proud of her hair), waves gallantly to all the women craning from the back of the hall. The groupies, gathered in a phalanx to serve, agree, admire, ratify, reinforce and reiterate, offer rapturous loyalty. What eloquence; what courage: they feel inspired, energised, connected to the life-force.

Mother-of-the-Movement gives of herself so wholly, so heartily, that she makes herself ill. She's frail by now, depleted by years of hard labour for love of the sisters. She suffers from chronic fatigue and migraine, allergies and eyestrain, pollutant poisoning and nerve sheath corrosion. She suffers from heat in the summer and cold in the winter, from all sorts of fumes: alcohol, petrol, cigarettes, tar-making, and oil-based paint. She suffers from earaches, backaches, and chilblains; she's prone to legstrain, handstrain, facestrain, shoulder-strain. I wouldn't be surprised if she developed footrot as well. She had a brief encounter with stomach ulcers but nipped them in the bud with strict dieting. Her eyes are half gone, her bones are brittle, and she wonders whether she's developing angina. She's had tests for diabetes, kidney stones, anaemia, emphysema and thyroxine imbalance. She responds positively to intimations of hay fever, diarrhoea, and insomnia, as well as to a range of modern viruses. On the other hand, she is always willing to point out that she still has all her teeth, has never had even the mildest venereal disease, shows no trace of alopecia, and despite her age, has not yet entered the menopause. Frail is only one way of looking at it: she could also be described as dainty, delicate, fastidious, vulnerable. In her own eyes she is clearly delectable, since she frequently announces that this one or that one is aching to bed her though she's done her best to be discouraging.

The groupies honour and succour, whisper and offer. This is sisterhood. This is what lies above and beyond money, status, grubbing and scrubbing, mar-riage and meniality—even beyond power. This is the reward of the cause. This is the personal made political. This is how to belong, because Mother never

scolds (or only with infinite care and gentleness);
Mother always comforts (or at least gives the benefit
of clear analysis); Mother elucidates how everyone
outside the group is probably mad or bad, and is
certainly misguided. "But we mustn't (she continues,
and this is essential)—we mustn't waste our energies
on negative actions or negative formulations by
answering back. We must get on with celebrating
our selves and each other and the things we've done
and the things we're planning (and the things we'd
do if we could, and the things no one else could do
if they tried). We must love one another . . ." and
she sips herbal tea, caressing each trusting face with
the gift of her eyes.

When she abandoned me, the groupies were embarrassed, and the outer sisters talked to me earnestly
about egoism. Babes began a whispering campaign.
The story went (by the time it reached me) that I
was wounded because she'd regretfully declined my
advances; and further wounded because she hadn't
asked me to chair meetings or write pamphlets or
arrange parties or take care of her when she was ill.
It was only (said the whisper) because I hadn't been
chosen. Where there's smoke, I could hear them
thinking. There was no mention, of course, of the
cash, or the legal file she'd "mislaid", or the doctored
minutes of meetings, or any of the other shady deal-
ings. And in any case, Annie told me recently, Babes
has a hit list of prima donnas and yes, I'm on it.

I've told all this to Sybil, not out of simple spite
(though there must be some of that, naturally), but
because I need someone to understand the whole
truth about our Mother-of-the-Movement: the complete

scope of her dissembling, her chameleon expertise, her utter plausibility, her superb ability so to manipulate the projections of her own image that reality itself can be changed. That (let's be honest) is genuine power; that is power of a profound and fundamental kind, because it can destroy women without their ever knowing what happened to them.

Sybil's sympathetic, of course, but she cautions me against hysteria. She reminds me that feminists proclaim no god (though they secretly hunger and strive with longing). She reminds me that in the sisterhood we have each other. "A feminist (Sybil proclaims) believes that the world is redeemable. The only enemy is the patriarchy; and to deal with it there are strategies, arguments, practices, visions." She even said all this once during a performance. I was taken aback, and extremely irritated. We always rehearse conscientiously and have agreed not to take chances with improvisation. I couldn't admonish her, there in public; I couldn't instruct her to stick to the script, though I was sorely tempted. I was forced to respond. "You're right, of course, in the abstract," I said feebly. "Though there are some problems, some situations . . ." But she interrupted me! I felt the audience hold its breath. The professional part of my mind gave grudging admiration to Sybil. She has a genius for creating excitement, for generating tension—audiences love that, as long as you can resolve it as well as you create it. Sybil's interruption was perfectly tuned. She pushed up her eyebrows, adopted her loftiest tone, said, "Even you don't altogether avoid the ways of men. Even you don't always hide your face, keep your own counsel, secrete yourself with the other women at the dark end of the forest, where there are no men, though you all invent them nevertheless. Sometimes you raise your voice, and shout and rage and accuse other women; and then, almost at once, you praise and revere them and crown them with rectitude. It's *inconsistent*, isn't it? (appealing to the audience, who shouted "yes, yes" fervently, gratefully) and it's *sentimental*, isn't it? (and they shouted "yes, yes" and finally broke into thunderous clapping). Sybil lowered her eyebrows and grinned. She was a big success. I let her stay up specially late that night, as an acknowledgment.

Professionalism aside, I trust Sybil's loyalty, in spite of the occasional disagreements we have. She warns me against excess. She says Babes is no devil, but only a mere mortal, a distraction, a minor irritant, an unimportant fool, an unpleasant obstruction in the scheme of things. "But not harmless," I insist. "That's the real point." Sybil rises to the challenge, says, "Look, so Babes plays bit parts badly, dances clumsily, sings her own praises out of tune. Is that unique? So Babes, being a toad, knows nothing of mountain tops or ocean spray in summer—is that so significant? So Babes, being a monster, is immune to the ecstasies of fire and ice. So what? Are you faithful yourself to the elements? So Babes might be an enemy: who hasn't got enemies? That's not a reason to kill her off." I can't let it go at that. "She *destroys* people (I rage) —at the moment she destroys them one by one, but soon it will be in pairs and groups, and then dozens and scores. If she isn't stopped, she'll destroy the whole movement, don't you see?" Then Sybil smiles at me slyly and shakes her head, and winks. "If Babes is made to meet her end, is the world therefore cleansed, and the sisterhood redeemed?"

. . .

Babes has perfected her survival techniques. Everything about her is disciplined, honed, calculated. Take the way she walks, for instance. She never strides— but she never minces, either. She's worked out a gait that's midway between airy and purposeful. And the corresponding politics she's rationalised are that self-preservation in the face of patriarchy requires a semblance of ordinariness that is never provoking. When the more ardent and impulsive (badgewearers, clone-dressers, handholders, kissers-in-public-places) accuse her of oldfashioned cowardice, she explains how there's no point casting pearls before swine and no merit gained from becoming a victim of patriarchal abuse. This theme brings out the strategist in her. When we're stronger (she argues); when there are armies of us; when we can't be picked off so easily —*then* we can flex our muscles. This way (therefore) she can avoid any accusations of closetry and can join any march or demonstration without problems. "I'm not interested in senseless exhibitionism," she announces, to drive the point home.

In discussions, she teases out all the implications. Not making an exhibition (she elaborates) is efficient on two counts: first, it allows us to slip through the fingers and fists of the patriarchy. But it allows us, also, to win friends and influence people from the inside. On the outside, that is, there's the threat of the patriarch, but on the inside, there's the threat of butch and femme. Babes says that butch and femme women are acting out unreconstructed feminist rebellion, since the true origin of these behaviours is the rejection of compulsory heterosexuality. It follows (she goes on) that the butch woman is more admirable than the femme, because the butch is obviously lesbian, while the femme can pass for a heterosexual. Consequently, the femme is much less brave than the butch and much less likely to get bashed, raped, abused or insulted.

Her real point (though it's obscured from the groupies) is that she herself has always been regarded as a femme. She once confessed that she concurred. How could it be otherwise, given her delicate frame and dainty features? How could someone as fragile as she was try to be a butch? She would be ridiculous as a butch. She wouldn't want anyone to think she was *proud* of being a femme, since butches are braver and take all the stick. But if you look like a femme, what can you do about it, other than refuse to cash in?

She always beams generously at the groupies during a discussion. No one's as small as she is. Compared with her, everyone's a butch, including me. It used to make some of us uncomfortable, being simultaneously praised for being brave and pitied for being big. Even though Babes apologises for being small, she can't help being pleased about it. She often confides that there are practical advantages: she can shop for clothes in the children's department, for example.

Babes has made *all* her tics into tricks. She can glitter through her teeth, for one thing. She's proud of her teeth, feels sorry for women who clack their dentures in discussions. She can glitter through her tiny fingers, as well: She gets a lot of satisfaction from undoing minute knots in cotton or string, or from picking out impurities in rice without making a mess, or from pressing the buttons on miniature calculators when the rest of us need to use a pencil.

There are differences, I know, between conceit and vanity; and between vanity and honesty. Babes takes the humility line. She glitters becomingly. A woman can't help it if she's born with glitter and it's crucial to accept the truth about yourself. How can there be liberation without self-knowledge?

The path to destruction can be slow and subtle. I wasn't the only one to lose confidence, feel demoralised, become insecure about ordinary things. I wasn't the only one to stare longingly at children's shoes or size eight T-shirts. I wasn't the only one to feel guilty about eating chocolate. And I certainly wasn't the only one to end up losing my cash, my partner, and the deeds to my house. The political is personal all right: I've learned that for good and all.

. . .

Sybil complains that I'm always negative these days, that I'm full of miseries and fears and theories. She tells me to cheer up, look on the bright side, pass beyond it. But when she says all this she seems to be laughing at me.

I know what's behind that smile. She thinks she'll just listen and watch, watch and listen. She'll be forbearing. Patient. Why shouldn't she be? She knows what side her bread's buttered on. She does her best to respect me, though that's hard when there's no pity. I don't mind very much—not seriously. It's my own business, in the end.

Long ago, when I had more important secrets, I told them to the stars, but the stars said nothing. Instead they made music out of my passions. The music was thin and wonderful, but it was only music. Though fires burn at the hearts of stars, I feel only the freezing white of their light, now that I no longer believe in mysteries.

.   .   .

A long time's passed between when I first thought of killing Babes and now, when I've decided to do it. And because my memory is as volatile as anyone's, I'm never quite sure whether I thought of it in a flash of rage, or whether it came in a sequence of clean and frozen sentences. I have the memory in both modes: sometimes the burn of hatred, other times the paragraphs of calculation.

Babes is not a nice woman, by any standards. But I'm not a psychopath. I know well enough that being a first class bitch doesn't, among sane people, incur the death penalty. According to convention, Babes doesn't deserve to die. But convention is patriarchal, isn't it? Designed to serve those in power, and keep them there? And convention aside, is there anyone at all who *deserves* to die? People just die, whether they deserve to or not.

Whether I remember the rage, or the sentences, what stays the same is the word *kill*. There are other words which should do as well—*homicide* or *murder* —but every time I go over it, it's always the word *kill* that appears. It's a cruel word: short and hard. It frightens me just to write it. It frightens me even more to take it to myself. But I took the word *lesbian*— that was frightening at the time—and I'm still here, living an ordinary life and not doing anything odd or remarkable.

I joke about it sometimes, to test the water (or to get in touch with my feelings, as they call it). But the sisters look blank. What reason? (Meaning what justification; or what motive?) They're curious about the narrative, I suppose: they wonder what might drive a person. Or they wonder what it would feel like (having an interest in the psychopathology). Probably what they actually wonder is what it would *mean*, since other kinds of killing seem rational enough: farming and abattoirs, for example, or wars and revolutions, or abortions and euthanasia. It's the one-to-one relationship that provokes anxieties. The individualism. The astonishing secret they must share in their totally enclosed universe of two: the killer and her killed.

(I know women are differently socialised and not on the whole capable. But there are limits, even for women. There's an intensity of pressure that can, at a fixed point, break open the flood gates, and the ensuing torrent will rage until it spreads itself thin and calm across forbidden territory. I considered myself superior. I had a woman's resilience to frustration and oppression; a woman's contempt for men who brutalised, rampaged, wrote eulogies to heroism and slaughter. It was men, after all, who played war and prostitution and sado-masochism and rape. And I had a fervent unbelief in what they called human nature. But Babes instructed me in a deeper wisdom. Babes unlocked Pandora's box.)

Apart from assassinations or mistakes, it's usually the case that the killer and the killed were once fond. Babes and I are no exception. We were friends, co-workers, fellow activists. But whatever lies she tells now, we were never lovers; that was never in the air. We had our own lovers, as friends do. These days, she has Portland Jo (who dumped faithful Annie to set out on the primrose path); and I have Ria. I think Ria senses what I'm planning but she doesn't inquire. Ria is even-tempered, likes to stay calm, tells me to be happy, cautions me against the pomp and circumstance of public issues and private mania. For Ria, the highest virtue is optimism.

I don't expect any sisters to approve, but is that relevant? Thatcher, for example, had hundreds killed in the Falklands, though none of the sisters approved. They say it's different if it's public policy—if it's nothing personal. But for us, the political is personal. We can't do anything, anyway, about the nation state. They say, as well, that it's different if there's a cause. Or a threat. I know all the arguments: capital punishment, pacifism, collective responsibility, collective guilt, elected representatives. But I did learn something new from the age of Thatcher: I learned the logic of privatisation. Killing, like anything else, can be privatised. In any case, I have a cause; I feel a threat. I must use initiative, take care of my own problems, must not rely on the nanny state.

Babes has not committed what the patriarchy would call a capital crime; and we feminists have shrunk from codifying any alternative. For us there are only men's crimes against women; women (of ourselves; left to our real natures) are incapable. That

Babes has poisoned our meat and drink, and that consequently we have slowly, very slowly, become ill, and that there is no easy remedy, seems clear only to me. The sisters are distracted, enthralled, secure that Babes directs their action and inaction.

But don't we (otherwise) burn or bury rotting flesh for fear of contamination, epidemic, irreversible corruption? Don't we discard the rotting apple to preserve the barrel? Don't we delimit pollution and obstruct the spread of entropy? If Babes flourishes, is that not the beginning of the end of everything we've sown, grown, built, believed in?

.   .   .

It being yet again midnight, with Sybil sitting up watching me pour tea, watching me practise difficult phrases into the mirror, I take heart from a good session's work and ask her to amuse me. She says she's not in the mood, though I can't see why. She says my arguments make her dispirited, unhappily reflective. I can have that effect, I suppose; but who can laugh their way to the brink?

I decide to humour her. Why shouldn't she say what's on her mind? "Then amuse me with melancholy," I suggest. "Everything has its place." She sits up straight and looks serious, pleased to have my attention. She says (quite calmly, as if she were reading out a letter, or dictating a recipe):

By now there have been hundreds of legends about me, but there's one I specially detest. It comes from the north, where forests of silver birch confine each freezing lake. They say that where I walk, and when I smile, dead trees bud with spring, whatever the season;

they say that even the fences sprout leaves and flowers.
They say such things.

I say that death is its own desire; spring is only a
promise of how things might have been. The world
grew old, and all the soils of the earth were nothing
more than bones and blood and other burnt offerings.
Where I walk is not forever spring; it is only a dream
of how things might have been.

"You're getting very solemn these days," I say.
"Can't you just enjoy being famous?"

"Thatcher is *famous*, Michael Jackson is *famous*,"
she counters; "and just look at what they're like! I'm
not talking about being famous."

"Lord knows what you're talking about." (I open
her box and settle her padding and supports. She
likes things just so.)

"Likewise," she snaps, and won't say another word
after that. She sulks like this every so often and it's
to be expected, I suppose. Artists aren't known for
their equable temperaments.

Some months back, despite her speeches about
solidarity and monogamy, Babes became obsessed
with Portland Jo. This was the Real Thing. It was also
one of many predictable results of being brainwashed
by American feminist imperialism. Babes was mesmerised throughout by American feminist glamour: Judy
Chicago, Adrienne Rich, et al. (at the arty end); Alice
Walker, Maya Angelou, Audre Lorde, et al. (at the anti-
racist end); Mary Daly, Andrea Dworkin, et al. (at the
polemical end). Younger glamour icons like Naomi
Wolf had less appeal, since the big bucks came to
them much faster than could have been the case in
the sweet seventies, and since the television networks

accepted them as mainstream. But at least their success proved the endurance of the message. Babes knew from experience that if you wanted to fill a major venue in Britain you could only do it with an American star. Home grown was humdrum, though Gloriana Hardy was determined to change all that. Portland Jo was no writer; but she threw her weight around and made a lot of noise and had useful connections back on the west coast where she came from.

For her part, when she met Babes and said this was It, Portland Jo was still living with Annie. Babes, being an autonomy and monogamy woman, wouldn't live with anyone; but nor could she allow anyone to have someone else, of course. Portland Jo was out of her mind with love and lust, but she had to keep up her half of the mortgage and Annie hadn't yet met someone else. Annie suffered from being working class and not wholeheartedly proud of it, though she went to "assertiveness" and tried not to sound middle class. She couldn't get the theory clear because she loathed her mother and knew she shouldn't. She was, perversely, very mum-like, which Portland Jo found a comfort, though she knew she shouldn't. They had long talks about it. Portland Jo thought Annie was gorgeous when she cleaned the bath, scrubbed the cooker, hoovered the stairs, wiped out the fridge. Annie made things nice. And Annie's flanks were nice, as well, from all that bending and kneeling and stooping and squatting. Annie had such a luscious backside (said Portland Jo); every time possible, Portland Jo would slap Annie's backside fondly, fully—even when they stood at a bar in a disco, talking about Babes. Annie is pure gold, Portland Jo told everyone.

And Annie could cook: acres of pastry, mousses and meringues, blue cheese dressing, stuffed baked fish, zabaglione, Chinese soups, Indian curries—it was a lot to give up, since Babes was funny about food, and the groupies around her were hard-core vegetarians who didn't mind half-cooked brown rice, cold quiche, spinach juice. Portland Jo, in bed with Babes as often as time allowed, sighed with pleasure at the thought of what Annie would cook when she went home later.

Annie had a friend called Sal who'd had a brief fling with Portland Jo, and Sal was a great solace to them both when Babes turned out to be It. Sal had escaped from New Zealand and wanted the lot. She'd taught in a school where women weren't allowed to wear trousers and Portland Jo had liked the feel of up and under her skirts. Sal was cautious and had building society deposits; she could handle workmen and bills and curriculum reports. Sal was sane, steady, sensible, and prepared herself properly for her Home Office interview. Annie and Sal did boring paperwork for the Women's Centre Fitness Series when the grants people threatened to show up for the twice-yearly review.

"Oh my eye, you can't be serious," wailed Annie, when Portland Jo broke the news about Babes. "We've been through all this. We went through all this with Su." Su had left the country, in the end, to drive lorries across Canada, but while she'd tarried in the arms of Portland Jo, she'd worked at one of the women's bookshops, helping herself from the till to top up her social security money. These days women need the equivalent of a business plan to qualify, but back then it was easy to get support, and no one checked up on anything except whether women were sharing toothbrushes with some man or men. If they'd known how many women were sharing toothbrushes with each other, they'd have saved themselves a packet. Su was neat and trim except for her overlarge breasts and her even larger cashflow needs, which were never less than chaotic and always utterly spontaneous. No one minded much about the till, since the movement was (Portland Jo explained) both democratic in itself and subversive with respect to the mainstream. Women were entitled, after all, to have enough.

Sal told Annie not to worry about Babes. There's nothing so calming as a mortgage, she told her, patting her hand and sharing the last of the angel cake. And Babes is famous for autonomy: she won't let anyone move in. "Don't you remember Morag?" she reminds Annie. Morag's a Scottish theologian who entranced Babes at a conference once and Babes was so besotted that she begged Morag to move down to London. No way, Morag said, because they'd just given her a congregation. After that, Babes had sworn she'd never be in thrall again and that the best way to start was to vow single occupancy.

They agreed, after a few exhausting weeks, that Portland Jo would move into a bedsit and Sal would move in and take over the mortgage. Just for a period, to see if it helped. It was different from the seventies. Back then, Portland Jo had believed in collectives and had a string of women to prove it. For women like Portland Jo, collectives were simply communes in the workplace, and the theory of collectives didn't rule out collecting—both cash and women. It was earnestly argued: the money really went to the cause, since women had to live; and the women all said that relationships were life-enhancing. Portland Jo was an optimist and had a ball.

When collectivism got dumped in the hardnosed eighties and serialism came back in, Portland Jo had Parminder, Kate, Pen, Buchi, Mary Beth from Nebraska, Rage, Nimity, Celeste from Bordeaux, Bunty from the aristocracy, cross-dresser Johnny, Lakshmi, Esther, Eva from Munich and Lillian the Lout, before she settled with Annie and bought the house. Then came Babes. Whatever's gone before, she told Babes (who told Annie, who told me), this is definitely It. In the beginning was or had been Babes; Babes was her was-been (she joked in public), having been had. Had was how Portland Jo liked to even up her bedtimes. Love is democracy, she argued, when it all boils down. To have and be had and be having and be had again. Gertrude Stein (she argued further) had understood it better than anyone else alive. And had gone to enormous language to make that absolutely plain. Babes was (or had been) a Gertrude Stein fan, and said she could raise her legs at the drop of a single present participle; and Portland Jo had plenty of them. It was rumoured that Babes had her vulgar side and wasn't beyond whispering expletives when the time came. Babes (said Portland Jo to whomever was listening) was made to go through life pubis first, and who was she to go against nature?

Sal took on Annie's distress and told her it wouldn't last. Sal was conservative at heart, and had never thought Portland Jo was a calming influence. But for

Annie's sake she soothed and consoled and told her to wait it out. (To me she confided her hatred of Babes, but what could anyone do? Women were free, after all, and no one could dictate. And no one else should try to protect: that would be patronising.) Who could do anything about Babes? Sal raged at me. Babes is in control. Babes has it made.

After Annie got over the initial shock, she got used to sharing the kitchen with Sal, and living the celibate life. I started visiting most weekends. Here were two good sisters mown down by Babes' designs. If Babes disappeared, they'd recover their confidence. Even Portland Jo would be better off, back with Annie's cooking and comforts. And I could be a proper sister and believe in justice again.

Once, after supper, I ventured my plan, just in the abstract. Annie and Sal were horrified. We all had fantasies, they counselled. It was good not to bottle things up. It was good to voice one's pain and anger. But in the real world . . . I didn't mind their reaction. It was a new idea for them, and in any case they hadn't spent as much time as I had contemplating Babes. They weren't as aware that Babes' demands and desires were bottomless. That since she couldn't or wouldn't put brakes on herself, someone else would have to do it for her.

Spending time with Annie and Sal took some of the pressure off Sybil. Not that she ever complained. But she hardly ever laughed any more, except in performances. She sang to herself, or else just sat. I started asking what would make her happy, but she insisted she *was* happy. I wasn't convinced, but there's a limit to how much you can interfere.

One night, when I felt particularly furious, I discarded the tea I'd made and drank cognac instead. Sybil started singing and crying and eventually said she was constructing a speech and would I listen to it and make comments. "Of course," I told her; "if I can be any help."

Sybil said: *"In the past, I held my women close and calmed their fevers. What did they give me in return? The comfort of their arms? The fiery embrace? The knowledge of tides and seasons? Or just their terrible secrets, bare as the bones they picked clean? Why did I calm them? How then could the truth be uncovered?"*

"God," I said (frightened). "Heavy," I said. But she swept on: *"Tessa, thorn among thorns in my withered flesh; tell me then the glories of your rage and pain, since you insist. But expect from me no affirmation or elucidation. The function of a god is to sit and listen and make only universal laws. The sisters pity only their own pain, never the pain of men or gods. You have permission to use me for your own ends, if that's what satisfies. I know better than you think the surge of longing while hope and faith remain.*

Make your case. Bring your dreams and break them open in front of me. Bring your memories and let me check them for veracity. Bring your prattle and your anecdotes. Bring your treasure-chest of failed intentions and sorry boasts. I am (after all this time) impermeable. I am (as you discern) unmoveable. I am, in my own time, transparent with emptiness. There is no river of regret in all the world that has kept its waters free from my immersions. Bring your libations. I can endure."

"I had no idea," (I was embarrassed and panicked) "that you found me such a burden."

"You promised your comments," she rebuked me, "not your responses."

"That's true," I acknowledged. "Let's see if I can get the style right:

'I, Tessa, named for the saints both good and bad, bring you what troubles me, though you wave me away. With raised eyebrows you admonish me. With a shake of your head you call me to account. With a flick of your wrist you dismiss me.

But who have you been? Above and beyond the circles of women, do you share ground with the men? Do you give me the sour taste of men's checks and balances? Do you tell me to live and let live? Turn the other cheek? Do you tell me I don't see what I see?

In the circle of women, love was no problem, though its coming or going was never examined. Love was a mystery, and also a principle. But justice? Where was justice? A word only in the mouths of men?'"

Sybil clapped her hands and giggled with pleasure. "You've got it, you've got it," she congratulated me. "Let's do some more."

"Sure," I complied. It was a change. Sybil said:

"Even I am capable of shame; can feel the ache in my joints from unrequited rage. Even I can imagine how everlasting silence can boil the blood and keep the vengeance singing. It takes two to make peace.

When I was young, in the days of goddesses and queens (and slaves—let's not forget; only the sun was ever golden), the ways of the flesh were less ambivalent. A goddess clicked her fingers and the rains came down; and another pouted and the bare twigs burst into flame. A queen waved her sceptre and the wine flowed all night long. Now we have women in suits

37

and ties who manage pension funds; and when they say shine, the babies come.

A woman taken in rage was sitting by a well. I asked her to emigrate and sin no more. She looked at my manicured hands and my high cheekbones and she spat on the ground. What would I know (she demanded) about ethics, or the twist in the tale about freedom?"

"Now *that* (I forgot the game in my excitement) we can definitely use. We can definitely weave it into the number about women in banking."

"If you think so," said Sybil sadly.

"But it's good," I assured her.

"That wasn't the point," she said.

"Look," I said, "no obsession is wholly possessing. Even Mozart made rude jokes; even Bach had choirs to train; even Blake, who sang purer than a bird, was visited by angels with beards and wings who frightened him half to hell. And women, who harboured the greatest souls on earth, did their baking, mending, washing, cleaning, bearing, rearing, between the hours they stole for love of pen or paint. I only ask that you listen."

"Okay, okay," said Sybil relaxing. "Let's work up whatever you think can be used. It turns into cash that way, if nothing else."

"Quite," I said gratefully, and reached for the file.

. .

There is Ria, after all: Ria who works at smiling and who regards happiness as the true religion. Ria makes passion effortless. I see her always as I saw her first: swirling under staccato lights burning crimson, cobalt, emerald, amber, fire, silver. She sought me also (though I never dance). Light fell from her eyes and I was bedazzled.

Liberty sighed the Liberty Bell from the corrupted sea bed. From the slush-mush, the dirt-murk, where no fish swim. Cast for blood's sake, then cast away. *Yield O sea* cried the Liberty Bell in memory of an antiquated age. But the sea swings where it wills.

Like everyone, I've travelled by ground and sought out flesh to flame with my touch, believed in the life-force, pursued the divine spark. To that end (I believed) we were born and saved and made what we made. In that context I've understood the rest of human affairs: the loss, the cost, the range, the grasp, the reason for inventing algebra. How else avoid the petty and intimate? How else discard the danger of death?

Because of Ria, everything made sense. Light fell from her eyes and I became consuming. Friends came and died and rose again in their second flesh, again and again. They burnt one another; they bled one another. They said (sometimes) she'd be bad for me. *Stay away,* they cautioned; *have some sense. Can't you remember?* They said (other times) *she'll be good for you; keep it light. Keep it sweet.*

When I think of Ria, I remember nearly everything, but mostly the sea, soft and deadly, yielding nothing. I remember my education: how, in idiot times, we were roused by bells and baubles, flags and emblems, maps and money, crescents, crosses, colours, conjurors. Now we know better and follow words.

Ria and I succumb to our own inventions. We tell each other intimacies, to become disfigured, and then transfigured. She loosens her blueblack hair, she loosens her clothes, she loosens her tongue.

I see her in gardens, her long hem flowing between hyacinths, poppies, unruly borders of bushes and herbs. I see her over my mouth. I remember for ever the heat of the rain at the equator. She asks what I remember but I am bedazzled.

Incipient to my condition is her condition. No one knows who starts these things. There are (they say) more important things. I agree there are; but who decides?

I never actually saw the Liberty Bell, but they pointed out where she lies and I heard (I imagined I heard) the muffling and sighing under the swish of the sea. I was young when I did my travelling and prone to atmospheres.

Light falls from her eyes because I expect it. I have accrued, from my reading and travelling, some priestly ways and know something about libations. I know how to tune my voice. But in this dance, who is the leader?

Bad women (I must confess it) are hardly rare, and if I must be among them, at least it can be part-time. I share women's vices: lying, thieving, betraying, self-regard—but can leave to men their own specialisms: bombast, petulance, bullying, boasting and cruelty. Few in number, though, are women like me, who can plan a kill without blood. The passions of bad women are strictly personal.

Ria, however, could never be evil, given her vitality. She finds frustration strange, and isn't tempted to bend the world her way. The sisters find her frivolous, but they mean she neglects them, and is unreliable about priorities. Who starts rumours anyway, apart from Babes?

Babes (I remember) built her power on a base of feminist ethics. Babes was always earnest about how women should and shouldn't live. Babes was first in line to affirm autonomy and fidelity and freedom of information. Over and over, in public, Babes has declared how important it is to analyse what women do. Babes has always been an expert witness when it comes to assessing who failed and who succeeded.

Ria takes no notice of what Babes says. Ria believes in ordinary life. In the piecemeal of the daily round, therefore, we do what everyone else does: we meet in restaurants, go to movies, swan in and out of pubs and clubs, sit in meetings, talk on the phone. We're not New Age, though it is a new age and it's London in a new age. No one any longer does opera or ballet or theatre or the South Bank. No one we know, that is. It's the hassle of getting there, the problem of parking, the dangers of the underground; and the high prices, the clothes, the smart people, the rip-off food bars, and the marketing. Like the other sisters, we're urban, which means excluded and excluding.

The sisters are worker bees, part of the great scheme that makes the rich even richer and the powerful ever more mighty. The sisters live in swelter-shelters: one-room flats with corners cut off for miniature bathrooms and kitchens. Or else they live in squalor-parlours, the old bedsitter in a lodging house now revamped, renamed, in the technical settings of re-housing programmes that are the nuts and bolts of privatisation. Well, not quite all the sisters. Gloriana Hardy has a big house, and Ria, being her oldest friend, has a whole floor to herself. These are dog-days, dog-years—post-socialist, post-feminist, post-idealist, post-modernist. Wars in the Middle East and spreading; famine in Africa and spreading; AIDS in the ghettoes and spreading.

"What are you thinking?" says Ria ritually, over some cup or glass in public, or over the cigarette ends piled in the ashtray at the end of the bath. And I say (more than once) "I'm counting nationalisms."

"How many are you up to?"

"Eleven; but I've only just started."

"Count them out," she commands, ogling and smiling, promising with her eyes all sorts of things, promising much, even everything.

"The IRA, Kashmir, the Palestinians, the Kurds, the Armenians, the Georgians, the Hungarians in Romania, the Turks in Bulgaria, East Timor, the Punjabi Sikhs, the Tamil separatists."

"You've left out the Balkans," she accuses.

"That's too deadly," I counter.

"Surely it's deadly anywhere," she argues.

"Well, I'll do all the old ones: the Welsh, the Québecois, the Tibetans, the West Australian seces-sionists—there are quite a lot not doing any killing at the moment."

"And you've left out the whole of Africa." She flirts with her eyes and I'm nearly distracted. But it's good to stay in control.

"In Africa (I instruct her) they call all the fighting liberation struggle and civil war since the whole carve-up was done by the imperialists."

Then we're fond for a while, surreptitiously, secret-ly, so that neither of us is quite sure. Soon, to deflect her eyes, I rant a bit:

"They all go on about freedom, but don't they see how freedom works? Freedom's being armed to the teeth, shackled by loans, mesmerised by porn, prostitution and McDonald's, manipulated by savages in pin-striped suits . . ."

"Calm down," she soothes. "The freedom fighters aren't after us."

"No," I agree, willing as usual to be seduced on the spot. Love, after all, is a satisfactory past-time. Draws no blood. Honours no principles.

She strokes me; whispers at my left ear, "Know what I like about you? You're so wonderfully old-fashioned. So beautifully preserved."

"All those books I read once," I murmur, conscious of her swinging hair.

She likes it when we count nationalisms, says all you can do is laugh, says all other ways lead to madness. I elaborate the game as we go along. There are good and bad nationalisms: then bad, worse, worst. We innovate sometimes to include religions and racisms. I argue with myself in front of her about whether it's possible to be hostile to Islam or Hinduism without being racist. "Obviously I can be anti-Christianity," I say rashly. But she interrupts: "Not so. What about the Caribbean version—the black churches, black theology, black evangelicalism, the black charismatics? They say it's an essential part of black culture."

"I give in," I say. "I don't know where I stand."

"I don't think anyone has to stand anywhere," she says, pouring herself visibly out of her eyes.

"Did you know," (she likes me to tell her things she won't have heard of) "that in Singapore they play this game in public?"

"Do tell."

"In the *Straits Times* of Singapore there's an ad for CableVision that lists a whole string. Judy sent it to me for my clippings file."

"Who's Judy again?"

"The one who went off to do community law."

"I never met her, did I?"

"You wouldn't remember if you had."

"What does it say, anyway, this ad?"

"I memorised it. It's a long column headed 'The Big Fight'; underneath, each on a separate line, it goes: THE CROATS vs THE SERBS vs THE MUSLIMS vs THE ISRAELIS vs THE LIBYANS vs THE AMERICANS vs THE JAPANESE vs THE RUSSIANS vs THE AFGHANS vs THE PAKISTANIS vs THE INDIANS vs EACH OTHER vs THE BRITISH vs THE CHINESE vs THE VIETNAMESE vs THE AMERICANS vs SADDAM vs THE WORLD."

"I suppose you can see it like that if you're a tiny speck of a country," says Ria loftily. "They're a bit out of date, don't you think, about the Indians and the British?"

"I like the bit about Saddam," I counter, not wanting to get drawn in again about the sub-continent. Ria went to Lahore once, and can get sentimental about Sufis.

"Not the sort of ad that would work here," Ria goes on. "People wouldn't find it funny."

"We do," I point out.

"But we're hardly typical," she jousts, grabbing with both hands the back of my neck, the better to draw me in.

And after that we tango, as they used to say, love being a mystery and imperious at the point of urgency.

There are other games. It's important to keep being inventive, since familiarity cancels out excitement. I'll do anything to keep myself alert, and not take anything for granted. I'll make every effort not to submit to becoming comfortable and jaded. Ria needs to stretch and dance; and I need not to be boring.

I manage, nearly always, to keep my plans for Babes to myself. Ria isn't interested in Babes, one way or the other.

Ria is entrancing. She casts spells and invokes apparitions. She manoeuvres plots and counterplots. She grew up in the days when people held dinner parties with the right cutlery and more than one wine. She says talking is what moves mountains, even more than money; and that money, anyway, is only the fastest form of talk.

What schemes, what strategies, what elaborations! Once she tried organising group purchases of stately homes. "A sumptuous flat each," she told everyone. "Acres of landscaped gardens. Just as safe, just as autonomous . . ." But they wouldn't listen, weren't impressed, felt more at home with a thirty year mortgage on a couple of basement rooms in the deadbeat bits of London. And once she tried to start up a periodical. Ten thousand women at ten pounds each would do it; or one thousand women at a hundred pounds each. A hundred committed, motivated, moderately comfortable women at a thousand pounds each. Two extremely rich women. "No call for it, you see," admonished the weary young women in the pubs and clubs, crying poor but shelling out plenty for an evening of double brandies.

Ria seems tremendously busy all the time, but since all the organising never comes to anything, she's actually always at a loose end. She jokes about it, not being susceptible to depression. "Some people can turn absolutely anything to gold: bulimia, oven-ready minimeals, UFOs, old school books. But maybe I'm not one of them." And she smiles wickedly, daring me to kiss her in public.

I resist. "Some people (I'm following up one of my own one-track ideas) can even turn other people's childhoods into gold." (I mean her best friend's rise to fabulous wealth; Gloriana Hardy's facility with bits and pieces of gossip, confidences, lovers' twitterings, incest survivors' declarations, memoirs from news-letters, and so on.)

"Anything between the covers of a book is legiti-mate fiction," says Ria sententiously. She isn't just being defensive on her friend's behalf: she's fresh from filling in for Helen, who's on maternity leave, and who's got her classes hot for post-modernism.

I didn't want to be brushed aside. "How would you feel . . . ?" But she cut me off: "And the nature of women's fiction (feeling with her righthand finger-tips all along my calf, back of knee, back of thigh), as you well know, is to write the body."

I should know better than to try teasing her about Gloriana Hardy, but it's like toothache. I have to keep poking to see if it's still there. Ria will never desert Gloriana Hardy, no matter what she does or says. Or writes. "What's wrong with narcissism anyway?" asks Ria. "She's just better at it than the rest of us." In my opinion, Gloriana Hardy's contribution preaches nothing more original than individualism, but Ria says what does it matter? If writing a few best-sellers makes you rich, what's wrong with it?

"I'm not saying it's wrong; I just question whether it's admirable," I say irritably.

"Well, I admire it," she says firmly. "I'd do it as well if I could. It isn't the books people admire; it's the success."

"The reviewers say it's the books," I point out.

"They have to, Tessa; that's how *they* earn *their* money. You're sweet when you're being naive." And she pats me fondly.

At least Gloriana Hardy is good for a laugh, which is more than can be said about Monster. Ria gets impatient if I go on about Babes, so I save all that for my chats with Annie and Sal. Annie hates Babes nearly as much as I do, and Sal joins in for Annie's sake. In any case, Ria doesn't like me to get too intense about things. She says it makes life complicated. She's always telling me to relax. She says if we're kind to animals and supportive to women, we've done all we can. We're not in charge, we don't run the world, we don't really bother anyone, so why fuss?

"But we *should* bother people!" I insist. "Feminists *should* be a threat! It's not all right to make no impact at all . . ." But then she always kisses me and tells me I'm luscious. Sometimes I wish I could be impervious, but I never am.

.   .   .

There are times when I'm alone with Sybil when I forget about Monster and talk instead about Ria. "Aren't you enchanted? (I ask Sybil): aren't you charmed by her easy airs, her languid drawl? Doesn't her poise give you pleasure? Aren't you filled with solicitude?"

Sybil scowls then, more often than not. I feel her adjudicate. I feel myself overwhelmed. I sense alienation.

"Let me tell you, Miss High-and-Mighty, Ria is no bystander like *some* people. She doesn't idle the hours with never a thought about justice or passive complicity. She stands with me. She sees what I see."

"Oh yeah?" says Sybil nastily. (And what shall I do if Sybil turns against me? If she stops up her mouth and pulls down her eyebrows?)

"Ria is faithful (I blurt out); she makes the sea rise and fall with her eyes; makes mountains shake."

"Oh yeah? (says Sybil): so where is she now? Why say all this to me? Who do you think I am?"

"A friend in need," I tell her, and put her quickly in her box.

On the following evening Sybil's usually penitent. She laughs a lot and makes silly jokes. Once, recently, when nothing placated me, she finally grew quiet, and said she'd been working on a riddle. "It isn't quite at performance level," she said, "But do you want to hear it?"

"Okay," I conceded. Work always mollifies, if nothing else will.

She declaimed, *"I went on a journey through cities full of women. They furnished each other's houses, birthed their babies in each other's arms, walked all night long through friendly streets. They asked me to preside and we invented ceremonies.*

But then they grew restless. They were afraid of the moon and relinquished travel by night. They were afraid of trees and pulled them out by their roots. They were afraid of me and brought me gifts. They sang me eulogies.

And then I grew restless and asked them where I had failed. What did they do? They sank to their knees and offered me anything I wanted.

Was this a great success? Or a terrible failure?"

"We'll use it for sure," I said. "Women love problems about guilt and leadership. We can make it an interactive piece."

"That's what I thought. I'm glad you're pleased," she said smugly.

. . .

Night and day I hear the words of the Liberty Bell. *Beauty is power*, it sings, over and over, repeating (requiring, as in all things seasonal and ritual) my glad acquiescence. And sometimes it sings *Power is beauty, beauty power,* as if those who could hear would prick up their ears.

The populace, born and bred to the new music of the added spheres, believes it's a fearful thing to die without comfort of religion. But that isn't the problem. The fearful thing is to love without comfort of religion. How then calm the rage of millions who cry without ceasing for acculturation? *Burn the imperialists,* they command. *Kill them. Kill.*

. . .

Ria has a child's capacity to rise fresh every morning, which provokes Gloriana Hardy to a clutch of characterisations. Well, they shared a passion once; after such knowledge, what forgiveness? Passion (they both know) is a great respecter of persons; and Gloriana Hardy in particular has an accretion of enemies, cast-offs and disaffections from an early beginning. Ria's motivation is differently constructed:

she always perceives in advance what might be useful and therefore useable. Power between women is well advanced, but its explication not yet attempted beyond the complex fantastics of theorists interested in female bodies and matriarchal motherhood. Ria knows better; and Gloriana Hardy was always a fast and expedient learner.

Not long ago (for example) I was at one of Gloriana Hardy's grace-and-favour workshops, and a German ingenue (whose conceptual audacity far outstripped her shaky English) had a question. The German was not yet familiar with the knowledge that enormous tranches of cash had been invested by the feminist core readership in its stars. "What do you do for your life?" was her question, meaning "for your living". Gloriana Hardy, whose social manner is as charming and femininely foreshortened as her name is illustrious (if borrowed, and for sound marketing reasons), declined the correction and instead responded, "I write for my life." There was spontaneous applause for this heroic stand. "And who to read your work are you wanting?" persisted the earnest newcomer. Gloriana Hardy swept the assembly with her grin. "The whole world. Everyone. I want everyone to read my work." Ria, by association, smiled. The whole world was indeed a fabulous market to go for. Look what they'd done with the Bible!

It's possible, given the distortions caused by the specific density of water, that the voice of the Liberty Bell is strained with agony. The words come without overtones, lacking resonance. They are embarrassing in the way extreme suffering always is. They come in such repetitions that Ria, who never fails to hear them, deduces the composition of ritual. *Beauty is power,* breathes the Liberty Bell. *Beauty is power, power beauty.* And Ria, in concert, wrapped in a bath towel or naked under a sari or shaking for pleasure her ever-ready breasts under pure cotton coverings, answers, "That is all you need to know on earth."

Gloriana Hardy has the upper part of the house, Ria the semi-basement. There's plenty of space: more than a dozen rooms, with an assortment of loos, baths, jacuzzis, kitchen fittings (though being women of means they only cook occasionally, for pleasure). One morning recently, when Ria had finished with my most esoteric parts (which mysteries remain coffined and confined within their Latin signifiers, I was thinking) and had begun again on my nipples, meanwhile allowing the palm of my hand to keep promising and promising, there was an insistent knocking and Gloriana Hardy's voice calling, "I know you're *in flagrante,* but it's the actress again and she's brought a posse."

"The one you swore eternal life to?"

"The same."

I was quickly dressed and ready for the fight. Like everything about Gloriana Hardy, this was a practised performance. We'd done it often.

"I'll take the back," I said, heading for the door to the garden, then round the side, shouting up from the bottom of the steps. The speech about nobody being a possession and nobody having the right to demand and everybody having the right to autonomy and everybody having the right to validate their own experience. Because of the monotony, I added on a cadenza about the self-oppression of dependence.

Meanwhile Gloriana Hardy and Ria headed up the main assault. It was precise, personal, beautifully paced: it conflated sneering, argument and threat. They had, after all, the power of the sentence at their beck and call, having spent a lifetime in its service. The actress faced a force of the highest class, posse or no posse. She had only her fury and pain, still embedded in the dumbness of her flesh; and she was trained, in any case, to speak other people's words.

After they'd gone, Gloriana Hardy made coffee and Ria instituted the debriefing. Gloriana Hardy had a weakness for black tresses and red mouths, but it wasn't sensible to have this commotion in the street so often. I said the whole thing could be avoided if Gloriana Hardy would only use hotels. God knows she could afford it. But Gloriana Hardy (as usual) was adamant. She had the right to live as she pleased and wouldn't be bullied and harassed by importunate women who should have better things to do with their energies, just as she had. She couldn't help it (could she?) if the right woman hadn't turned up yet. She wasn't even forty till next year and there were a lot of women in the world.

"It's not efficient," counselled Ria, "to bed them all."

"True," said Gloriana Hardy, "but I haven't, have I?"

I stared again as I had so often. It was beyond my capacities. The flat chest, the rakish grin, the spindly legs, the hint of South London terraces in the accent, the bulge of the overlarge brow. "She hypnotises them with the force of her will (I thought for the hundredth time); or she's amazing in bed." But it couldn't be that, since she'd have to get them into bed in the first place before they could know. "Or they adore being wooed."

"What are you thinking about?" Ria intruded.

"The tedium," I lied. It was a secret from Ria. Once upon a time, after all, Ria had fallen likewise.

Gloriana Hardy made ready for her latest fray, invigorated after a long night on her latest obsession: a popular masterpiece that would simultaneously boost her bank accounts and enhance her literary reputation. Gloriana Hardy had always been on the way up, no matter who it took.

I don't, from personal knowledge or acquaintance, know any more about the *Sturm und Drang* of the literati than anyone else who reads the Sundays and watches the books programmes. It's Ria dropping me bits and pieces that makes a tapestry of sorts. Ria dreams in and out of this or that contact by proxy, because of Gloriana Hardy's packed calendar. Ria is value (I've worked out) because she has no desire whatsoever to leave even a sentence for posterity. She doesn't even own a word-processor. That gives her a different kind of glamour, the more enhanced when she refuses their sexual advances. "You're a free spirit," Gloriana Hardy tells her, half believing it.

Ria's view of women's creations is untypical, to say the least. Not for her the conflation of sales with quality. She sees the unholy mix of capitalism, art and the Cause, then pities the futility of trying to do what rich men do bigger and better. She pities the confused devotion of readers and followers, who behave unconsciously like everyone else, buying what's made visible enough and extolling what's fashionable. She pities the collusion of writer and

53

publisher, who tell each other again and again that they suffer meagre money for the sake of women everywhere, while silently hoping that this time, this book, this formula . . . "Just look at Gloriana," she says. "She's always been on the make. She's got what it takes: a hard head and no heart."

"You can't," I tease, "have thought that when she lay panting between your legs."

"Oh but I did, I did," insists Ria. "It was the nakedness of her ambition that matched the energy of her flesh."

"But what use were you to her?" I was intrigued.

"Well, I knew people," says Ria vaguely.

"Movement people?"

"Among others. But movement people were essential, when she was starting. She sensed what everyone had missed up till then. She knew she could invent herself by making lesbianfeminism exotic and fun and fashionable and safe. There's a lot of money in that, as you can see from the results."

"Everyone else being so solemn, you mean?"

"Everyone else being so keen on rage and pain. Gloriana, you see, having no heart, never felt any pain. Ergo—write down your grip on life and watch them all get throttled by their own envies. After that, count the cash."

It's all plausible enough, but makes me uneasy. Is cynicism a neurosis? "But what about Babes?" I counter. "She never tried to be rich and famous."

"Babes (explains Ria, as if to a five-year-old) could be a much more serious matter. She can actually lust, with the pure white light of rectitude, after power. She lusts to change the world, to remake everyone in her own image. Which means laying waste to whoever she's got her hooks into. She's the wolf in sheep's clothing: beguiling, moralising, full of affect and portent, full of endless promises. Babes isn't a woman with no heart. Babes has a corrupted heart, able to go after what she wants with gallantry, *largesse,* love and gratitude. You're not the only one she cheated and crushed. Give me Gloriana's egoism any time—she couldn't care less what ordinary mortals do or think."

I adore Ria when she agrees with me, but I don't say so. Instead, disingenuously, I fish for names. "Who else has she done over, in your opinion?"

"There's Gloriana, for starters, as you well know."

"But you've never told me why."

"You must ask Gloriana herself."

"It's not like you to be priggish. What's so secret?"

But Ria can't be swayed. She protects Gloriana Hardy even against me. Why does someone who has no heart need protecting anyway?

"I can't believe Babes ever did anything to threaten Gloriana Hardy's famous career," I snap. "She wouldn't keep that secret. At the very least, she'd put it in a book."

"But she might have tried," says Ria meaningfully.

"Oh come on—do tell," I wheedle.

"Look," says Ria impatiently; "who gets money and power isn't random, you know. It isn't an accident. Nothing is successful, including books, in some other universe which runs along by itself without cause and effect and manipulation."

I'm not convinced. Even if I were convinced, Gloriana Hardy's secret weapon, capable of neutralising the Monster, is clearly not to be shared with the rest of us. What does it matter, then? Let Gloriana Hardy be rich and famous; let Babes and the groupies promote the Cause. I have my own agenda—and it's personal.

"We've got each other," I say, attempting seduction.

She smiles, kisses me with her tongue, cups my breasts. "You imagine (she whispers) that you've changed the subject. You'll see, though, that it's the same subject."

But I'm already at sea in the rush of arousal, the flight of logic, the instant re-arranging of the day's schedule. A small and vanishing part of my mind wonders for the first time whether Ria owes her magnificence to precisely those features she discerns in Gloriana Hardy: a big head and no heart.

That night Sybil glares at me while I make tea. I suppose I've neglected her these past few days. "We should work on the new number," I tell her, having decided to be businesslike.

"Now that you've got nothing better to do," she says nastily.

"Don't let's quarrel," I tell her. "It doesn't get us anywhere."

"So what's the score?" she challenges. "More doom and gloom?"

"Women want us to explore where the movement's heading," I instruct. "It's not our fault if things look depressing right now."

Sybil says, "Things follow where they must. I'm bored with blame and guilt and legislation. I'm bored with bad music and jaded rituals. And I'm hellishly bored with bad women—you included."

"You *are* in a sulk," I say patronisingly.

"Look," says Sybil. "I promised to listen and I promised to help. I never promised to agree with you. I can't help it if I see all the patterns when you're so blind. Just because you see decadence all over the place, it doesn't mean I have to pronounce benediction."

"Don't be absurd," I tell her. "Go through your natural woman bit you said you were going to work on. I want to hear how it sounds."

Sybil raises her eyebrows, faces to the front, recites: *I'm a mere woman, my sisters, a mere woman. Just like you. Just like all of you.* (I hear the applause. Grateful sisterhood. Togetherness. Collective comfort.) *Like you, I have no ark of truth or crock of gold or sacred muse or moving finger. I have my long hair, and the memories locked inside my thighs. I have had, like you, sight of the emerald sea with her girdle of cypresses and her lover the sun descending. Like you, I feast on the blood of poppies, drink from the necks of lilies. I sit alone, and am therefore beyond temptation.*

But Sybil (I say, entering into the spirit) *if you remain aloof, what shall I do? I shall be scorched by your silence. We must stick together and overcome.* (The audience murmurs here and a few women clap.) *You know the glory of glamour and victory. We all do, from experience or by proxy. We've felt the white of stars on our faces and have cherished the future. Are you astonished that women might crave a share of the glare, the pride, the prestige, the fame and the fanfares, the wealth, the power to influence? Is it all the property of men and gods and women voting ourselves unworthy?*

(Sybil turns to look at me and lowers her eyebrows half-way.) *In the early days we believed in each other. We believed in equality. We believed in democracy. We scorned men for their systems of rank and dominion. We gave up hierarchy and sat in circles. And then we grew stronger and saw that the world must have its ways. We adopted the language of money and markets. We needed some of our number to rise and shine. Instead of kings, we thought of queens. What else could we do? Is it surprising if we are no longer equal?*

(Now the audience is silent. We have their attention. They feel warm and regretful.) *Sybil* (I pat her hair) *you're pretending to be shocked. You're pretending to be weary.*

(Sybil pushes away my hand, says irritably) *In the absence of other authority I've crowned myself. Look, Queen of the May. Or August, or anything you like. No one objects. No one objects, do you? Do you?* (And the women shout "No, no, of course not, why should we? Go ahead! Right on, Sybil!" And she does go right on, says) *Power is a past-time born of frustration. It need not be exercised.*

My turn! (I say to the audience) *I also have visions. I see a garden where the apple season never ends, where every Eve is satisfied, where there are never stories about serpents, where there's no weakwilled Adam* (roars of applause) *and no wrathful patriarch.*

(Sybil interrupts) *But the dream turns pale and sour. The harvest fails, the women hiss and squabble, construct delusions, invent seductions. The apples are left for insects to inhabit and the seasons change. Left to ourselves* (she appeals to the audience) *women want more than gardens. There may be no end to what we want!* (Storms of applause) *In another dream, what we want above all is to be forever wanted.*

I don't want Sybil to have the audience eating out of her hand all the way. I don't want to be a mere stooge. I ask her *Doesn't love conquer all?* but it doesn't work. The women shift restlessly, and some murmur. Sybil answers *I had my reasons, once, for rejoicing in the love of women. I thought peace could prevail. I thought our tears could salt the earth, that our grief could placate the selfish gene and pacify the commands of evolution. I believed in commonality. But when the flesh built conquest upon conquest, and I looked back at crops in the wilderness, the breeding of herds, the spread of cities, the walk on the moon, I set up my bench on a mountain and considered the sea, where all change remains hidden.*

Depressing (I comment softly, trying sideways to get the audience back on my side) *and more poetic than realistic. See us all here! Ordinary women!* (There is brief applause.) *We eat and sleep, go out, make love, read books, do politics, argue about right and wrong and money. We only want peace. We only want to be happy.*

Then put away your dreams (exhorts Sybil). *If I were kind, I'd tell you about the beams in your eye, but I stop up my mouth. Gaze at your navel, as I've gazed at mine. Sing at the stars. Leave me my solitude, since that is my choice. Leave me rocks and stones. You take the slings and arrows, since you're fond of life, and ignorant. All I crave is silence. I've watched the feminists march and shout and I've shouted with them. I heard them sing and sang myself, in the beginning. I heard the talk and read the books. But I'm still waiting for the charity.*

Now she's slipped up and I've got my chance. The women don't want a life of silence. They want success. *There's one among us* (I declare) *who must be cast away. She makes us docile. She tells us we can take for granted all the bloodshed in the world, since it's manmade and not our fault. With her gone, we could give up hypocrisy and face the truth about fame, fashion, famine and human error.*

"Who? Who?" shout the women, eager, willing, wanting a solution.

It would spoil everything (I tease) *to name names and take the easy way. Look at it this way. The sisterhood is disordered and can be undone.* (The audience sighs and nods.) *Sages say, if the tree is diseased, take the axe to its roots to save the rest. But we sisters have been sentimental. We've carried the banners of peace, worshipped all trees, found our faults petty and unworthy of blame. And the worm in the garden, the worm that turns, the worm of corruption, we've watched or eaten with equanimity.*

Sybil cheats me, panders now to the women's pride, says rudely to me *A sister's sin is a man's story. We women, scarred and broken from misuse or neglect, can't easily forget our pain just because the sun leaps upward every day and bursts with joy in the spring. Any sister may fall and falter because of the pain; and therefore we should all be reconciled.* (The audience stamps and shouts with endorsement, gratitude, relief. Togetherness is even better than a scapegoat.)

Under my breath I whisper to Sybil that I'll deal with her later. "It's not my fault," she whispers back, "if they like me better. Just because you want inter-vention, arbitration, absolution, or whatever it is you do want, it doesn't mean anyone has to agree with you. I certainly don't. I like saying what I like and being applauded for it."

We leave the stage and the women file out to the bar. I'm angry with Sybil, despite her success, and put her straight in her box without even a thankyou. She smiles nevertheless, content with a good night's work. Meanly, I insist on the last word and say, as I close down the lid, "You've forgotten all about Babes!" But it doesn't do me any good. I know exactly if I took her out again she'd say "Babes is your problem, remember? I never said I agreed."

And so, alone, I forget about rehearsing and per-forming, about improving the dialogue, about how to do up old problems in a new format. I even forget about Ria. I think about Babes: how she might dis-appear between one instant and the next. I think about the killer and her killed. And after cleaning my teeth, I stare in the mirror and say out loud,

Violence is never the answer
Violence is what men do;
Violets are sweet
And so are you.

No one need know, after all. If anyone knows, it could be put down to boasting or seeking attention. It's important to keep the motive pure. And why shouldn't I be sweet? It's part of ordinary functioning. I still have to earn and eat. And if the movement is cleansed, we may all have a future.

AllyPally says it's always a problem doing *Hamlet* with young people. They erupt when they get to page four. They complain that it isn't fair, and she says she always has to put the book away for a whole lesson and talk about whether things are fair or not before they'll let her explain that the point of the play is what you do with what you're given, irrespective of what anyone thinks is fair. It's hard for them, she says, to imagine a time or a place where fairness is irrelevant. "No historical imagination," Ria responded once. "You can't do anything when people are illiterate." But AllyPally, soft-hearted to the end, defended her flock, said reading *Hamlet* was part of the process of becoming literate. "Well, good luck," said Ria dismissively. Ria has no patience with young people and gets easily bored by AllyPally's school stories, as she calls them. I wasn't so bored myself. I quite see that if I'm the one chosen to remove Babes, it's no good complaining about whether it's fair or not. "A girl's gotta do what a girl's gotta do," teases Ria, often enough, when we're at the point of no return on some bed or other. What's the point in resisting these things? Better to accept, do what has to be done as well as one can. And even better to stay sweet. I don't want to lose what I have. And anyway, in the end, the sisters will be grateful and relieved, whether they know how Babes died, or not. By then, they won't be in the least interested in who did what to bring it about, or why either.

Annie, cooking up a storm, invites us for a huge meal: Ria and me, Sal, AllyPally, and two new women she met at Greenwomen Gastronomes—one's called Fred, for some reason, and the other one's Annabel. Not Gloriana Hardy, though; she's just a bit grand these days for spending an evening in Annie's kitchen.

Most of the chat's about food, in one form or another, but then, out of the blue, Ria says to me, "You don't talk much lately about Babes."

Given that my embers smoulder day and night, almost without ceasing, I say back, "That doesn't mean anything's changed."

"I was thinking (she goes on, choosing to go down into the pit) that you've always been right about Babes."

"Now? You think that now, after all this time?"

"Who's Babes?" asks Fred.

"No one you need worry about," flusters Annie, who doesn't want the atmosphere spoiled.

"I didn't want to pursue the logic," says Ria. "The movement can't get anywhere with leaders like Babes."

"There's no plural about it," I counter. "There aren't any others like Babes. I'm not a terrorist."

"Oooh," gushes Annabel at Annie. "You didn't say you knew any terrorists."

"I don't," snaps Annie. "That's what she's saying. She *isn't* a sodding terrorist."

"I don't think this is the time and place," I say firmly to Ria. What's she playing at? Is it a flirtatious tease? Or a bit of impromptu aggression?

Sal, ever-tactful, says, "It isn't much fun gossiping about someone we don't all know."

"Sure," Ria capitulates. "Why don't we talk about Thatcher then? We all know what *she's* like."

"Oh good," says Annabel. "I like a bit of intellectual conversation over a good dinner."

Annie, calmed now, busies herself with serving and passing, spooning and dabbing. Sal watches the wineglasses. Ria, never bored when the subject is Thatcher, waxes witty and anecdotal. I wonder, not for the first time, how long I shall manage to keep one foot on the ground, and the other in the world.

"We should face facts," asserts Ria, while Annie clatters back and forth with coffee and halva. "Our politics bear no resemblance to big league players. In their case, popularity is only achieved through cynical manipulations and dispassionate strategy. Real power demands the screening and secreting of the self behind invincible barriers. We could never be like that. We're open to each other; we value friendship, offer genuine support, build our politics from a base of actual experience. We're utterly personal about everything."

"That means, though, that we're not serious in the least about ever wanting real power," says AllyPally. "That isn't right, surely? If we didn't want change, we wouldn't be in the movement. If we didn't believe what we do is authentically political . . ."

"I haven't said (Ria is impatient) that we're not involved in politics. I've said that the way we do things would never work in the big league. It wouldn't work if we had real power. It couldn't."

"We'd have a different agenda, obviously," says AllyPally, "if we had real power. To start with, we wouldn't have the problems of oppression to deal with."

"If we had real power," contributes Annie, finally allowing herself to sit down and sip coffee, "we would be different women. Very different."

"Some of us," I say, "might be quite like Thatcher, given the chance."

Execution

Then out of the west rides young Lochinvar—or so it seems: Riva, most dashing; Riva swathed in cloth-of-gold; Riva stepping out of a bas-relief, or up from a year-long meditation, or down from a steaming white stallion. Riva, pure of heart, steadfast, motivated. Riva can scarify, rip apart the curse (root and branch), tear out the heart that poisons, declare ended the reign of Babes the Bountiful.

I've taken six months off, for the sake of my nerves; cancelled the tour of the north-east and Scotland; put Sybil to sleep in her box in Ria's half of the attic. I didn't plan on Riva, but I knew if I changed direction for a while that something would turn up.

Annie, grieving after Portland Jo, has gone to ground in the west country, desperate for greenery and the simple life, though she writes once a week to Sal, knowing that you can't invent your life down the telephone. She's taken a terraced house in Exeter, and a ten till six job in the Oxfam shop, sorting their secondhands and smiling at the poor or well-meaning who pick everything over. *Bread for the world* says a board nailed up over the counter. The deserted wife who collects embroidery for the shop had it done by a professional signwriter. It's a conversation piece.

According to Annie, Riva (both donor and customer) is different from the rest. Annie doesn't make such judgements lightly, being used to eccentrics and derelicts, self-indulgent seers, experts in every kind of prophylaxis, chronic victims of instability or misfortune. Riva, says Annie, is none of these. Riva exudes charm, exhales confidence, rides any storm. And her clothes are superb: tight enough to show the muscle, flowing enough to enhance grace. Annie's quite captivated, tells her about London life. And Riva says, after a while, that it sounds as if plenty of work's on offer there.

So Riva comes to London and settles near Sal, who's working these days at a new women's paper. I notice after a couple of weeks that Riva's advertising all over the place—not just in the paper, but on women's centre notice boards and in all the bookshops. She even leaflets the clubs and pubs where women hang out at the weekends. And soon she's scooping up all sorts of strays, disconsolate in refuges, or drunk at singles nights, or passed over by friends who can't cope any longer, or dumped by lovers who've lost patience. She's even started training helpers.

After three months she sets up formally in rooms above the King's Cross helpline. Ria and I call it the Tea-and-Sympathy-Shop, sceptical in the extreme about the byways of therapy. Half the women we know are purring again and looking round for nest-mates. Ria and I are immune, of course. "Therapy subverts politics," declares Ria. "Therapy is conservative," I agree. "Therapy postpones responsibility. Therapy is no substitute for ethics."

But Riva in the flesh is harder to dismiss. At Ally-Pally's redundancy party, I meet her front on and have to succumb to her flair, so skilled she is in every social operation. And when we meet for lunch later in the week, I'm telling her in no time flat about Babes.

Her splendid eyebrows rise and fall; her earrings dip and flash. "You should take no notice," she says. And after I add several more paragraphs she says,

"It takes two to make trouble. What's in it for you?" Finally, after I've done the threats to feminism, the contagion of malice and spite, the vices of power, the evil of letting Babes go on and on and get away with everything, she says rage is irrelevant. "If you're serious, you have to put emotion aside and *be* serious", she declares. Meaning, I think bitterly, put your money where your mouth is—but I don't say so. We're silent for a while, until I blurt out, "She should be cursed." Riva sips at her wine, looks at me calmly, and asks, "Do you know a good curse?" I'm taken aback, ask her what she means. "Curses, like anything else, can be done well or badly. So do you know a good one?" I admit that I don't. "Shall I tell you one?" she offers. And of course I agree. Riva drains her glass, refills it, leans back, stares intently at me, pronounces:

> *Curse the rivers with their insecticides;*
> *the disease-carrying tides;*
> *the burnt pastures and their mutant sheep,*
> *carnivorous cows, adulterated wheat;*
> *curse the dying children, covered in sores,*
> *the campfollowing whores,*
> *the enfeebled old men with their parched lips,*
> *and the whole Apocalypse.*

"It's not very feminist," I say, feeling confused. She shakes out her long hair and replies, "But does it help?" I say automatically, "I don't want to be helped. But I suppose, given your profession, you have to help. And anyway, you're committed to the bright side, aren't you?" She nods. "There's always a bright side for someone. It depends who's looking."

We go on meeting, always for lunch, and always

to gossip and argue. I forget entirely about Sybil. I miss all the protest meetings about Gloriana Hardy's plans for a professional harem. I start drawing up plans.

Riva's fond of shellfish and chilled Loire whites, has no guilt about consuming what her income allows, gives me the still air of quiet restaurants with their starched table linen and obsequious waiters. My wizened middleclass soul opens and ripens, cries out for joy. Now I can think clearly. Now I can do battle on my own terms. Riva asks, "So how, exactly, do you want to go about it?"

Out of all my plans, I have my favourites. "Off a cliff. At night." The Gothic image appeals to me. Riva pats my hand. "You're such a sentimentalist," she rebukes. "Wouldn't you rather she knew? Don't you want her to suffer—psychologically, I mean?"

She has a point. The satisfaction of shared retribution—shared between Babes and me—I've left that aside. How good to have that to remember . . .

Ria's jealous, despite my explanations that it isn't like that. "Like what?" she demands. She storms and sulks. "Like what? I'm not a child. There's more than one way."

"There isn't," I say firmly. "I'm not looking for another lover."

"You never know what you might get when you're not looking," she mocks, "and in any case, you don't know what else you might be getting into." She's right, in a way. But I have to go on.

Riva says, over coquilles St Jacques in a crowded wine bar near Leicester Square, "I know Gloriana Hardy's beyond the pale, but I like her latest book.

It's so driven by self-importance that I think it's unique. She's out of her time. She should be living in the sixteenth century, carving up enemy invaders or running witchcraft trials."

"They didn't let women . . ." I begin loftily. But Riva isn't interested in history. "Listen to this," she says, opening a copy she's brought with her: "Be more willing to hear than to construct sacrifices. Be careful when you string words, because dreams are threaded through waking thoughts, and multitudes of dreams are threaded through with vanities, and multitudes of vanities have one source, namely, the seeking after perfection."

"You mean, she thinks she's god," I say.

"Well, why not?" says Riva. "You can't get on without confidence."

"You think anything goes. You think everything's all right. You never find fault."

"It doesn't matter what I think," she points out. "You're the one obsessed with an immoral bad dream."

"You mean the Banishing of Babes, do you? I see betrayal, apostasy, corruption, hypocrisy, and the destruction of women's lives—and all you see is an immoral bad dream?"

"The thing is," says Riva, "are you capable of making a good plan? Or is it all just talk?"

"You've never said before that it's immoral."

"Right and wrong isn't my business," says Riva. "But I know a lot about dreams."

"So I should write down my dreams?" I taunt. But she's already intent on calling the waiter.

In *Tikki's Tavern,* wide and vacant, moaning in the gloaming, with a dry fade on the bread and the ice in the bucket gone to water; in *Red Rose's,* when someone starts hoovering the back stairs; in *Peter's Palace,* with the fake chandelier turned up hard to become disenticing; and in *The Water Garden,* where they say, disingenuously, that they've run out of tea . . . my torrent of talk never falters, and Riva smiles on and on and pats my hand. I wonder how old she is, but she won't say. She's secretive about personal things—says it's a professional habit. Me, on the other hand: I tell everything. She thinks I'm a hard case. She thinks I'm a new cause. I'm a statute of limitations, arguing expedience.

And who, all these times, pays the bills, Ria wants to know, huffing and puffing round the kitchen, sloshing in and out of the bath, grabbing me on and off the bed. "The love of money is exact," I say naughtily, liking the clutch and squeeze, resenting the proprietorship. Because, of course, Riva pays. I'm eating, drinking, talking my way through the balance carried forward of incest survival, battered wife syndrome, relationship break-up, loneliness, despair, neglect, grief, obsession, projections and introjections of every possible hue and cry. Rape, even: though I can't be sure. Riva is always professional and never discusses her clients or their fees, though her card says sliding scale, according to means.

"Why do women want therapy?" I ask, over and over. She always says, "For friendship. People have to trust someone."

"Don't they know you can't buy friendship?" I say sanctimoniously, feeling well-tended, letting something new and delicious roll round my mouth, slide down my throat. "You can buy anything at all," she remarks. "If it exists, you can buy it."

Ria, bored with fuming and fretting, takes up yoga and karate with the dual aims of self-control and power. She teases me about Babes. "You can hire me when I'm proficient," she offers. "I can push Mother-of-the-Movement off the white cliffs of Dover, into the everlasting arms of the English Channel. And while I'm doing it, I'll be able to meditate at the same time."

"Very funny," I counter.

"Well isn't that what you want?"

"I'm quite capable of looking after my own wants . . ." I begin, but she interrupts me, cupping my breasts, probing my left ear gently with her tongue. "Oh really?" she whispers. "Are you sure?" she breathes.

"Not now." I push her back, striving for control.

"But you do seriously want to get rid of Babes, don't you? I could help."

"It's up to me what I do."

"Nothing to do with feminism, then? Just personal?" she teases.

"Personal is political," I retort bravely. But it bothers me. Is it really just personal? But isn't anything anyone does *just personal?* How do you make people identify and say, there but for the grace?

"It's a good game," says Ria undressing, "but don't start taking yourself too seriously. You would, after all, have to convince other people. Starting with me." She pulls me towards the bed, though I'm still fully clothed. "Here I am, ready and waiting, in the best possible position for being convinced of anything you like."

"You're laughing at me," I protest, trying to resist, but already giving way from the neck down.

She traces my eyes with her tongue, fingers my shoulders and back, pushes my T-shirt up, says, while I help her undress me, "People can be convinced any time, before or after the event. Take wars, for instance . . ." But I'm beyond taking wars, or anything else, into account. There's a time and a place, after all. So it goes on, for everyone: in and out of agreement, in and out of bed, in and out of society. Women fit in as and where we can.

Riva only phones when she's found a new restaurant, since otherwise we make the next date at the end of lunch. This time she's found *Cochin Cave,* a genuinely original concept she says: authentic South Indian coffee and dosas, everyone sitting on cushions and carpets, and you can only go by invitation from a list of subscribers. "But we won't be private," I point out nervously, realising that for me, tables and chairs make a room of one's own. "You're being Eurocentric," she laughs. "I've agreed Thursday fortnight with them, if that's okay at your end." Any time is all right at my end, which she knows but never mentions. I move everything if there's lunch with Riva.

I feel uncomfortable and irritated sitting cross-legged in a large circle of strangers, but Riva seems quite at home. I'm not at my most charming, but you take liberties when you think someone knows you well enough. In any case, I want her reassurance. Ria these days has taken to shutting herself in a back room to play with a word-processor Gloriana Hardy has declared obsolete. I'm only allowed to stay over three nights a week. She says she's reconstructing her realities.

I'm aggressive towards Riva, though I try to be subtle. "That stuff you quoted last time, from Gloriana Hardy's masterpiece. I thought about it. It doesn't make sense. Did you mean to tell me that a plan is a dream? Bishop Berkeley, Hinduism, Plato—all life is illusion and so on?"

"Not so simple," says Riva, scooping a dollop of coconut chutney with a chunk of dosa she's folded into an exact square. Riva's mastery of eating conventions makes dining a performance art when she gives it her full concentration. "You've left out the unconscious." She's clearly intent on being good-humoured, however provoking I might be. How can anyone make friends with a therapist?

"I'm a materialist," I claim. "What about common sense? A plan is a plot, as in research, strategy and scheme. So where's the prevailing vanity? It's the working out of an alibi that's the hard part."

She takes the bait. "So what have you worked out?"

I've rehearsed it over two days and recite, parrot-fashion:

"1. Buy a week's package to Paris (by air).

2. Book into Paris hotel. Collect passport on second day, take train and ferry back to London. Arrive evening.

3. Stay in cheap London hotel overnight.

4. Spend morning in Harrod's getting hair cut, re-styled and coloured; go in afternoon to Databasics. Wear hat, scarf, dark glasses etc.

5. Beat up Babes; tie her to chair; set fire to office.

6. Take train to Dover; stay overnight in cheap bed and breakfast.

7. Take ferry and train to Paris. Arrive evening.

8. Spend next day collecting as many receipts as possible and change some to show previous two days' dates.

9. Bomb around Paris for remaining time before flying back to London."

Riva chews barfi and says nothing for a while. No one else takes any notice. Suddenly I lust after red wine, a rich dark claret, purple with body. We're in the wrong place. "You haven't said anything about my plan," I accuse her, feeling aggravated. "Can't we go to a bar now?"

She smiles. "But it's not a plan, is it? It's a fantasy."

I say nothing. What's the point? And then, to complete my degradation, she fishes in her large handbag and pulls out the same copy of Gloriana Hardy's book that she'd brought last time. "Listen to this bit," she says: 'If we watch the disenchantment of the many (remembering that poverty and powerlessness are synonyms) and if we notice that justice is a perversion of sane reasoning, then we can never be surprised, since the creation of beauty is hardwon and requires blood sacrifice.' Now that's to the point, don't you think?"

"For god's sake let's get to a bar," I say rudely.

"You'll have to accept," she says on the way out, "that things are only possible through acquiescence. You can't ask for consensus. Equity is an idea, you know; it bears no relation to sweat and flesh."

Is this, or isn't this, an endorsement? If justice is a perversion of sanity, then is disposing of Babes a perversion? So what, anyway? Riva's perhaps only provoking me back.

I spend the next week reorienting. With Ria being so volatile and Sal off for a holiday down with Annie, I'm at a loose end. I want to firm up my plan for Babes, but it's hard to concentrate. Riva seems so obstructive and where else can I find inspiration? For relief, I throw myself into external activities and decide to help out in the Women's Computer Centre for a few weeks. They always need volunteers to send out flyers and make tea.

I notice after a few days that a young woman turns up at lunchtimes at the entry to the pedestrian precinct. She wears a sandwich board that says, front and back, *God is dead*. She doesn't do anything except walk a few steps up and down for about an hour. She has a hat on the pavement and a few people throw coins into it out of habit. She looks about twenty-three. I go up to her one lunchtime and ask her why she's standing there. "I call it job creation," she says. "I don't see why I shouldn't get paid for telling the truth."

"Philosophy is certainly an ancient profession," I agree. "But you can't earn much this way."

"Twenty quid a day," she says defiantly. "I don't need more."

"Would you like to come back to my place for supper?" I ask on impulse.

"If I can bring Ashok," she replies. "He never gets asked anywhere. And my name's Sarah, by the way."

They turn up as arranged. Ashok's about twenty and is classed as a mute, Sarah explains. He gets an invalid pension, though none of the doctors knows what's wrong. He just never speaks, so it's assumed that he can't. She made friends with him in the library and he painted her board for her.

I like having young people around me for a change, even though Ashok only nods sometimes. Sarah, anyway, chats enough for two. She walked out of college after an argument with her father who she says is only interested in being proud of her. "I think people should care about the truth," she says. "Don't you?"

I'm not so sure, I tell her. When you get older things don't seem so cut and dried. "For example," I hear myself starting, "take murder. What's the truth about that? What if someone's obstructing good works for their own selfish reasons? Or what if someone's prospering results in other people's misery and disease? What if you're being menaced to the point of insanity? Don't people have a responsibility to their own survival?"

Sarah laughs. "That doesn't make sense. If that followed, people would go around butchering each other all the time."

"Well, they do, don't they?" I point out.

"I mean, even more than they do."

"You can't argue from majorities," I say. "Look at your own case. How many people agree with you?"

"Twenty quid a day," she reminds me. "And when it's most people, that will make it true beyond doubt."

I seize the crack in her defence system. "You mean you just *want* it to be true that god is dead. You want to *make* it true, because you're not really sure."

"It's no different," she argues, "from what you're saying about murder. You just want to make it all right because you're not absolutely sure yourself. That's what everyone does, isn't it?"

After they've left, I phone Riva and tell her about Sarah and Ashok and the conversation. "So you see," I instruct Riva, "the success of the plan depends on conviction; and conviction depends on persuasion; and persuasion depends on assertions in the face of doubt. I rest my case."

Soon I'm seeing quite a lot of Sarah and Ashok, mainly in the evenings, although Sarah sometimes seeks me out after her lunchtime witness, usually because of the drizzle, on damp days, but also when the bornagains turn up to do a street mission. "I can hear them praying for me," she complains. "It makes me desperate for a coffee." Ashok spends every day in the library, mugging up particle physics and esoterica.

Sarah has problems with her mother, so it isn't surprising that she uses me for ears. She moved out of home when she left school, but her mother still comes to the housing co-op once a fortnight, with a carton of tinned soup, corned beef, tuna steaks and assorted veg. Sarah says there's no point trying to explain to her mother that she doesn't live at the North Pole because her mother only bursts into tears. After she's gone, Sarah always takes the carton round the corner to the Salvos. She's faddy about food and only eats the most delicate concoctions. After their first couple of visits I leave any food preparation to her and Ashok.

Sarah's a wonder with a vegetable knife. She can shred cabbage more thinly than any machine; and tiny radishes and fennel and chicory. She won't eat meat or dairy, except for homemade yoghourt, which she's shown me how to do. She says to leave it over-night in a large-throated vacuum flask in the airing cupboard, which I do. She's started growing mush-rooms in there, as well. She makes hummus and fat-free dressings and dumplings done out of soya flour. After a while she starts beanshoots of various sorts on cushions of waterlogged cotton wool. Then there are dried peas, mung beans, and lentils of every colour soaking in plastic buckets all over the kitchen. Ashok has fine-bladed scissors for snipping chives, and a collection of brass pestles and mortars in different sizes for crushing the assorted seeds and grains that now line—in neatly labelled jars—the bench space along three walls. Given the tending the plant life needs, I suggest that they move in.

I'm fascinated by all their knives: small, large, all-purpose, long-handled, and so on. I spend two lunch-times window-shopping, looking at fishing knives, hunting knives, flick knives, sheath knives. I send off for a couple of mail order catalogues. I draw some diagrams of different types of blade. Maybe knives are the answer.

Riva says Sarah and Ashok are charming and that it's healthier to have young people around than all those cats women use to act out their maternalism. I haven't before heard Riva giving way to sentimental-ity. It makes me feel superior. On the other hand, she doesn't take at all seriously my current conviction about knives. "It's still all fantasy," she insists. "You've only thought about what sort of weapon. You haven't spent a minute thinking about using it. You haven't said a word about tearing into flesh, about how hot blood is, about how to react to the screaming. And you haven't thought, either, about how to handle the resistance. She's not just going to stand there with her arms out, is she? You haven't even worked out where to strike."

That's true; and it's humiliating. "I'll get around to that," I say sullenly. "I've never done it before, after all." Riva raises an eyebrow. "And you might spend some time thinking about whether that's relevant, as well," she comments.

For some time I've suspected that the unspoken reason Riva has for not taking me seriously is her lack of comprehension about Mother-Monster's crimes. Next time we meet, I explain again, this time trying to cast the whole problem in a theoretical framework she'll accept. "Look," I tell her, "feminism is essentially a model of reality that's fundamentally different from the received ones because it takes a female human being to be the norm."

"Agreed," she says, looking affectionately at the bucket of steaming mussels we've decided to share.

"Therefore it follows that the whole ideational system of crime, punishment, justice, and law—being patriarchal—is as much in question as gender identity, sexual conduct, the structure of the family, and the organisation of labour."

"Hypothetically," she concurs, pushing to the bottom the mussels that haven't opened yet, and ladling over the rest spoonfuls of hot spiced wine.

"How are laws about war crimes or international trade relevant to women? We decide nothing about such things. We'd never make war anyway. And laws about divorce, or private property, or rape—we'd never make them the way men have."

"What's any of that got to do with Babes?" she says calmly, serving mussels on to both our plates.

"You have to understand the context," I say impatiently. "Take Salman Rushdie: he's unjustly condemned to live in fear and people say how dreadful. But we have to live like that all the time, all our lives, and no one says how dreadful, except feminists."

"Sure," she says. "So what's new?" She prises the first mussel from its shell and pops it cleanly into her mouth. For politeness, I begin eating as well. But I'm not silent for long. I don't mind at all if Riva eats most of the mussels. I want her to understand.

"Babes knows what she's done, however much she fools everyone else with her justifications. She knows; and I know. No one else cares. If they think anything, they think about the "facts": did she really do whatever? How can it be proved? And anyway, proved to whom? How can anyone prove the degree of destruction she's caused in so many women's lives? Even if it could all be proved, she can't be held to account because we don't have any system: we don't have depersonalised ethics; we don't have any external code; we don't have any jurisprudence; and we don't have any tribunals. Since I'm the only one who accepts responsibility for dealing with these things, it's up to me to do something about them. In the end, it's me who's in the mirror. She can't be allowed to get away with it, because if she is allowed to, then everyone else will be allowed to, as well."

"Including you, of course," Riva remarks. "What puts you above the heap? Women aren't perfect. And who can decide, really, whether Babes has done more damage than some other woman has."

"I can," I say. "I haven't the slightest doubts about it."

"What's more," she continues, "if you believe in justice, you've got a real problem. Justice is a dualistic notion: right, wrong; good, evil; all that. What's important is how things are."

I should be used, by now, to Riva's non-directive style. Maybe all she's after is a quiet life for everyone and each to her own. Maybe I have to face the possibility that no endorsement is feasible, beyond the agreements forced by co-operation and expedience.

That night, on impulse, I decide to ask Ashok what he thinks. He's male, so he won't understand; but he's an outsider, so he will. I tell him the essentials and he scrawls me a note saying he'll write out what he thinks while he's sitting in the library. Next evening, he hands me some closely written sheets which say:

"Professional psychobiologists often rely on experimental findings taken from laboratory rats. For example: to correlate operationally defined behavioural phenomena with specific areas of the rat brain, the procedures detailed below are recommended. In order to execute them, the following apparatus are required: n number of matched subjects (rats); a rat atlas; a set of electrodes; a rat microscope; a rat maze. A rat atlas is a set of photographs of cross-sections of the rat brain done at a few microns apart. Each photograph gives measurements in three dimensions for the location of the cross-section. This means that if the experimenter wishes to examine structure A of the rat's brain, then this structure is located in the index, which refers to photograph number n, page n, which in turn gives co-ordinates so many microns up/down, in/out, and sideways, which co-ordinates correspond exactly to three-dimensional measures on the rat microscope. The rat microscope is constructed so that an anaesthetised rat may be placed on a tray above a device which implants electrodes. The device is set so many microns up/down, in/out, and sideways, so that the electrode can thereby be implanted in the exact structure of the subject brain indicated in the rat atlas. Once implanted, the electrodes may then be stimulated at different points in the experiment where particular behaviours are to be monitored. Most such experiments involve observations of how quickly or by what strategies the rat subjects can work their way through a rat maze. Motivational parameters are set by starving the rats before the experiments occur and by placing pieces of cheese in the chosen end of the rat maze. Accurate stimulation of implanted electrodes clearly offers great scope for conditioning stimulus-response mechanisms such that experiments undertaken without pieces of cheese may yield important results. All data derived are analysed according to accepted statistical methods and are thus found to have significance of a measured order. In case of dispute, however, the experimental results can always be validated beyond doubt by killing the subject rat and dissecting the brain to establish observationally that the electrode was truly placed in the structure specified in the experiment."

I'm shocked, initially, but then intrigued. "Is this true?" I ask. "Is this the sort of thing psychobiologists do?"

Ashok grins. He writes on the back of the soya flour packet, "Science is objective. Science is verifiable. Science will save the world. Science maps."

"But what's the point?" I persist, "if you have to kill your subject in order to prove your findings?"

Ashok nods, and writes "quite". Something occurs to me. "Are there human atlases, do you know? With cross-sections of human brains?"

He doesn't know. But what if there are?

Ashok's offering is ambiguous. Is he suggesting that my only reason for killing Babes is to prove a point? Or that all means are justified by the pursuit of truth? Maybe he thinks that the pursuit of truth is always the excuse trotted out when people want to do something dreadful. Or that working something out logically, rationally, to the last detail, just leads to the absurd. He might even think that an electrode placed in the bit of my brain that wants to remove Babes would remove the want. Anyway, who is the rat and who the experimenter?

Ria says she's going down to Exeter for a week to see Annie. I agree a lunch date with Riva and scribble some notes for her. They say:

Five Deaths. An Exorcism

1. A woman who started a fire in the office of a former friend, intending to choke her victim to death, was given a twenty year sentence at the Old Bailey. She admitted arson but declined to give the court any reason for her action. She expressed regret that several antique chairs had been destroyed beyond repair in the blaze.

2. A woman who gagged and bound another woman before beating her to death with a brass doorstop

was found unfit to plead and was ordered to be detained at Her Majesty's pleasure in a secure unit for the criminally insane. The dead woman's office safe was found to contain a great deal of cash. Robbery was not thought to be the motive for the attack.

3. A woman who pushed another woman under an oncoming train during rush hour in the London Underground pleaded guilty to manslaughter at the Old Bailey. The Crown prosecutor accepted the lesser plea in the absence of reliable eye witnesses, though evidence connecting the two women, found in the deceased's papers, together with written material obtained from the accused, proved sufficient to obtain a conviction on the lesser charge.

4. A woman who had spent ten years planning the murder of a former friend was told by Lord Justice Scholes that he had never in his thirty years on the Bench been forced to listen to a tale of such callous hatred, malice and evil. "It may be thought inappropriate," he concluded, "but all I can think of saying is may God have mercy on your soul." Sentencing the accused to a life term, he thanked the jury for their conscientious and rigorous attention to the difficult forensic evidence offered by the prosecution witnesses. The victim had been buried alive in her own garden.

5. A woman who drowned a former friend in her bath was found strangled while in police custody in Notting Hill, West London. Two other women held in the same cell were last night helping police with their enquiries.

Riva is in reflective mood and hardly comments on my notes, but she doesn't smile, either. "You're really getting into it," she says. That makes me feel better, though I would have liked to explore the implications of these cases with her. Maybe she thinks I'm too dependent.

Later, back home, I'm surprised to see Ashok appear before closing time at the library. He comes in with two huge shopping bags completely stuffed and dumps them on the floor. Sarah takes hold of his skinny shoulders and dances him round the kitchen, yelling, "Chutneys and fruit; chutneys and fruit; chutneys and fruit." She turns to me. "Ashok's found these sugar-free recipes in some old book from the war, so now we can do preserves." The next few nights are taken up with peeling and chopping. Sarah's got an old preserving pan from the Salvos and the two of them scrub it for hours before piling in pounds of fruitflesh and spices. I've no idea where all the jars have come from, or the wax for sealing the tops. The smell of fruit stew is thick and heady and permeates everywhere, even into the pillows.

"Frankly, I'm surprised," I tell them. "It's rather old-hat, isn't it? You can buy this sort of thing in the health shop. And we can't possibly eat it all." The growing rows of glugging jars are oddly dismaying. Ashok smiles. Sarah says, "They're not all for us, if that's what you think. We're going to sell them in the market. I've got us a stall."

"Do you think people will buy them?" I'm doubtful. I never buy such stuff myself.

Sarah is earnest. "You'd be amazed how many people would eat sugar-free if they could get it. We'll sell the lot in a couple of hours. You'll see."

I'm expansive next time I see Riva. Maybe the cooked fruit's gone to my head. In any case, I've established that I mean to do it, and not in ten years' time.

"This week," I tell her, "it's mainly drowning I've had on my mind. It's fairly quick and there isn't any blood or screaming. What's more (I add nastily)—you don't need any technique or special knowledge of anatomy."

"But it's still the case," she says evenly, "that what really interests you is the before and the after. You still can't face the act itself. The discipline's lacking."

That makes me bad-tempered. What more do I have to say to convince her? "Last time I gave you five different scenarios. This time I think of a sixth. You haven't talked through any of them with me."

"Why should I?" she says. "It's your life. Your choice. What do you expect?"

"I thought we were friends," I point out. She looks at me intently, then says, "Being a friend of yours can be dangerous."

"That isn't fair," I say.

"Perhaps not. But you must see that listening to someone planning a murder is rather nerve-wracking. Most people . . ."

"Most people (I interrupt) wouldn't have let me get this far."

We eat and drink in silence for a while. Then she says she's decided to go to the Conference after all. That's very cheering; we talk about restaurants in Brussels and what price the wine might be in the hypermarkets. Neither of us mentions Babes. She'll be there, of course, setting up seminars about what other women should do to secure a feminist future.

On the evening of market day, Sarah and Ashok celebrate their sales and plan how to make profits on wholewheat pastries. I'm taken aback by their margins—just on seventy per cent. They have no interest at all in the Conference and never mention Babes. I feel left out. "Sometimes," I say sulkily, "I think you young people have no values whatso-ever."

"Don't be absurd," says Sarah. "We collect values. Haven't you noticed?"

I dream of Jeannie with the light-brown hair. I dream of Gretel in a leather arm-chair, flicking through *Harper & Queen*. I dream of Esmé, who never knew her mother. And then, clearly, etched, it comes: the push in the back in the dark, and over she goes. The waves close over, or the rocks record a direct hit. I see nothing of blood or splintered bone, hear no thud. She falls as everything falls: thirty-two feet per second per second. Even if you don't believe in death (whose sting? whose victory?) you have to believe in gravity. In my end is my beginning.

It comes on a cliff-face, or else (given the prac-tical problems: given the confines of credibility) it comes on a platform's edge in the rush hour (but won't she see me? People aren't so somnolent that they never turn round, that they never shift from one restless foot to another. And the coincidence? How to make sure she stands right at the edge? Only a few choose the very front row at the cinema.) Or it comes at the top of a stairwell (but then she'll certainly see me).

Next time I have lunch with Riva she refuses to discuss it, except for saying, "If you're determined to do it, then do it well. Conviction must always control circumstance."

"I'm still confused about the method," I complain. "I can't work out how to be sure."

"And that proves your ambivalence," is all she'll say. There won't be any more lunches, either, for a while. Not till we get back from Brussels. She says she's jaded and needs to be alone for a while. She wants to read and think, have space, take stock. I don't argue. I'm taking stock myself, after all. And absence makes the heart regret its absence.

It's hard to choose a method when I have no experience. The aristocrats went meekly to the block, heads full of consensus about the vainglories of this mortal coil. And in Paris they went under the blade by the cartload. And in movies they're bashed, shot, strangled, stabbed, poisoned by the score. Babes won't keep still. It's necessary to arrange a meeting on a cliff-face in the dark.

. . .

Babes is a hit at the Conference. She votes with her mouth for third world venues, third world agenda-contextualisation, anti-imperialist prioritisation. Riva smiles all the way through the opening plenary sessions, remarking over coffee how Babes is widening her constituency. Gloriana Hardy is packing them in for her two televised sessions on "Near-Fiction: post-feminist impressionism and the supramodernist umbrella". She excels under the arc lights, oozing sincerity and purposefulness, expounding the uniqueness of her texts in a fugue of perfectly formed sound bites. Women are beside themselves with adoration. Here, at last, is a real star who has never set foot in the USA. Ria goes off afterwards with the entourage, but I go with Riva to a glitzy cabaret where we can enjoy champagne and canapés in relative privacy. I say, when we're settled, that I've reduced my list of precedents to the bare essentials.

"Which are?" she asks.

"First, Lady Macbeth: 'Come you spirits, that tend on mortal thoughts, unsex me here . . .'"

"Written by a man," she interrupts.

"But embedded in the language, and therefore the culture and the socialisation," I counter. "If that's a valid objection, you may as well tell me I can't have any precedents, since all of recorded history is patriarchal."

"Not to mention the motive," she sweeps on. "Greed? Personal advancement? And the victim practically a saint?"

"A poetic device, Riva. You're distracting me. My first point is that it's necessary to discard the idea that murder doesn't fit the average female psyche. My second point is *et tu, Brute.*

"Same male writer," mutters Riva.

"It doesn't matter who wrote it. Brutus had been Caesar's friend, but saw that the state had to be cleansed."

"Dante puts Judas and Brutus at the very centre of hell. Dante says betraying a friend to death is the worst possible crime."

I'm not going to let her sidetrack me, so I go straight on. "Thirdly, there was the generals' plot against Hitler. That, too, was about restoring health to the body politic."

"That," protests Riva, "was an attempted *coup d'état* with the same motives as any other coup. Not to mention having an eye on self-preservation. Anyway, these are all men so far. We might live in a men's world, but we don't think or feel like men, so how can we act like them?"

"Apart from political history, there's the entire religious history of half the world."

"Which half?" she says, needing only a nod of her head and a practised wrist to order another bottle.

"Martyrdom. Burning heretics. Stoning, crushing, drowning—any number of torments were done to stamp out false teaching."

"It isn't half the world," Riva argues. "It's localised to Europe and the Middle East and comes from a cultural psychosis that channels sexual energy into sado-masochistic fantasy. Are you really saying you want to make a martyr out of Babes?"

"Of course not. I'm saying that thousands of people before me have realised that if you really care about your belief-system, you not only have to be ready to die for it: you also have to be ready to kill for it."

"You may as well make sacrifices to the rain gods," says Riva contemptuously. "Honestly, I thought you had more brains."

"We have to clean up feminism," I say, starting to sulk.

"Who says?" she responds. "Let feminism clean itself up, if it wants to. You'll have to face the fact that if you really intend to murder Babes, it won't clean up anything. It will, maybe, bring a personal gratification to you, but only you. And even that won't last long, because you'll have to keep justifying it to yourself in secret. You won't be able to tell anyone. You won't get a prize."

"I thought you understood," I say.

"I do, I do. I understand better than you think."

There are always bombshells at conferences: the latest in anti-racism or lesbian marginalisation, anti-censorship versus anti-libertarianism, the problem of post-modernism, the interface with legislation . . . at one of the most recent gatherings it was even feminism itself ("isn't the concept *passé*? Shouldn't we dump it and call ourselves women?") This time it's market forces. Babes says, in a meeting of groupies held unofficially in a bar, that she doesn't personally mind Gloriana Hardy being rich and famous: she just wants women to think about whether Gloriana Hardy should give some of her cash to feminist businesses, especially given the truth about how she got started. Annie tells us about it after the meeting, says everyone's seething with rumour. Some are terribly grateful that Gloriana Hardy's so famous and don't want her reputation reduced in any way or for any reason. Others wonder whether such a lot of cash couldn't be spread around. Yet others say that attacking a fellow woman is despicable and distracting. Feminist theory about money isn't anyone's main interest and is never on agendas, so a lot of women are bound to get upset.

"What's Mother-of-the-Movement claiming now?" asks Ria.

"What she's claiming," says AllyPally sourly, "is a piece of Gloriana Hardy's action. She's hardly likely to get it. They're as bad as each other, if you ask me."

Annie can't remember every detail of what Babes said, but the gist of it seems to be Babes' contention that she, after all, introduced Gloriana Hardy to Beatrice Brown, whose lover at the time was Angelica Rowse, who worked for Giovanna Bianca, who was the sales and marketing director of the publishing house that took on Gloriana Hardy's first book. Networking, claimed Babes, is how women help each other. Gloriana Hardy has a debt to women as a whole which she should now honour. No woman is an island, and so on.

"It wasn't like that at all," says Ria hotly. "Babes only knew Beatrice Brown because Sal introduced them at Linda Lewis's CaveNight. In fact Beatrice and Angelica were breaking up, as I remember. And Gloriana had already sent her book off before then, because Giovanna talked to June Wellesley about it at one of the Sistren Suppers we used to have when I worked at the bookshop."

"Sounds like you should have been at the meeting," says Annie.

"What's the point?" I say. "Babes tells any number of lies and no one can do anything about it."

"She wouldn't dare say it if Giovanna was still around," says Ria.

"But she isn't," I point out. "Babes makes sure she can't be caught out as easily as that."

"But did Giovanna actually read it?" persists Ally-Pally. "Just because she was . . ."

"Oh do leave it alone," says Ria wearily. "Let Babes stir things up, if that's what she wants. It won't touch Gloriana."

"It sure as hell won't get her to part with a few pounds," says AllyPally aggrieved.

"Still," says Ria speculatively, "I wouldn't have thought Babes would be stupid enough to take on Gloriana."

"I don't know that it's so stupid," I say. "Gloriana Hardy's had most of the media interest all week, as well as packed venues for all her sessions. Babes has to keep her profile up."

"Do you think that's why she's been wooing the ethnic vote?" AllyPally asks. "Do you think she's been planning a challenge to Madam Superstar?"

"Babes never does anything without planning," I reply.

But whatever Babes has planned is shattered by the next day's news. Everyone forgets about Babes versus Gloriana Hardy. There's talk that someone in the oldest and biggest women's co-operative in Germany has been murdered. An emergency plenary's been called to discuss it, but no one can wait patiently for that. We all rush round trying to find out what happened. As usual, Annie beats us all hollow: she tracks down Hilke in a coffee-and-cakes place near the main square. Annie tells us Hilke's a linguist who's lived in the co-op from the beginning, some twenty-five years ago, long before they moved to their present site near Göppingen. They've been growing all their own food since the move, and still share all their worldlies, take collective responsibility, rotate all the jobs, and so on. "Sounds like a nunnery," I say. I always thought group living was carrying things a bit far. On the other hand, Germans are better than most at applying principles and following the logic of a position right through to the end.

Hilke's told Annie that eight months back they finally managed to buy an entire house, on the edge of town and right next to the farm. It cost over five million marks, which is a guide to how profitable they'd become. Twenty individual rooms, cooking and washing places, cellars, library, sauna, jacuzzi with indoor pool, and a giant *Wohnzimmer* for meetings. They got settled in and then trouble started, mainly about aggression theory and power ethics. It boiled down to a confrontation between Brigitte, who was in charge of the market gardening for that quarter, and Edeltraud, who was developing their *Sozialarbeit*. The set-up was that women householders in the town got discounts on produce, and single parents got one free case of veg every week. Edeltraud wanted to increase the concessions by linking up with a new women's merchandising *Gemeinschaft* that had just been set up on the other side of town. Brigitte opposed this passionately: how could they possibly contemplate dealing with women who traded in meat?

Edeltraud argued that the world couldn't be changed overnight; insisting on ideological purity wouldn't win the unconverted. And in any case, hundreds of people struggling to survive would eat anything they could get. Wasn't it more sensible to make their produce even cheaper? If it was cheaper, wouldn't women buy more of it?

Hilke said Brigitte raged and screamed. It was that cow Gisela who'd caused all this trouble. It was Gisela who'd persuaded the others to include butchery in their deals. She was a charlatan, a collaborator, a recidivist, a materialist, a Judas, a vampire. Edeltraud

shouted back. Real people mattered, not only ideological purity. Why should the poor do without, just
to preserve the spotlessness of Brigitte's soul?

Brigitte wasn't having it. She told them they must
choose. If they dealt with Gisela, she'd leave; and
take the market gardening contracts with her. Edeltraud yelled back that that was unconstitutional: their
collective agreement was binding—no ultimata, no
blackmailing, no withdrawal of labour. Brigitte had
agreed, along with everyone else. Power had to be
negotiated; consensus was always possible.

At their next meeting, Brigitte had agreed to
compromise. A discussion with Gisela could be put
on the agenda for the following meeting. Nothing
happened for a few days. They had to have their
monthly meetings with the writers and accountants
who handle the promotion side, and with the interface committee which deals with the enterprise
budget. Enterprise cash comes from a development
agency of the provincial government and gives them
a three year cushion. The business plan apparently
projects fifty linked corporations by the end of the
decade.

Then, Hilke told Annie, on the following week-
end she was turning over part of the potato crop.
She called out for the others to come. She lifted her
garden fork. Everyone stared in complete silence
until Hilke said, "That's fingers." The others variously
whimpered, swore, groaned, screeched, jabbered;
and then started digging. It was a body.

We're all mesmerised and fill in time waiting for
the plenary with coffee and speculation. Sessions are
abandoned, and even the bookstalls are deserted.

Annie's taken on looking after Hilke, who's alternately defiant and depressed. At last it's time to file in for the plenary, which is, as expected, completely packed out. Everyone cries out for Hilke to speak. As she comes to the lectern she looks vulnerable and confused, but her words are clear and precise. After explaining the details of the co-operative's constitution, and the confrontation between Brigitte and Edeltraud, she adds: "I'd never before seen a dead body. The face was blue and purple and looked stuffed. Lumps of soil were stuck here and there. Idiotically I waited for her to brush them off. Then someone said, 'Mein Gott—das ist Gisela.' And it was. All I could think was 'This is the end of feminism I'm looking at.' Everyone just stood there, staring."

Hilke stops speaking but doesn't move from the lectern. There's complete silence in the auditorium. Riva, sitting on one side of me, whispers, "Still think it's all right?" I say nothing. I feel strangely smug. Now, finally, women will have to find something to say beyond the platitude that women don't kill each other.

After what seems like a very long time, Hilke begins speaking again: "Ingeborg told us to cover it up again. She said we'd have to have a meeting. I protested. I yelled at her, 'That's a dead body. We can't go away and have a meeting. That's a dead body!' But she shook me by the shoulders and told me to calm down. 'I know it's a dead body,' she said. 'The world is full of dead bodies. Get control of yourself. It isn't your dead body, or mine. We have to work out what's best for the whole community, just as we always do.' So here I am. I was chosen to come here and say what happened and ask for solidarity and support."

She sits down. There's a buzz; then a swell. There's shock and shouting. The platform has trouble restoring order. Gloriana Hardy beats Babes to it for the first question. She speaks evenly, with only the barest minimum of theatrical emphasis: "We haven't yet heard the end of the story. What happened to the body?"

There's a frisson as she says the word *body*. Hilke waits for a few seconds, then says, "We made a ceremony. We made a bonfire in the garden. It was a funeral pyre as they have in India. But we had no sandalwood. We made a stretcher from poles and sheets and rubbed the body with oil. Not the head, though. The back of the head was all smashed in. We dressed her in clean things and put everything on the wood. Then we lit the fire. Brigitte threw something from a bowl onto the flames, but I don't know what it was. Some of the women started chanting. It was very awesome and frightening. We had to keep feeding the fire. The whole process took hours."

Gloriana Hardy persists: "And no one came? No one sent for the police?"

"Of course not! (Hilke is astonished.) Why would we bring in the patriarchy, to victimise us further?"

A young woman in the front row shouts out, "What did the women chant?"

"Various things," Hilke replies. "We'd agreed that everyone should say what made sense to them. Some women said things they'd known from childhood— ashes to ashes, that sort of thing. Other women said power to the goddess and so on. Brigitte said 'the personal is political.' I sang some verses of *Where have all the flowers gone*."

Babes asks, "Then no one knows what happened?"

"We know," responds Hilke fervently. "We know. And now all of you."

Ria stands up. "Do you know for sure who killed her?" There's a terrified silence as the word *kill* falls from the air. Hilke says nothing at first; then, stiffly, she pronounces, "We are a women's community. We share responsibility. That's why I've come here—to discuss the implications."

"But we're not terrorists," argues Babes piously. "We don't get rid of women just because we disagree with them. Some women are bad women—it has to be faced."

"None of us," Hilke is emphatic, "is a bad woman. We have worked hard; we have worked together; we have built something important. Life is not perfect. We should not let everything we've achieved be sacrificed to the patriarchy." This affirmation is followed by a storm of grateful applause and relief. Babes knows when she's lost an audience—knows when to stop. She sits down, biding her time.

The platform announces that we should break into discussion groups and reconvene the plenary session at the end of the Conference. My spirits are high. "Do you realise," I tell Riva as we jostle our way out, "that Brigitte or Ingeborg or whoever actually did it has got away with it?"

"Maybe they all did it," says Riva. "That's happened before."

"But no police; no prison; no wasting the rest of one's life!" Riva stares hard at me. "The point is, was it worth it? Is the cause advanced?"

"You must be joking," I say. "Rooting out corruption? Of course that makes a difference. All the difference."

"Like the Inquisition?" mocks Riva; "murdering anyone who gets out of line?"

"Don't be absurd," I say. "We're not talking about policy and systems. It isn't a mass movement. We're just talking about one or two extreme cases. When a movement's as small and radical as ours, we have to keep it clean. One or two maniacs can destroy everything—put us back decades, if not centuries. In any case, as women, we have to work out our own ways of dealing with problems. That should be obvious. I have thought a lot about this, as you know."

"That," sighs Riva, "is undeniable."

That night Ria and I meet for a drink, away from the other women. "So how does it feel?" she asks me; "someone else's obsession?"

"I identify," I say happily. "I am, as they used to say in CR groups, affirmed. When things are distanced a bit, away from our own patch, I see there are situations where there's no other way."

"Maybe," says Ria, looking preoccupied.

"What?" I ask her. But she shakes her head. "Nothing. I was thinking about something else. Actually, I was thinking I'm sick of politics. Let's have a party when we get back. We haven't had one for ages."

"Okay," I agree. "But where?"

"At our house, of course. It's plenty big enough."

"Everything's always at your house," I say petulantly.

"Oh come on. It will be fun."

"Who would you ask?"

"Everyone we owe, for starters. Myra and Ruth, for example. Kim and Parminder. AllyPally and whoever."

"Who's AllyPally with this week?" I want to know.

"Haven't a clue: but whoever it is, it'll be someone else by the time we have the party."

"What about Naseem?"

"Maybe . . . but Ruth's Jewish and what if . . . ?"

"Ruth doesn't defend the West Bank, though; and Naseem isn't a bigot."

"I know; but Ruth's family is a remnant, and she won't sign that paper the Palestinian women want signed—the one saying the State of Israel shouldn't exist."

"They won't talk about that," I insist. "Especially if it's a big party. Anyway, Naseem doesn't go to the Palestinian women's group any more. And we're going to ask Fatima, surely?"

"That's different. Ruth and Fatima have known each other for years."

"Let's go through the patterns." I want to flirt with Ria and this is a good way. There's always some glamour to be found over drinks with a lover in a foreign city. If the form is right, the content will look after itself.

Ria recites: "Myra, Ruth and Kim are musicians; Gloriana, Naseem and Eve are writers."

"Why are we asking Eve?"

"We have to. Anyway, she's talking to AllyPally now."

"Since when?"

"Since she took up with a Welsh sheepfarmer called Myfanwy. All is now sweetness and light."

"Where did she meet her? Who told you, anyhow?"

"I thought you knew."

"All right, Eve, if she's not in Wales. Where were we?"

"Ruth, Eve and Naseem are mothers; Parminder, Myra and AllyPally have been co-mothers; Naseem, Ruth and Parminder are non-Christian; Myra, Kim and Gloriana are apostates."

"What about Riva?" I remember.

"Riva's a therapist! She wouldn't fit in," says Ria with finality. "Anyway, who's she with?"

"She isn't with anyone," I say. "You didn't tell me it was going to be a pairs party."

"Can't we have one single hour, one conversation, without that woman's name coming up?" says Ria spitefully.

We endure a sullen silence. So much for flirting. I say feebly, "What about AllyPally? Shouldn't we have a few teachers?"

"There's all Gloriana's lot. Half her fans are teachers."

"We don't want a fans party. She can organise that herself. And if it's too big, the groupies will hear about it and wonder why we're not asking them."

"We *are* asking them," says Ria. "Why do you always want to make trouble?"

"But not Babes!" I'm horrified.

"Babes will cry off. She'll be sick with something— she always is. For god's sake can't you leave it alone about Babes?"

"I wish you wouldn't argue about everything. We never used to argue so much."

"You're no fun any more since you took up with that therapist woman."

"Come back to my place," I wheedle and tease. "Let's do what we do best."

"That's all I am to you, isn't it?" snaps Ria, slamming down her glass. But I persuade her in the end. Who wants to mope all night on their own?

. . .

Afterwards, unexpectedly (since I've laid my not-sleeping head between Ria's very familiar breasts) I remember Kit. Suddenly, vividly, she's in front of my eyes: Katherine/Kathy/Katy/Kath/Kit—super-lover, beached after high tide. Katherine, come what may, as far as her mother was concerned. Kathy to an array of kith and cousins who were friendly enough, however outrageous she was. Katy to the fierce young matron at her boarding school who'd had four Katherines already. Which had led to Kate among the other girls, sophisticated about name-calling. Kath to a couple of elderly who'd known her for years: Mr Hall the postman and Mrs Postman; Miss Ryan at the corner shop who ironed her aprons and had damask on her bed. "Nice bed, good bed," Kath had said grotesquely, patting the damask that first time. Kit appeared under cover of intimacy, not to mention Kitten, which came naturally.

Snug between the bedposts, dreaming, thinking, dreaming. The vehemence had been unusual. With Kit, it was always the first time, passing understanding: the first time, the only time, the best time, the time of times, whose girlhood had been watched over by so many concerned adults that their collected observations would take a century to read. Kit could leap from bookcase to bookcase, crouch on each top as still as any predator. Kit could screech like a cockatoo. And sing, also.

Kit of the proud thighs, of the wondrous breasts, giving and taking in handfuls, gulping them, glorifying. Her dreams spilled out through her fingertips. She never waited to be hungry; there was no need. Between the bedposts was Kit, always coming or going, whatever the interventions. Kit of the magic belly and bone, waisted, large-jawed, generous-mouthed, muscled shoulder to wrist. Kit disclosing: "But we always say we'll get up and we never get up. So just this once, if we get up, we can actually make the kitchen before noon. For a novelty. What do you say? What do you think? We could cook something." Me, grinning and pouting, unable to resist; Kit, already at sea, hands soft as water, but strong as trees, laughing out loud: "Shall I tell you what I think?"

I was never sure whether the sound of her felled me, or those matchless hands. It went on for a long time, longer than ever, longer than is usual. And how the friends teased; how they were curious, prurient, ambivalent, censorious, patronising, envious. "What's the secret, Kit? Tessa? How can you still—?" Since we'd break up and make up as everyone does. But in the end, couldn't settle. We must have been too young.

Most of all I remember the bedposts—the rest is vague: work and money, movements, meanings. Friends said, "There's more to life. You'll find out." But I forgot everything once her tongue was in my ear, on my neck, in my mouth. Maybe there was more to life. I still don't know. Ria lies there peacefully and says nothing about the Liberty Bell. Everyone moves from Kit to Ria—it's only time passing. Sometimes you can hear it, but mostly not.

Ria wakes and makes tea. "About the party," she says, "we'd better not have middleclass music."

"I gave up that struggle long ago," I say. "You do the music. I'll think about the food. Riva's an expert about food."

"Always that woman," Ria starts.

"Be rational, Ria mine. Give up the formulaic. Riva isn't what's called 'the other woman'. She simply knows a lot about food. Patterns need organisation, you must admit." I lust after the spirit of the dance that breathes life into puppets. "The mere formulaic computes to absolute zero, which produces homogeneity."

"I just want to make a party," says Ria sourly; "not a work of art."

"Well, of course," I cajole; "of course," I soothe, letting the palms of my hands take their accustomed course, letting my mouth brush and caress. "An evening of poetry with no prose allowed. No campaigning and no confessing. We'll drink nothing but champagne. We'll have canapés with crabmeat and caviar."

"Who's going to pay for all that?" Ria can be practical when a chasm of luxury is about to open under her.

Then it comes to me, bold, clear, floodlit. "And of course," I tell Ria, firmly, sincerely, "of course we must ask Babes. And of course she must come. The ultimate celebration. A world of women, articulate, elegant, politicised, proactive—and right at the centre, Babes the Bountiful, Good Queen Babes, Babes of the Hundred Faces."

Ria sighs and pours more tea. "What are you plotting now? Honestly, sometimes I feel I don't know you at all. Sometimes I feel as if I've never met you; as if you're just some crazy woman who's come back for a drink after a meeting. Sometimes . . ."

"Sometimes?" I prod.

"No, nothing," she says.

I get busy washing and dressing, needing to hide my elation. We go out to eat. Ria feels chatty, tells me this and that gossip, this and that manoeuvring. "Gloriana says she won't come to any more of these jamborees unless they set up a filtering committee. She's mobbed wherever she goes—armies of women with manuscripts wanting her to do something."

"I can't quite see Gloriana Hardy as a patron of the arts," I say. "But times are hard and feminist commerce is even harder. You can't blame them for clutching at straws."

Ria laughs, "I don't think Gloriana's self-image includes being a straw."

I laugh back, "Or the Pied Piper of Hamelin. But self-image is only one kind of truth—even she must know that."

"There was one woman she rather took to. A fulsome admirer, like the others—but older. She learnt English in a prison somewhere and writes dystopias."

"You mean Gloriana Hardy's actually read some of this stuff?"

"No woman is an island," Ria admonishes. "Being

famous is one thing, but establishing yourself at the summit of a literary school is even better."

"I can see it now," I agree; "histories of literature finally universalised: the Elizabethans, the Victorians, the Modernists, the Feminists—Gloriana Hardy inaugurating the great Crypto-Classic Age of the third millennium."

"One person, after all, can't be a movement," Ria points out. "Look, she gave me the woman's card. It's interesting." She sorts through her wallet and hands me an embossed card, shaped like a bookmark. It says *Maria Francesca—prisoner of other people's consciousness* and under that is an address in Chile. Then it says:

> *Good women bow with the weight of their virtue*
> *Wicked women eat other women's passions*
> *Wise women bear the fool's apron*
> *Angry women build mountains*
> *Silent women break open rocks to find water*
> *Timid women marry and burn*
> *Bitter women ride the winds*
> *Broken women beat their hearts into pruning*
>   *hooks*
> *Brilliant women make their hands into chains*
> *Ambitious women give birth without pain.*

"I see what Gloriana Hardy sees," I say. "Moral vision isn't her long suit. An alliance with this sort of writing would add some gravitas to her reputation."

"I don't think that's all she has in mind," says Ria defensively, taking back the card.

"Don't be naïve. Gloriana Hardy knows better than most that love and knowledge are the same thing. What you can't do yourself, or haven't got, or never can imagine, you have to acquire from someone else."

"Let's not argue again," pleads Ria. "I'm too tired."

"Didn't get enough sleep then?" I tease her.

We part for different meetings and workshops. The concluding plenary added to the end of the Conference because of Hilke's story isn't due till tomorrow evening. I feel unaccountably restless and take myself to the bookstalls for diversion. Nothing there attracts, either. Eventually I give way to whatever enzymes or hormones are insisting, and go back to my room to sleep.

Lying alone, the familiar cycle of rage and despair begins. Shining and burning at the heart of it all is the sacred oil, the red altar-light, the fixed point of contemplation, the promise of the incense of salvation. It burns and shines; I have no power of resistance. I hear the drowned pealing of the Liberty Bell, its broken cough distorted by sea and wind. *Purity is power* it breathes, as best it can. *Purity is power; power is purity.* I wonder whatever happened to beauty. Beauty, purity, they can sound the same under the waves.

On either side of the cross were two malefactors, the story goes. But one of them was good. The simple message is, it's never too late. The complex message is, yes—do it, and it may still never be too late. Macbeth, afterwards, was only troubled by the Shakespearean world order, which has long since passed. When I was a girl, I had a teacher who said "If you were sorry you wouldn't have done it." The verbs aggravated me; I was only fourteen. Am I sorry and therefore do I decline to do it? But what is my puny sorrow compared with the greater good?

The concluding plenary is packed out: women stuffing the exits, jamming the gangways, crushed against the platform, squashed together on the stairs. Everyone who is anyone in movement politics is stacked side by side in a row of chairs on the platform, drenched in lights and half-hidden by a bank of microphones. Babes sits third to the left from the Chair. Despite the enormous crowd, there has been a meticulous exclusion of press and media; and the Chair announces that anyone seeing anyone using a tape-recorder is to indicate the matter immediately to the platform.

As the Chair taps her mike, the buzz hurtles full throttle into a funnel of deep silence. Ria on my right hunches forward eagerly; Riva to my left purses her lips. My own heart bumps painfully. Who is the enemy?

The Chair launches efficiently into the order of the meeting and various women on the platform pour water from their jugs. Then, one by one, the discussion groups report their views. I wait for Babes. The rest is nothing new: women can't; women don't; women shouldn't; women are for what's life-enhancing and against violence; women cultivate positive energy; women suffer internalised oppression; woman against woman is unnatural; woman against woman is a product of patriarchal misogyny. No one says anything about law or morality. Then comes Babes. Her voice is thin and high: "We repudiate this appalling act committed in the name of feminism. Some women —we must face the fact—are bad women, untroubled by conscience (here she flings back her long hair), unfettered by the demands of the greater good of all women. What is absolutely essential today is for us to condemn this act as a completely personal and private matter. The fact that it took place in a women's community is deplorable and embarrassing, but we must be quite clear that that is an irrelevant coincidence. Anything which turns women against one another is not feminist and has nothing to do with women's real needs and concerns." She goes on in this vein for some time, responding graciously to outbursts of applause and carefully lifting her voice for more abstract sweeps of rhetoric. Her cadenza is a call-to-arms: fight the good fight; focus the true enemy. Mother-of-the-Movement pleads for constancy, co-operation, positive visibility. She sits down to storms of grateful applause. Feminists can be let off the hook. It's not our crime; it's not our way.

Hilke speaks last, breathless with the strength of support, overwhelmed by the power of the sisterhood. She's had word that Brigitte has been given permission to leave the community. Peace will be restored. Gisela will not have suffered in vain. Ingeborg feels nourished. We will all feel strengthened by this solidarity. Riva mutters that a bit less strength and a bit more clarity might be useful, but Ria glares at her for whispering into my ear.

At last the meeting is open for discussion. The fever of babble takes some time to die down. Woman after woman endorses the speakers. My heart knocks harder. Is no one going to say it?

It's Riva in the end who says what's obvious. She addresses Babes. "I don't like to sound negative," she says calmly, "but how does all this fit in with our conviction that the personal is political?"

The unrest this causes threatens to break into uproar. Babes smiles and waits. Ria is furious, but controls herself. Babes quietens the audience by raising both her arms in invocation and blessing. "But of course," she soothes, "of course," she croons, "the personal is political. That is our bedrock. That is the inspiration for all our planning and longing." The audience sighs with solidarity. All is not lost. "The personal struggle is the blueprint for our strategies. The personal struggles of every woman here are the evidence for our analysis. All our experiences are experiences of struggle. We can't build our politics on negativity. Negativity is insignificant. Negativity is the result of mere self-indulgence." The rest is lost in an outburst of cheering and clapping. Babes knows when to stop. Women in the grip of each other's praise and acclamation can remove mountains, especially mountains of doubt and suspicion. Even Riva claps, though her smile is full of ambiguity. Ria says to me, "Quite a performance." And I say, "Nothing is what it seems."

I stare across the sea of women. Mother-of-the-Movement is in her natural element. She rests her small chin in her small hands. Small is beautiful. Small is delicious. I, with my small Swiss knife, could end it all. I with my bare hands, possibly. Or, like the Indigenous Australians, I could point the bone of my desire, no violence necessary. Point the bone and the transgressor goes away to die. But it takes two to believe: it takes consensus. How much does she know? Does two count as consensus?

The Chair thanks Babes and then everyone else; Hilke thanks everyone and then Babes. The meeting is closed; women disperse; the mood is buoyant, upbeat, gratified. The Conference has been yet another milestone on the way to a feminist future.

Back in London I phone Ria about the party. Then sleep, sleep. Even in an English June, even in London, there are sometimes red clouds at sunset. Riva has given me freesias from somewhere abroad. The red light, the heavy scent—how can I be ungrateful?

Riva phones next morning. AllyPally's called a meeting to discuss the ins and outs of what happened in Göppingen. I know Ria's going off with Gloriana Hardy to look at a cottage someone has to sell in Lincolnshire. Despite my need for a couple of days to myself, Riva insists, says she has my best interests at heart. Adds, too, that we could go on afterwards to the *Flambé* for seafood crêpes. That I certainly don't want to resist. So I go to the meeting. What Riva hasn't told me, though she must have known, is that Babes is part of the party, solemn and sympathetic, centre stage as usual.

No discussion can start, however, because another event is in full swing. Mother-of-the-Movement is soothing a sobbing sister, holding the unhappy head carefully against her sinewy chest. I wonder if such bones are more brittle than is normal: whether such delicate structures shatter into shards like fine china. I notice a pair of lower ribs outlined through the thin lilac cotton of the T-shirt. A children's size, clearly; not made to last.

AllyPally's in the kitchen doing her best with coffee and cold quiche for twelve. She tells me about sobbing Myrtle, impressionable, afraid, who's a friend of a friend and who's finally fled a battering husband. "I set up this meeting before we all left Brussels and I definitely didn't invite Babes. Julia told her. And then, into the bargain, I get back to find Myrtle on my doorstep. There are times (she glares at the drooping flans whose crusts are too flabby to cut cleanly) when I feel I can't bear to hear another word about women's problems."

"Battle fatigue," I say cheerily, taking the knife from her and easing the sodden dough from underneath. "Why don't we heat them up and just take in the coffee for now?"

"She's been crying all night," complains AllyPally.

"We'll help," I offer. "You take a back seat." Though sitting with the others I can see straight away what's bound to happen. Lovely Babes will soothe and smooth; and pitiable Myrtle will adore her instantly. I'm so detached I can watch quite clinically. It always happens. Babes told me once how she keeps all the letters and poems filed under name, age, date, and outcome—part of the archive of the movement, she said—women of the future will need to know these things. The personal is political.

Myrtle is unable to contain herself and brims over with the comfort and cossetting she craves, folds into the nurturing arms, rests on the dear bosom. She'll recover in the end; one day she'll find a sensible woman with a job and a flat and they'll live happily ever after for a year or two. Mother-of-the-Movement will ask them for dinner and they'll feel flattered. That's if Holy Mother is still around.

I could, of course, do it right now. I with my small Swiss knife. In the movies they find the spot instantly

—somewhere special at the base of the neck. Easy with a script and the camera angle just right. Strangling, even in the movies, takes a bit longer. I can, though, add Myrtle to the list of tormented souls. There are so many who must live with the anguish of rejection.

AllyPally brings in the warmed-up slabs of quiche. Myrtle goes on sobbing; the others chat and gossip. I think about the ebb and flow of power. The King is dead; long live the King. Rupture or rapture, death is incarnate—of the flesh, fleshly. But a rupture only of the ordered course: the Shakespearean order, a landscape in which it was no sin to make all human life a metaphor. Rapture as in mystery as in consummation as in destiny as in the end of dreaming as in the end of ends. The end of all ends is the beginning of knowledge. Everything works together for good for those who love god and entropy. The marriage of earth and flesh is the birth of light. Let us consider phoenix rising *and arising and arising* . . .

"What are you thinking about?" Riva asks.

"Entropy." Which is enough to focus attention. The meeting begins. Babes holds court and AllyPally sulks, finds pretexts for going in and out of the kitchen. It must have been Brigitte, everyone agrees. Babes wants us to write something for the newsletter. But it must be abstract. Nothing of this should be made available to the patriarchs. Riva disagrees, says we're having the meeting to discuss the issues brought out by a particular situation. Babes says *exactly* and *quite* and reiterates what she thinks about the issues. I say nothing; it suits me these days when I'm in a group.

Riva says, "First, does it make a difference if Brigitte had a pure hate, since purity atones? I mean, there was no personal gain—for her it was a matter of principle. Or did she have a ruthless coldness, since only power can enact? Or was she dissociated: standing watching while her arm and hand achieved what all her words had been incapable of getting? Or was it an accident, a force miscalculated: being in the wrong place for the wrong reason? After all, being crushed by a falling tree in a hurricane is called divine intervention, not human intention. I mean, is murder proved?"

Babes is reproving about the word *murder.* "This isn't a court," she patronises.

"Well, that's another thing," Riva continues. "We don't have courts. There's a meaning in that."

Inwardly I laugh and clap; I dance for joy. It's sweet to hear my case outlined by someone else. AllyPally joins in, energised by opposition to the Rule of Babes. It may not have been Brigitte, after all. It could have been Edeltraud inventing a scheme to win the vote on a wave of sympathy and outrage. Outmanoeuvring Brigitte was, after all, her main goal. Practical politics demand illusion, deviousness, manipulation, sleight of mind. You should always look at who benefits. In this instance, it's Edeltraud, surely.

Annie says, "Everyone always jumps to the most melodramatic conclusion. It could have been suicide —I mean, being in the right place for the *wrong* reason. Gisela could have purposely provoked it, thrown the dice at martyrdom. She might have had cancer or something and decided that as she had to die soon anyway, she might as well make her death have some political value, just as life insurance gives dying a commercial value. Then again, it could have been a passionate collusion with depression, given that her side was losing the argument."

"If you're going to go in for psychoanalysis or metaphysics," says Lakshmi impatiently, "you might as well argue, on the one hand, that it was an ecstasy of masochism brought on by accusation and mockery; or on the other hand, that it was the only possible resolution of the logic that had been set up—like the death of Socrates. We don't know anything about what sort of person she was. She could have been a little Hitler; or a Joan of Arc; or a Thomas More; or an Edith Cavell . . ."

Annie interrupts, barely concealing her annoyance: "Or a Rajput wife, a freedom fighter, an anti-terrorist terrorist . . ."

"Girls, girls," croons AllyPally. "She could have been a schizoid, closet-vegetarian, lateral-thinking, incest-surviving, market-led mother. So what?"

Annie says, "It makes a difference whether she brought it on herself or whether she had it visited upon her." That makes me giggle: "Nominative versus accusative? A matter of mere grammar?"

Babes is angry by now. "We never have, and we never should, talk about women bringing things on themselves. Think about rape!"

AllyPally wants to get back to the specifics. "It's obvious who benefits," she says. "One, Brigitte, since her opposition is removed. Two, Edeltraud, since she gains righteousness and credibility. Three, Ingeborg, since her grip on the leadership has been strengthened. Anyone else?"

117

Me, I think gleefully: I've been given an objective correlative. But I say nothing.

Annie brings up another worry: "We only have Hilke's version of what happened. How can we decide anything without someone else's version?"

"Exactly," says Riva. "All facts are inventions of one kind or another, depending on whose point of view is accepted as central. We can't know what really happened. There isn't anything useful we can decide about it, except whatever we want the rest of the world to think about it."

"Even that can't be controlled," I say. "One thing's certain: it will sure as hell turn up in Gloriana Hardy's next book. Why don't we wait and see what her verdict is?"

Babes glares at me full on, and says—slowly, patiently, sorrowfully—"That's an excellent reason for putting something in the newsletter right now. If our politics are to depend on Gloriana Hardy's twisted views . . ."

But I flash back: "I don't see that her views are any more twisted than anyone else's."

Riva says, "There's no point arguing like this. We can't write something collective for the newsletter. It's too soon. We need to discuss everything much more than we have so far."

AllyPally, always eager to enact democracy, says, "But if anyone here does want to write something, we shouldn't try and stop them."

"It's always better," says Babes, with preacherly confidence, "to have support. But one way or another, what needs saying must be said, even if it's left to me alone to say it."

Myrtle looks lovingly at Babes the Brave and I'm made to realise yet again that Babes will never be alone. There'll always be a Myrtle or two, not to mention the groupies. I feel depressed. Will no one rid us of this pestilent protagonist? Does it really have to be me?

Riva takes me to the *Flambé,* but it isn't up to much. I'm out of sorts. For the first time I feel bored by Riva's talk about the short cuts taken by chefs who produce this kind of menu.

Back home, I walk into fresh kitchen smells and find Sarah and Ashok hard at it making chutneys. I fill them in about the Conference and the dead sister in Göppingen, but they're only half-listening. They brighten up much more at the news about Ria's party plans. Sarah says she wouldn't dream of coming, given that Ashok wouldn't be welcome; but they're both keen to help with the catering. "We'll cut our profits back," Sarah offers, "since it's your friends." I'm relieved. I can tell Ria I've decided not to ask Riva to deal with the food.

Ashok has taken some books out of the library for me and has also prepared some typed pages. I take all this up to my room, longing for solitude and sleep. Ria, I notice, hasn't phoned and there's no card from her either.

The typescript is headed *Recent developments in brain-browser software* and reads: "A three-dimensional map of the rat's brain is providing a model for plotting the workings of the human mind. The browser, developed by neurobiologists at a military research foundation, already holds nine-tenths of what is known about the rat's brain. The system shows a picture of the brain segment with text describing the properties of the neurons at each location. The principal researcher, Dr Harold Loewen, explained last week to the scientific press that the brain is like a globe of the earth, given that if you put your finger down on the surface, the computer will tell you not only the name of the place and its geographical co-ordinates, but also the kinds of people who live there, the food they eat, the television programmes they watch, and even the cars they buy.

Obviously the next steps will involve mapping more complex brains: dogs, chimpanzees, and eventually, humans. This superior mapping will have to take account of individual differences, which are of less account with the relatively simple rat brain than they are with human brains. Dr Loewen reports that software developments are already being planned in this area. The research programme, branches of which are co-ordinated internationally, is called the Human Brain Project; it aims to build a three-dimensional human brain map whose segments will be accompanied by a huge database of information about what functions neurons at each junction can perform.

In the future, human brain mapping will clarify and codify how we think, imagine, improvise, and learn, as well as detailing what goes wrong to cause dysfunctions such as mania, dementia, hallucinations and delusions, memory distortion and loss, and a range of other pathologies."

After reading this, I sleep easily. Maybe it's true that science will solve everything in the end.

Next morning Annie arrives for coffee and chat. She's off to Exeter but wants to tell me Hilke's phoned.

Edeltraud's sun has set and Ingeborg's moon has risen. Ingeborg has got things back to normal by insisting on routines and commitments, and by pronouncing that when there's a threat it must be removed. The work is what matters and it must go on. The seasons wait for no woman . . .

I remember Hilke's face: the wide sculpted square of the Teutons, cheekbones high and arching like a Valentine's heart, the skin leathered from outdoors vigour. I remember the hard eyes, blue as flowers, and the flat white hair. Hear no evil; speak no evil. We are all sisters. Some likes and dislikes we inherit; they are not personal. They run down our veins with the rest of our toxic waste. So I remember things I shouldn't remember; I remember the history of human nature. But out of what remains, who will describe the features of feminist human nature? Once upon a time, in Germany, a wicked witch pursued to the death a heroine on horseback, whose valour in the causes of women was legendary. Once upon a time, in London, a wicked step-sister killed the bright star of the holy sisterhood. What do German women know, that we have only imagined? I remember, years ago in Tübingen, standing alone in the Stiftskirche among the tombs of the Dukes of Württenberg, their effigies clear and clean despite five centuries of breathing and staring. I felt the dreadful longing for space: the menace of all the Russias on the right, the leer of mighty France heaving from the left, and here between, just a handful of bishops and dukes, quarrelling and skirmishing, suspicious and jealous, their petty fiefdoms ripe for ravage. Thrones and Dominions, Principalities and Powers, the armies of Satan and St Michael ready and willing to ransack all the earth. Give me space; give me room; let me speak some language other than English.

Annie laughs when I ruminate about *Lebensraum*. "You're in a time warp," she tells me. "Who needs outward trappings when you have the Deutschmark? The Göppingen women have land and property and big contracts. This is the new Europe: free trade, mobility of labour, a market-place of hundreds of millions. Hilke says Ingeborg's running rings around the local bureaucracy. And she's persuaded Gisela's *Gemeinschaft* that Gisela went back to her family in the east because of all the frustrations caused by the negotiations."

"What about the cheap meat?" I ask.

"Not an issue any longer, since Ingeborg's taken over. The two groups have just agreed to keep separate for a while, till they see how their sales figures look. Money talks loudest, in the end."

"If that's so, why didn't they buy Gisela off in the first place?"

"You're forgetting passion and principle," says Annie, "and in any case, they're not the Bundesbank. How could they promise to buy all that meat, ad infinitum, and not sell it on? You can only have idealism when you can afford it. Otherwise, we're all left with expedience."

Sarah and Ashok are chopping up garlic and ginger, measuring out herbs and spices, stewing tomatoes, peppers, lime rinds. I like the scented steam, the casual sounds. I want to feel clean, clear, strong, but it's an uphill battle. Whoever keeps faith feels nothing wicked because the wisdom of faith discerns the right time, the accurate judgement. No woman has power over the day of her death, the means or the motivation. Until—maybe—the brain map reveals this last of all secrets: the off-button, already programmed. Meanwhile there's the endless invention with the fruits of the earth, the flush of green fields, the seasonal sun. Sarah and Ashok think only about recipes and profits and do not mind the worm turning.

Above the sink Ashok has rigged up a cork board for notices, memos, and other ephemera. Pinned to it is a postcard of a piece by Praxiteles, man holding baby, found at Olympia. Next to that is a written list:

1. Hot tomato chutney sales needed for greenhouse deposit—50.
2. Get white radish seeds.
3. Time can go backwards in quantum theory.

To the right are printed circulars about car boot sales and street markets. In the bottom left corner is a pencil drawing of an onion, made by Sarah. Underneath it she's written *O Breath of Life*. I'm not sure, staring at it, whether it's a joke or not. The petty round, the common task—that makes the world go round, say bosses and property-owners who understand wealth creation and the justice of their cause. Love and sympathy—that makes the world go round, say saints and poets who are elevated above the sweat and toil of fields and factories. Righteousness and terror—that makes the world go round, say godfearers and earthshakers, adoring the divine right they nourish in themselves. Solidarity and sisterhood—that makes the world go round, say feminists. So round it goes —round and round. It spins like an onion on a chopping block.

"Dearest Ria," I suggest when we meet, "I know you're above women's bunfights, but do you really think it's wise to have Gloriana Hardy and Mother-of-the-Movement in the same room?" I have, of course, my own plans for the party: well-laid plans, the apotheosis of Babes the Bountiful. I shall set Babes free for ever and ever.

"Why not?" Ria is bored.

"After the rumours that went round at the Conference. About Beatrice Brown and the rest."

"Oh that." Ria's dismissive. "Everyone's forgotten about that. They're all still going on about what happened in Göppingen."

"Gloriana Hardy won't have forgotten."

"She hasn't mentioned a word about it. Anyway, we can hardly ask her not to come to a party in her own house. And it is only a party. They don't have to leap into bed together."

"If you say so. She's your friend."

"I would've thought it's more problematic having Portland Jo in the same room."

"True. But it's not worth risking one of her outbursts. She'd gatecrash it anyway, if she wasn't asked—and likely wreck the place as well. Though I must say it's surprising how she's kept low this past couple of weeks. Annie's talked to her nearly every day and says she's coping surprisingly well."

"Can we get on with the details?"

"There are no details. Sarah and Ashok are doing the catering. Cut price."

"Well that's a relief. I thought your pretentious friend

would be saddling us with crates of vintage booze and a bill to match her lofty ideas of the good life."

"You don't have to get nasty," I say. "She's never done you any harm."

"Want a bet?" flares Ria. I hear the Liberty Bell. It sings in pain—a doleful note. Time isn't the only thing that passes. Ria is evasive: there's work to do, people to see, and it's the middle of the morning. But I persist, against my better judgement, say "I remember, even if you don't, when it didn't matter what time of day it was: the gilded mirror, the answering machine on for the duration, you flat on your back hell-bent on all you could give and get— you past caring about the morality of money or the aesthetics of success or the durability of coupling."

"You've changed," she says sullenly. I go on flirting, regardless. "So you don't want my body? You can do without my long-drawn-out, passionately attentive, wildly precise (drawing the fanned fingers of my right hand slowly from outside right knee to inside right thigh) embraces?"

"Cut it out," says Ria. "It isn't funny."

"Have you forgotten already how we fell on each other? How you glowed and gloated? How the joss sticks ribboned the whole room, tracing temple and church in a perfect meld . . ."

"We're not adolescents."

"We're forever young. We can have joss sticks any time we like. And red wine, candles, moonlit terraces, nights at the opera . . ."

"Not by bread alone," she says severely. She's not to be moved. I have to go home, though the phone is silent and there are no messages on the machine.

It's all very well being self-employed and fancy-free, but what if there's nothing distracting to do? I look at the books Ashok got for me. I may as well improve myself. I may as well know what I'm not capable of knowing.

The three books are different versions of quantum theory, particle physics and cosmology, written in English for people like me who can't read mathematics. Still half-thinking about the computer model of a normal human brain and what they might do with it, I start on *Reversing Time?* which says that human flesh is made out of the remnants of ancient stars. Every atom in a human body, except for hydrogen, was made in stars that formed and exploded long before the solar system existed. Nuclear reactions in stars burned hydrogen fuel for billions of years until temperatures increased to the stage where the next heaviest element, helium, was produced. At higher temperatures still, the helium burned, and heavier elements, oxygen and carbon, were formed. And so it went on: the hotter it got, the heavier the elements that were produced. And at temperatures of billions of degrees, the stars exploded and all the elements went rocketing out into the universe. "The earth and all that therein is," says the writer, "including ourselves, is literally made of stardust."

Not, therefore, earth to earth, ashes to ashes, but incandescent light—unimaginable burning. What matter the motive or the cause? What words or threads, what thoughts, can circumnavigate the majesty of fire? Nothing can match the power of the act. Philosophers say the concept of cause is a language trick, a shared illusion, a composite collusion. Two events are merely linked by time and contiguity and constant conjunction. In any case, if stars burn hotter and hotter, something different is bound to happen, so long as there's someone around to notice. I can choose from an endless stream of metaphors both lived and written: the avenging Furies; Kali who cleanses; Artemis, hunter; Vandals and Visigoths; Philistines, Saracens, Mongolian hordes, Cossack avengers; Aphrodite who never tires; St Michael Archangel who speared the serpent; the Assyrians bearing down from the hills; the battered wife who stabs her spouse; the raped woman who shoots her tormenter; the abandoned mother who throws her screaming child from the top floor, the river bank, the high cliff-face. All, all, results from the evolution of stars, cycled, recycled, burning and bursting. Babes will explode in a flash of light, in a pillar of fire, between one instant and the next. And then I, likewise; stardust to stardust, sequinned along the curve of time, the arc of existence. And the one-eyed god whose only function is to see whatever can be seen rests for ever in the dark behind the light.

.   .   .

Sarah and Ashok come back from the street-market with empty cartons. Everything sold. But they bring with them a girl called Flo who they say is homeless and has no money. My protests are weakwilled: I've got a lot on my mind. Conventions collapse in the face of an actual victim. She can sleep on the sofa for a while. She's young; she'll move on. Someone was bound to end up on the sofa so long as it remained unoccupied. I don't like to admit it, but having people in the house does let me out of the cleaning and cooking. The power of property, the power of money, the power of power—the less I do, the more choices I have; the less I do, the more I like it. I'm sure Sarah knows how I feel though we don't discuss it. I catch her eye sometimes and feel embarrassed. I'm not so sure what Ashok knows: Ashoka the Great, who massacred the Kalingas and who afterwards converted to the Buddha's eight-fold path; Ashoka the Great who sent out missionaries to preach moderation; Ashoka the Great who had pillars built all over India for the sake of truth. A change of heart is a change of mind.

Flo sleeps, or follows Sarah round like a puppy, eyes large and moist and full of worship. Sarah teaches her pounding and measuring.

After a couple of days, Ria finally phones and sounds cheerful. It's the party in three days' time. She outlines procedures for fetching and carrying booze, food, glasses, crockery, mini-disco lighting, music stands. Everyone's coming, she tells me happily. Even Eve's friend from Wales.

"And Babes as well?" My heart's in my mouth.

"Babes as well."

"How come she isn't ill with something?"

"She wants to add names to her piece for the newsletter. It's a perfect opportunity."

"How did Gloriana Hardy react?"

"She's preoccupied with agents and solicitors about the cottage. Anyway, why should she care? From her point of view, Babes is a woman of no importance." There are times when I feel my entire

128

universe is only a black hole at the edge of Gloriana Hardy's glittering space.

"And since Babes is definitely coming, I've asked Jade," adds Ria. "You probably got introduced at her organics stall in Brussels before she got together with Babes, which Annie says only happened at the end of the Conference, when all the fuss was over. Anyway, she says she met you there. She's already started at Databasics, wouldn't you guess! Babes invented a job for her."

"What about Portland Jo?"

"She's shrugging it off. She told Annie, Babes is as faddy about women as she is about food; that it's just a passing *tendresse*.

"Doesn't sound like Portland Jo."

"Well," says Ria, "she's been getting support from Morag—you know, Sal's Presbyterian minister who can have a congregation so long as she stays in the closet. Morag's been giving counselling sessions down the phone."

"That's not very loyal to Annie, is it? Why should Sal want to help Portland Jo stay with Babes?"

Ria sighs. "You're a bit slow these days, Tessa. Sal's worked out that Babes keeps Portland Jo on the boil with a hint here and a hint there. Jealousy's a wonderful motivator. If Portland Jo can be weaned off her automatic reactions, Babes will get unsettled and start to change roles: start to put pressure on Portland Jo. Given how much of a predator Portland Jo's always been, that's bound to turn her right off. Annie, of course, will be waiting in the wings."

"Very devious. Does Annie really think it will work? Is Morag in on all this?"

"Don't be ridiculous—Morag earns her bed and board doing universal love. She's always telling Sal how politicals are unhappy because they think too much. She dreams of green hills far away and flocks and shepherdesses. Perfect for Portland Jo. Mind you, it's taking a lot out of Sal. She's spent more time in the last week sitting on British Rail than sitting on anything else."

"What does Annie think?"

"Annie's had her mind on the German women. Hilke's been phoning two or three times a day."

"But she's coming up for the party?"

"Definitely."

"So tell me about this Jade person. Do you think she's really interested in Babes? Or did she just want a stint in London?"

"Can't tell."

"What was she doing before retailing organics in Brussels?"

"She's Australian, originally, but seems to have moved round all over the place. AllyPally says she was helping with Judika's translation of the Dutch Muslim women's oral history project—you know, the one they got all that EU cash for. Don't you remember? Some of the groupies went over to Amsterdam to work on it at the time, when Babes took over Databasics."

"So she knew Babes already?"

"Only by reputation," says Ria. "Who doesn't?" We ring off then, having made all the practical arrangements. Now I have nothing to do but wait. Sarah's humming round the kitchen day and night, teaching and mothering Flo, who creeps to and fro like a bird with a broken wing, looking at me sideways. Ashok is spending more and more time in the library, since there's another pair of hands to chop, grind, stir, pour. Maybe, as well, he feels unnecessary now that Sarah has someone who'll talk back. Riva's got appointments booked solid because of taking time off to go to the Conference. Annie's down in Exeter, and AllyPally's at her wits' end coping with the sobbing Myrtle. I sleep as much as I can, but it's difficult. Who sleeps well for the thirty-six hours before an execution?

Between thinking and dreaming are memories and images, shapes of past and future superimposed, echoes of the same sounds, outlines of the same scenes, notes of the same scripts. In the end is the beginning, so that the myths explode in endless sequence out of the mouths of mothers and gods. I read one story and lived another; and read some more, and lived out others; and mixed and matched like everyone else. Now I can remember whatever's necessary.

What, I asked him, years ago (the only man who was ever a real friend, and even that doesn't last— it never can; even that is doubletongued); what is the prevailing female image? Men have Man the Hunter, the pursuer and victor who woos and wins *la demoiselle du lac*; but who is she? He said (straight as an arrow from the id's primordial slime), "Woman is The Entrapper: void, vortex, centre of the spider-web. Perfect Woman waits and entraps." At the time, though I'd done humanism—philosophy, art, music, literature, history, (and the history of history), I hadn't done feminism—life, liberty, and the pursuit of justice; so it didn't occur to me that the hunter who woos and wins is the same hunter who kills and devours. It didn't occur to me, even reading "Whoso list to hunt, I know where is an hind . . ."; even seeing the sword between Tristan and Isolde; even seeing the logo of our own time, handheld phallus cocked and primed, with triggerfinger ready and bullets issuing in endless streams, obedient to the fateful law of Onan. *Spill not your seed uselessly upon the ground.* It never occurred to me that Man the Hunter waved his magic wand and thus created spiderwoman who entraps, and doe-eyed *demoiselle*, and greasy Joan who keeps the homefires burning once progeny's ensured.

I know the difference between wooing and feeding, between loving and hating, between sex and babies, between equality and authority, along with all the other women, however highborn. We belong to the outer-caste, slaving or playing in the shallows, prevented or protected from conflating rage with libido. I'm no hunter, have inherited no furious bloodlust. But Babes will never remove herself; and I am part of what will change the world.

Therefore, given the imminence of laying waste a temple of the gods (who was once a suckling, once a darling girl), I must perform ritual ablutions, so that I can forgive myself; and must rehearse the contract made with my mortal soul; and must demonstrate my knowledge of the inventory of implements. Then this cleansing will not be compromised by any of my personal flaws and failures.

.   .   .

My arranging and preparing come easily, naturally. There are no problems with ordering and timing, no interruptions, nothing distracts. It's three in the morning and the moon has two more hours of falling. There is a sense of fitness, and the beat of blood at my eardrums, which usually measures the silence, recedes as if it had never existed. And when the words come, they sing in my membranes with the same cold joy I hear when ghostly choirs in shattered cathedrals emulate the wings of a dove.

I, Tessa, in the presence of what can never be seen or conjured, spirits of earth and air, daughters of Demeter waiting underground, sirens of rivers and oceans, and the burnt hearts of all the dead who waited without hope; and in the presence of Our Lady the Moon; and within sound of the Liberty Bell sighing at the bottom of the sea; and being in full possession of my wits and senses;

and in consideration of such terms of justice as are agreed between those inner requirements residing from the beginning in the individual, and those exterior strictures whose imposition imputes authority to lawgivers and lawkeepers who embody and enact the fears and phantoms of the people;

and with earned knowledge and experience of the existential compromise between that sweet state of being offered up and that sweet state of being withdrawn;

do promise and contract with my mortal soul a pure intention and a firm will, which being before-times coloured or clouded by seasonal changes and random influences is now emptied of all sentimental inhibitions, whether great, petty, conventional, occasional, or individual.

[Here sounds the Liberty Bell three times and I wash with clean water my eyes, ears, nostrils, lips and hands.]

Wherefore, to show earnest of my preparation and conviction, I offer this contemplation of the list of implements regarded and discarded, it having been necessary to construct an inventory by class and method of operation;

namely, first, by blade:

there being the finest honed slim instruments which enter by the point, such as skewers, syringes, stilettos, and a range of tools used in various crafts;

there being next the sharpened instruments both common and exotic which cleave, cut, slice or saw, such as axes, swords, all manner of knives, and a range of household tools;

and next, by noose:

there being lengths of fabric of myriad kinds, including hemp, cloth, cord, and all woven stuffs;

and there being wire and other lengths of pliable metals;

and next, by crushing:

there being infinite possibilities of falls from buildings, cliffs, shafts, wells, and pinnacles of every kind;

and there being any number of blunt objects able to be wielded;

and next, by suffocation:

there being all poisonous gases, and all means of covering nose and filling mouth with pillows, plastic, sacking, soil, or a multitude of natural things;

and next, by electrocution:

there being many methods;

and next, by fire:

there being many scenarios;

and next, by drowning:

there being any number of places, both wild and domestic;

and next, by projectile, ancient or modern:

there being arrows, spears, boulders, and every kind of bullet;

and next, by explosive:

there being all kinds of bombs and other devices;

and next, by torture:

there being absolute deprivation of food, drink, sleep, or sensory information; or gradual impairment or removal of vital functions.

All these I have regarded and discarded; and for all others which I have through ignorance or idleness left unresearched, I make apology, and with compassion, do forgive myself.

[Here sounds the Liberty Bell three times and I wash with red wine my forehead, my belly, and the soles of my feet.]

Whereupon, to give clarity to my chosen means, I here declare the most efficient and most possible aid, having given due thought to the minimising of physical pain, mental dread, and the shedding of blood; and that is the ingesting of a lethal substance extracted from a plant which feeds some part of creation, but not our own;

the queen of such plants being belladonna of the bellshaped purple flowers and the deadly ovoid berries, black and fully glossed; *whoso list to hunt, I know where is a greenhouse;*

and the necessary preparation having been discovered in a book of arcane herbalism which is among the kitchen scriptures shelved by Sarah and Ashok next to their noticeboard.

So let it be.

[Here sounds the Liberty Bell three times and I wash with white wine my breasts and inner thighs.]

I, Tessa, collapse to a single point my memories, longings, pleasures, ambitions, and welcome the instant when I shall vanish without effort into my own desire.

[Here I celebrate silence, drink what remains, put on my clothes, and stare for a long time at the sliver of moon passing implacably through clouds.]

In the moaning, in the gloaming, in the meantime, pretty dreamtime, come requests from the body, ordinary demands, eating and sleeping, laughing and talking, though I remain hidden in that single point, that instant which is nearly, nearly, but not yet.

The day of the party wears the drab clinging heat of a windless London summer, all stale petrol fumes, caked dog shit, dry litter strewn in gutters or bunched under overflowing bins; but we'll forget the sweat and the stubborn sun once night falls and the crisp cold fizz is poured. I have my special canapés ready for their final spread—just a careful few on a handsome wooden plate, tucked out of sight behind the mixer in the cupboard next to Ria's sink. I know how to make sure no one else partakes. It will be easy to appeal to Babes' vanity about her very excluding diet.

Riva arrives first, to help Sarah cart in the food. And then AllyPally with a newly muted Myrtle. Gloriana Hardy has a dozen fans grunting over ropes of cable, a mixer board, and a jumble of lights and speakers. She looks more relaxed than I've expected, greets me warmly, waves at me a bottle of green fizz with a bright green label. "Look what I've got, just for Babes," she boasts. "Bury the hatchet and so on. An organic, non alcoholic sparkler, fresh from the vines of deepest Kent. It's only been on the market for a fortnight. She can toast her piece for the newsletter."

"Remarkable," I say. "It's not like you to forgive and forget."

"Life's too short," says Gloriana Hardy grinning. "Babes is a woman of no importance. And this is a party, after all; nothing heavy or political."

"Sure," I say. "But even so . . ."

Ria interrupts to get me fetching and carrying. There seem to be hundreds of chairs to be unstacked and placed carefully to maximise both chat and dancing space. I do my best.

When fifty women are already snacking and drinking, Portland Jo turns up, with Sal on one side and a couple of tightly shorn, bright pink heads on the other. "Gracy and Rager," she says by way of introduction. "They've been tarting up the stairwell at Databasics and can do with a decent rave."

Gloriana Hardy and Ria are stuck on the other side of the enormous room, and in any case, no one has said anything about gatecrashers. It's not my business who's allowed in or not. Portland Jo is clutching a paper plate holding a peculiar-looking piece of bakery or pastry, rather like a stuffed pitta bread, but not exactly. "Funky, isn't it?" she says, seeing me staring. "I got it from that deli called Ancient Alexandria. It's for Babes. She'll hardly eat anything these days that doesn't come from there. I didn't want her to go hungry while the rest of us pig out."

"That's hardly likely," I say defensively. "Sarah and Ashok have done all the food. Nothing but home-made, strictly vegetarian, preservatives and additives-free. Babes isn't the only one with special needs."

"But she *is* the only one with *extra*-special needs," responds Portland Jo aggressively. "It's my job to make sure she's looked after properly." She glares at me. "Is that bitch Jade here yet?"

"I don't think so. See for yourself. You're not going to start a fight, are you? This is a party . . ."

"Keep your knickers on, Tessa. I know you all think I'm straight off the farm, but I can pass for civilised if I want to." She pushes past, flanked by the pinkheads. Sal stays to chat with me. Babes makes her entrance an hour or so later, accompanied by a short slim woman with braided dark hair and wearing a loose skirt and embroidered waistcoat. This must be Jade. I watch her head off away from Babes, who herself heads for Portland Jo. Jade starts talking to Riva, which makes me wonder if they've met before.

The music bangs on and on; the heat and talk increase and increase. I'm in a jungle. I can feel a headache coming. When will the women thin out a bit? I spend my time pushing in and out of the kitchen. Babes is holding forth from an armchair to groupies and newcomers and the inevitable Myrtle, all of whom have pulled chairs as close to her as possible, though some have simply taken to the floor to sit at her feet. She's enjoying herself. She never needs to dance to attract attention.

Eventually the music slows and quiets down, the sequence of lights calms, the women melt in groups or pairs into other rooms, into the garden, on to the balcony. Now it's time. Babes is just finishing a glass of Gloriana Hardy's green wonder and has put down Portland Jo's offering half eaten, while she goes through her piece for the newsletter yet again. I've watched her all evening as much as possible, and as far as I can tell, she hasn't taken a bite of anything else. It's part of her image to be abstemious, so I can't believe I've missed some uncharacteristic gobbling. Now it's time. I fetch my plate from its sanctuary and approach.

"I haven't come to interrupt," I say nicely. "Just to add my name to the piece." She's surprised, but wants to be gratified in front of the admirers. Myrtle fishes for the sheet with the list of names. "And I've made you something special, as a token. You always go to all this trouble and most of us never show any gratitude."

"I'm charmed," she says graciously. "But you know I'm on a *very* restrictive diet. Most things, I'm afraid, I can't eat at all—and even what I can eat has to be in very small amounts."

"I know," I smile. "I checked it all out with Portland Jo." She begins to frown, and the threat of imminent failure inspires me beyond myself. "And Jade, of course. I met Jade in Brussels."

She relaxes and beams. "Did you? So did I. She's wonderful, isn't she? She's only been at Databasics for a week and already it's obvious she's going to make it hugely successful. She knows such a lot about absolutely everything. She even knows about diet. I've been better this last week than I have for ages." Myrtle looks brave and sorrowful. I push my plate forward. "I know," I coo. "That's why I talked it over with her at some length. These are just for you."

She takes one of the six delicate squares. "What is it?"

"Hand-ground garlic and black currant purée, smoothed with goat's yoghourt and spiced with basil and coriander."

She looks pleased. "I can have all those things," she says, satisfied. "No salt, though? I can't have salt."

"Not a speck," I say. "And the yoghourt's really fresh. Sarah got it from a stallholder she knows who keeps goats somewhere in Barnet."

Babes bites and eats and I stand there between that instant and the next. Mountains groan, the sea throws off all its froth, the fiery rocks begin to melt. From the other side of the room, Riva catches my eye and comes towards me. Babes takes a second square, then turns back to her entourage. I keep hold of the plate and head for the kitchen. I've removed and disposed of my plate of dainties from the cupboard next to the sink before Riva catches up with me. She's suspicious, but doesn't want to say anything. I ask her to dance. Ria is busy with AllyPally out on the balcony, and I feel like dancing the night away.

It's about half an hour before Babes starts retching and choking. I don't notice particularly at the time, but I remember later that Portland Jo has an odd look of calm on her face as she rushes to tend to Babes; and I realise long afterwards that the look of bliss on Gloriana Hardy's face can't be due entirely to the music, or to the chunky flesh of the pinkhead she happens to be holding at the time.

It's Myrtle who galvanises everyone. "Turn off that racket," she commands. "Where's the phone? She's having some sort of fit. Get an ambulance. Fast!"

I take care not to look at Babes' face, especially her eyes, so that I won't have to remember too much detail. I know she'd be screaming if she could. As it is, whatever gasping or pleading she's doing is drowned out by the hubbub of rush and panic.

The ambulance comes quickly. Some women fade away; others are agog. There's an unseemly crush and squabbling about who will go in the ambulance. Strangely, it's Myrtle who wins out. Riva avoids speaking to me and offers to drive Jade to the hospital. Portland Jo came with the pinkheads, so her motorbike's still at home. Neither of the pinkheads is anywhere to be seen, so Sal says she'll take Portland Jo to the hospital. Some of the groupies cram into a third car. "It's enough," says Gloriana Hardy. "We can't all go. There's no point. Let's clear up here." She subsides into the armchair Babes last sat in. The half-eaten bakery has disappeared, and so has the bottle of green wonder and the glass. Gloriana Hardy's fans start packing and stacking, clearing and tidying. Everyone is very subdued. Ria is nowhere to be found and I conclude that she's gone with the others to the hospital. I tell Sarah we should go home now. In any case, I can't trust myself to anyone's gaze until I feel ordinary again.

Le Déluge

I'm not in the least. (Why?) should I? It's not as if. Apprehensive, that's natural, because of the—(anyway in the vast scheme of things the void the spaces not much suffering not days and weeks like the rest of us not years (there are times when you wouldn't even know. Driving fast at night, for example, and a hard bump against a kerb or a bollard. Once it was a badger but it could have been anyone. (no dreams at all last night not one not at all no clanging and clacking no ringing no talking no people I ever met no colours no music what are dreams anyway? Why would dreaming mean anything? Who wouldn't rest all night after such a day and all the other days I never counted them (whenever it started. Who could remember that? Not entered in a diary. Not an appointment or a happening, not an event, not remarkable. Even the universe just started somehow.) Not why did I what did I who did I how did I when did I? With what? On whose account did I repay? In classical logic even randomisation is ordered by the software—in classical logic there are no middles no in-amongst no colours no dreamtime no instinctual adjustments no Mozart-is-better-history-says-so no standing in the aisles. Theology is excluded whatever Anselm said now we know all about algebra. In classical logic there are rules to fit any occasion so long as you fix the occasion so long as you state clearly so long as you can be faithful to the design) not I, said Cock Robin not I with any bow and arrow any plaything any known intention. I have an alibi.) never again the. Never the small beech saplings rust then green, the hedgerows. Never the acorns. Never the calendar of snowdrops, primroses, bluebells, queen anne's lace.

So benign a landscape it can be deceiving it can be a sentiment. better in memory than in the seeing. Remembering can change everything from how it was and how it might have been to how it seemed to be and how it really was.) Not at all. Not in the least. Not the slightest. No one knows the. No one has. Even not I. The sky said Chickalicken is falling in. We all fall in. Not days and weeks like the rest of us. Not years.

Not iniquity abounding (heaven forfend!) Not round and round, on and on, for ever and forever (heaven be praised!) Not the water cycle the nitrogen cycle the photosynthesis cycle (O heavenly father-and-mother, sister-and-friend, lord-and-lady, honourable majesty, prime origin, first principle, spirit of life, creator, redeemer, sustainer, maintainer, director, destroyer! O!)

Art is a start. In art you can have worms or not have them. You can have the nitrogen cycle without worms if you want. Worms gobbling the aqueous humour of eyes, the thin cornea that makes it all possible, the retina. They leave the lens for a while. Tougher. Maggots greedy and burrowing. Gone, all gone. Eyes that beheld. Eyes that could look at algebra though it never existed. Leave out the worms and maggots. Just have.

Renew in me.

(If you were sorry you wouldn't have done it.)

146

Done.

Done.

Not I. I have an alibi. Time was when time departed and the band played on. The ship sank the plane fell down the cricketer came up to bowl and sank like a stone the patient said "Oh doctor" and died the priest walked into the fire the peasants were sliced in two by the force of history (see the blade ascend and fall, rise and shine, knit one, purl one, cast one off) and the queen said bring me a sword I have married a throne.

(Did you want a blindfold? Did you want an alibi?)

Worms can be sliced and still go on. Now there are two. We might, nevertheless, be able to replicate the nitrogen cycle if we understand enough algebra. Worms in theory could become extinct.

If there could be torments, if there could be questions, if there could be rainbows, if there could be sweating and arguing, if there could be ethics without additives without pesticides without toxins without immemorial elms. Without doubt. If there could be pure intention (mothering the universe) pure devotion. If pure meant more. If there could be prophylaxis, if there could be what's observed. *Pure is cure* says the Liberty Bell; *pure is protonatural*. On the front bench is the leader, the coach, the repétiteur, the Queen of Hearts, the governor, the Field Marshal, the archbishop, the producer, the bank manager, the chief, the ringmaster, the mother superior, the gold medallist. The Fool. Mr Justice. Mrs Minister.

Now we can have Question Time. Answer Time. Story Time. Book at Bedtime Time. We can have reflection, discussion, debate, research, deduction, exclusion, meditation, proposals. We can have crime versus punishment. We can have real time. We can Vote!

When were sages and soothsayers? Waverers? Truth-tellers? When was the sacred site left empty? When did the home team triumph in adversity? When did they make honest policy?

When did the walls of the temple tremble? Not I. I have not. No dreams, no regrets, no fantastic irruptions, no demented allusions. Done, now; forever done. Can time move backwards in some algebras?

The Queen of Tarts is above ammunition, erudition, emancipation. She does what someone has to do. To fulfil. To survive. In the aftermath, she sits in her counting-house. Who should fling the first stone? Who has the answers at question time?

(If you were sorry you wouldn't have.)

Done. And not done.
Done quickly and well.

Well-done.
Over-done.

The moment in the rose garden is very personal (there are no consequences) and therefore timeless (no frame of reference, no reason, no relativist preclusions.) *I'm very sorry m'Lud I don't know what came over I don't know what I could have been thinking of I don't know what could have made me I don't know why on earth, where on earth, how on earth. And m'Lud says, "You don't know much, do you?" And I say, do I have to know more—is that required? And m'Lud says, "Do you know the difference between right and wrong? Did you know at the time?" And I say, what time? whose difference? And m'Lud says, "Do not be so impertinent. Do not waste the Court's time." And I, humble, contrite, remorseful, filled with penitential ardour, say, Do to me what ought to be done to you and to all of us. And m'Lud says, "You knew what you were doing." And I say, who can ever really know that?*

Moments in rose gardens being three-a-penny (everyone has them) and judges being paid for their nine-to-five, and prophets saying there's no hope, for a long time there's been no hope, for a long time many have known there's no hope and now nearly everyone knows: the idealists, the illusionists, the gendered and engendered, the rich and the envious, the feckless, the foot soldiers, the furnace-keepers. Now the feminists know also.

Not I, says Cock Robin, not I says the Queen of Hearts, not I says the solicitor, the surgeon, the currency dealer, the curriculum adviser. We do our best. We mean what's best. The obstacles (after all) are insuperable. We are not responsible for every little maladjustment. What is not designed is necessarily chosen. People, that is, have free will. Make their choices. Chickalicken is falling in *on purpose, deliberately, with malice aforethought.* Chickalicken has *chosen* to fall in. We must therefore understand and adjudicate. Much (after all) appends. *What if everybody?*

There are many ways of deciding. But if choosing is not designed, is it random? How can moral order include randomisation? *Tell me that, m'Lud!* But m'Lud is reflecting, refusing. *"This is not"* says m'Lud, *"this is not a debating chamber! You should have thought of all that beforehand. If you were sorry you wouldn't have done it."*

How much difference does sorry make? Is sorry a proper punishment? But if I don't, is it because I can't? The design (after all) which I may have engineered, or part-engineered, or not engineered in the least?

Is sorry only a feeling? And if I can't, in the least? Cut off their heads, says the Queen of Tarts, and we all wake up. Dreams (after all) are fictitious. The priest and the judge are fictitious. Their roles, by definition, are uncontaminated by their ordinary human lives. Therefore the stone can be cast by the roles, pure and simple.

My role, therefore, is and has been responsible. No stirring of the heart has been involved. It's the best we can do, given the absence from all proceedings of the great architect, may her Name be praised!

But if you were sorry you wouldn't have! Couldn't have!

And if Chickalicken is falling in, will she become a singularity? Disappear within a massive force which turns matter into time? Will she begin the world all over again, spontaneously, without intention or design?

If you must do it—says the god to Arjuna—then do it as well as it may be done. Do it dispassionately. No —says de Sade to Marat—if you must do it, at least do it with passion. Passion is what's human. No— says Marat back—if you must do it, do it for principle. Principle is what's human. No—says Jahweh—you must do nothing at all: I will repay. No—says Sartre —whatever path you take is the only path you could have taken. You can never say if.

But if (nevertheless), before all this, my heart was a golden-oldie, trained by television to processed cheese, double-glazing, hope and faith, personal pension plans, death by disaster, package holidays— I mean the democratic consumerism of everything— this golden-oldie pumped right on when Thatcher reigned because she said, as she sent them off with ships and guns to do kill and swagger in the South Atlantic, she said "peace-with-freedom-and-justice; peace-with-freedom-and-justice". It has a certain rhythm. You can hear how it might be set by composers who still do tunes. This golden-oldie never rose up out of me to shout to all the world Enough! Enough! Enough! Too personal. Of what account? To whom power comes, let them eat cake, for ever and ever, amen.

Otherwise, heartless according to convention, there is no mystery. There is no *how could you?* I could because I did. One minute is no different from any other; it can't be.

The Liberty Bell is sunk without trace. She doesn't mind. She sings on regardless. She sings whatever takes her fancy. She has no belief in corruption since it can't touch her, hidden, helpless, happy in her watery ways where human hearts are meat and drink to any creatures who care to partake.

If I would have (if I could have (if I had imagined (if the cost had been too high) I might have) I had let it be) nothing would be changed.

Whether by whim or by strategy? Who will decide?

If it is discovered? If I accept prosecution, because they ferret out my secrets and translate them into common speech? But what is translation? Some say it's a version of an original but not the original itself; others say it's a creation of a creation; or it's a rendition of a creation; or an interpretation of a meaning; or an approximation of a meaning. That's how they run the world. It roughly means this, or it roughly means that; it can't smoothly mean what it means. So (if) they say *we know why she did it and it's unacceptable* then have they approved their translation because of whim? Or stratagem? *Was there malice aforethought?* they want to know; *did she intend it? Did she know what she was doing? Does she know the difference between right and wrong? Could she help it?* But the cry beneath, the desperate longing to know that can't be rendered in the original, approximates to *how could she? How?*

152

Done. Done. Done as can be.

(If you were sorry you wouldn't have.)

Let us suppose she did know what she was doing but isn't sorry. Then? Let us suppose she didn't know what she was doing and isn't sorry anyway. Then? Or, she thought she knew what she was doing but she was mistaken; or, she knew indeed what she was doing and is truly sorry; or, she shows no understanding of what she's done and is sometimes sorry and sometimes not. She *appears* to be sorry; but can we be sure? She suffers dreadful remorse but can't show it because of her upbringing. How can we know whether she's sorry?

How can we know whether she did or didn't know what she was doing?

Forget why. Why is irrelevant because it can't be known. Think about how. If how can be known, and she did it, then that is enough. It doesn't matter why. How is what we can deal with. How doesn't need algebra or philosophy or poetry or what the gods said once upon a time. So how is what we need to know.

If how is undiscovered, then nothing was done and everyone is free to be sorry or not sorry, according to choice, taste, conscience, convention, relationship, impact. Sorry is personal. *(All deaths are disasters. By anyone's death we are all diminished. It is yourself you grieve for.)*

Only I know. Therefore it is utterly subjective. I can be sorry with the others since sorry has a social meaning.

But did she know what she was doing? Knowing is subjective. It can't be passed on in the genes. That is why all deaths are particular disasters. *But if they find the genes for knowing?* Then one day they will know whether she knew what she was doing and whether she was sorry.

.   .   .

Things can be hard to bear when you can't talk to anyone; when you have, with your own consciousness, committed one half of reality to secrecy and sent into oblivion with Babes the Banished your capacity for intimate connection. Ria, that is, has moved instantly into the middle distance, now slightly out of focus, necessarily out of touch, out of tune. She wonders why I seem to her so solemn, so withdrawn, so preoccupied, so over-controlled. She loves me less, now. Secretly, I have to insist on that; but I tell her it's natural that way. It's been a while. People corrode each other. Everything passes. Everything changes. Tell me a story, I ask her, over and over, to break the silences. Let's pretend I'm convalescing, I tell her; be my head nurse. Soon, when she gets into gear, she tells me a story, the same story, changing it slightly each time, varying just the odd detail or the cadences. That interests me, how the meaning shifts, according to how it's told. It's only three days since the party. A lot can change in three days, even everything.

Ria says: Once, in the queentime, there was a beautiful princess, the only daughter, the heir. Her spermbanks were ready for her calculations and the noble lady knight who was her chosen consort had only one last test to complete. She must ascertain who, in all the world, could provide the future queen with the one gift she lacked. This gift could not be named since the heir, according to the Constitution, possessed all gifts. All libraries, databanks, directories and research abstracts were made available to the lady knight. She had only to reason. The princess, anxious to secure the succession, waited impatiently. After undergoing the permitted period of fasting, meditation, consultation, and the construction of theorems, the lady knight requested audience. "I remain your vassal," said the lady knight; "I remain faithful, constant, happy in your service, pure in body and mind. I offer you the gift of my absolute surrender." Whereupon she made as if to fall on her own sword. The princess angrily intervened. "That is not the right answer," she rebuked. "What help is it if all my people die?" The lady knight replied, "But die they will, all of them. You may not prevent it." The princess sighed. "Then why should I be queen? Who would want to be queen of corpses?" The lady knight smiled. "They're not dead yet," she pointed out. "They might live long enough for you to enjoy being queen." It was obvious then. "I can abdicate," said the princess. "I am the person with the gift of gifts. I can vanquish myself." The lady knight looked puzzled. "But then," she protested, "you would lose all your other gifts. Most of all, you would not have access to the spermbanks. And who would rule?" The princess stepped down from her high place, took off her ring, her robes, her miniature crown, her royal sash, and adorned the lady knight with them. "You can," she replied. "I would rather be a vassal." So it was that the lady knight became the heir. She gathered together the fairest and boldest of her knights and set them the tests whose successful completion was required of a consort. The queen all this time looked on benignly. It would all work out, she consoled herself; duty would triumph. When the lady knight who had come through the lists presented herself for the final test, the new princess slew her on the spot. "I need no more gifts," she proclaimed. "I have power enough. And I need no consort." The old queen nodded and smiled and, after a customary period of mourning, died. The able heir ascended the throne, was blessed by the spermbanks, ruled wisely and well, and explained to the people that after her death they must rule themselves. In her learned discourses she expounded the explosive new theory of the one-person State, the development of which—she argued passionately— was crucial to the future history of the world. "Proceed by contract," she instructed. "Consult first your conscience, then the past, then the future, then your fellows. Give no one power to command or condemn you. Give no one authority to shape what you should shape, or to be who you should be. Your labours are your own; so should be your rewards and punishments." After some time, there was talk of insurrection. People murmured; people were restless. How would the one-person State work? Who would control it? Who would defend it? Contracts were time-consuming, difficult to work out, open to argument and interpretation. Petitions were mounted; there was a march on the palace. "We want a new queen!" demanded the populace. "Give us a queen! It is our right!" So the queen abdicated and the crowds appointed her daughter, who ruled despotically and created much misery. "If only we'd kept the old queen," muttered the masses. "It's unconstitutional," said the intellectuals, meeting secretly at night. "She doesn't have all the gifts." And the revolutionaries planned the destruction of the spermbanks. Eventually the bad queen was assassinated by a posse of handpicked lady knights who swore to serve the people and the Constitution. The dead queen's daughter was examined for gifts and pronounced worthy. For a while things were settled enough and the people grew prosperous, but the queen became lazy, forgot to sign documents, watched old movies when she should have held audiences. "There must be an answer," wailed a solitary poet whose works were unpopular. "It must be possible to evolve a system capable of withstanding corruption." She wrote, thought, worried, meditated. She found a desert and went there to solve the problem. Sages say she never died, but can still be consulted on important questions if the seekers concentrate hard enough. She threw all she had to the bottom of the sea—bell, book, and candle—they lie there still. On quiet nights she confronts the stars, the passage of time, the secrets of pain. Her devotees worship her from afar. She sees no one. The queens, meanwhile, have retired to the background from whence they rule through puppet administrations of various kinds. It amuses them to try different combinations of ideas and systems, principles and practices, bureaucracies and Constitutions. The people are contented enough. The people are not yet ready for responsibility. While they wait for evolution, they are content to pool their resources in their common cause: the quest for the one and only, true, original, authentic queen. "We are all so ordinary," they murmur happily; "she could never be one of us. Everyone we know, everyone we have ever heard of, is so ordinary, just like us. Some seek power, some are ambitious, but that is not the mark. That is just human. The true queen will be above all that." And although they waited with all patience, with the best will in the world, the people were not idle. They invented religions, art, intergalactic networks, love, law, glory, and the speed of light. They discovered they had invented the entire universe. And those who were faithful, which was nearly everyone, through age after age, heard their hearts singing, *the true queen will come, will come, will come; the queen, the queen, the queen will come; the true, the queen, the true will come; whenever she comes, whoever she'll be, however she is, she'll come, she'll come, she'll be the true, she'll be the queen.*

I like this story nearly as much as Ria does. If you hear something often enough, you can believe it.

Although it never occurred to me before, I know now that I can't stay here. I can't make a seamless web of my life when one of the threads has been broken. I have to change the scene so I can change the scenario. It's not only because what's done is done (whether or not I'm sorry and whether or not I knew what I know); it's also because of Sybil.

So my house is in perfect symmetry, or in equipoise between the completed past and the unopened future. Sybil, necessary witness to this continuous present, sits propped in her box, which I refuse to shut, either day or night, despite her mute protests that it's impossible to sleep sitting upright with her eyes wide open. My workroom is given over to the past; there I sort files and papers, jettisoning most, packaging the rest for storage. My bedroom is given over to anticipation; suitcases are half-packed, travel company brochures lie ready for sifting. There's a lot to do. Ria makes no protest; she has never believed in personal protests. It's already end-game between Ria and me. It's come so fast and I didn't predict it, but you can adjust to anything if you have to. Ria in particular is well-adapted, abundantly adjustable. It helps that all my lusts have shut themselves up with my secret.

So far, scandal hasn't arisen. Babes has made the newspaper shorts, and I've collected all mentions I've seen. The *Guardian,* for example, says, "Feminist activist Veronica ("Babes") Veruschi, aged 52, collapsed suddenly at a private gathering on Saturday night. She was rushed to The Royal Free Hospital, Hampstead, but was pronounced dead on arrival. Friends and admirers, who were guests of celebrated novelist Gloriana Hardy, at whose house the party was held, expressed shock and dismay. Police say there appear to have been no suspicious circumstances." Mentions in *The Times* and the *Daily Telegraph* are similar, though neither uses the word "feminist". *The Times* says "well-known speaker" and the *Telegraph* says "a proponent of women's rights." The tabloids all make sure they get in the word "lesbian", and the *Sun* even has an old photo of Portland Jo, laughing her head off at some priest or other who looks angry and is pointing his finger at her. It must have been taken on a demo somewhere. The *Sun's* caption reads "Babes Veruschi's lover, Joanne K. Pocock, said to be 'devastated'" Well, maybe. I have my own reasons for thinking the photo is apposite—the *Sun* very often doesn't understand its own position. I like the *Independent's* piece best so far: it says, "Veronica Veruschi, known to her feminist following as 'Babes', was fatally stricken on Saturday night at a party given by best-selling author Gloriana Hardy, who was unavailable for comment yesterday. The feminists had recently been together at a conference in Amsterdam, though police sources say there is no evidence of any drugs abuse taking place at the party. Veronica Veruschi was known to suffer poor health, and statements made by friends at the party, although expressing shock and regret, indicate that a sudden collapse of this kind was not altogether unlikely. Results of a post-mortem conducted at The Royal Free Hospital, Hampstead, are not yet available."

Sybil won't speak to me. She hasn't said a word since I got back from the party and told her it was all over. I can't tell whether or not her silence is sympathetic. I have no way of knowing. I feel disconnected.

When Ria phoned me early Sunday morning to tell me Babes had died, I tried to sound appalled and concerned, but I must have failed. There was an edge in her voice which I mistook for nervous reaction. When I tried to be soothing, she yelled down the phone, "You've got what you want now. You've all got what you want." I remonstrated, but she said she had to go. She said she couldn't leave Gloriana on her own to deal with the police and the press, even though Gloriana was being brave and sensible and telling her to go and rest. "She's right," I butted in; "you sound as if you need to. Gloriana Hardy's perfectly capable of handling the police; and she's used to the press, after all." This was clearly more than Ria could bear. She just hung up on me, which she'd never done before. It was a serious rift, but what could I do?

"Life just goes on, Sybil," I said, patting her head. But she didn't reply. That really unnerved me. Who am I without Sybil? "We'll go to Australia," I said to her on impulse; "the history fits (attempting to jolly her out of it) and the movement there isn't so jaded (appealing to her vanity) and I'm sure they don't have their own ventriloquist act (tapping at her self-worth) and we can put all this behind us (letting my vulnerability show), so that's what we'll do." None of it worked. She stared (glared?), made not a single sound. "So sulk then," I told her; "it makes no difference. Australia's as good a place as any. We can be safe there."

I don't know how long I'll be away—whether I'm leaving for good, or just till things settle down. It isn't important. I'm dealing with practical details: making sure there's a year's mortgage arranged, putting the gas and power in Sarah's name, going through the household file with Ashok, telling the Post Office to forward my mail. It's very hard to extricate oneself from the bureaucratic spiderweb, and I have to do it systematically. I don't want some petty fraud attracting official attention to me. I'm not young enough or mad enough to run away to Brazil, or wherever else they don't have extradition treaties. I'm going to Australia, where they speak English (more or less) and where it's easy to get lost, or just become someone else. There's a good gay underground there, as well, so I can marry an Australian national if I have to.

But it's all not yet. Too much co-incidence if I don't leave it a month or so, just in case they come up with "suspicious circumstances". It fits my known profile, anyway, to buy the cheapest air fare possible, and for that I have to wait for the cheap season to start— 4th October, the airline said. Sybil won't mind, one way or the other; she's always bored by travel plans.

Ashok's left a packet of paper for me which I'm just now considering. More of his closely typed sheets, with paragraphs of newsprint pasted in every so often. His note says he's been working on this material for a couple of weeks, which in my time-scale means both BE and AA (Before the Event and After Apotheosis). In his timescale, though, it's just any old two weeks, I suppose. He writes: "Mary, a lowland gorilla, communicates with researchers through a sign language of roughly one thousand words. She can paint, draw, tell jokes, tease kittens, and recollect the past. She grieves when friends die but is uneasy referring to her own death. In addition to her thousand words of sign language, she can understand several thousand words of spoken English, though in common with other primates, is limited by her larynx from uttering them herself. Mary's prowess is recorded, along with other stories of chimpanzees, gorillas and orangutans, in The Great Ape Project, in which anthropologists and philosophers ask for apes to be treated as our moral equals. The Project's originator, an Australian professor of bioethics, argues that the mental and emotional capacities of the great apes justify their inclusion in a 'community of equals' with human beings. Because they are unable to defend their rights to life, liberty, and freedom from torture, he asks that human guardians be appointed in the same way as they are for human infants or the mentally disabled. In support, an American physiologist points out that human beings share 98.4 per cent of our DNA with chimpanzees: more than chimpanzees share with gorillas (97.7 per cent), or with orangutans (96.4 per cent). Molecular biologists calculate that our common ancestor lived some five to seven million years ago in Africa.

"Meanwhile, the US Patent Office has just accepted the hundredth transgenic animal on to its files since 'Oncomouse', the first genetically engineered bio-product to be registered. Oncomouse, developed in 1988, initially sold for $100, but improved techniques have brought the price down to a current $15. Oncomouse carries human cancer genes and can therefore mimic human cancer, guaranteeing to develop the disease within 90 days and to die soon after. Initial sales were to research laboratories and pharmaceutical companies for the testing of anti-cancer drugs, but sales to schools and colleges soon became widespread. Variations on Oncomouse have been used for some years in AIDS research, but recent commercial developments have swung away from medical investigations towards more general applications. Well-known British entrepreneur Ernie Fisher, for example, has built up an extensive trade with the former Eastern Bloc by selling genetically altered poultry on to the open market. Chickens with leg-sized wings, ducks which reach maturation only seven days from hatching (which means they can be transported as eggs and sold for meat only a week later), and miniature turkeys, have all proved extremely popular. Profit margins are high, and shares in Ernie Fisher's new export subsidiary have jumped fifty pence since the company went public last month. French geneticists, instructed by worried politicians to come up with viable alternatives for angry fishermen, are working on an 'amphifish' which will combine characteristics of tadpoles and fish. The creature will thrive in great numbers in relatively small ponds, will grow more quickly and eat less than commercially farmed trout, will have the exotic taste of frogmeat, and will be easily bred. One twenty-gallon tank or pond, it is promised, will be able to provide up to a ton of flesh a week, and there will be virtually no collateral expenses. French fishermen of the future will no longer require boats.

"A report from Kuala Lumpur seems relevant here:

A Malaysian businessman out hunting shot dead a tribesman sitting high up in a tree, mistaking him for a monkey.

Police and firemen, using ropes, took several hours to bring the man down from a tree 18m high in the Petaseh forest reserve, about 120km south of Kuala Lumpur. The businessman fired his shotgun at a figure on top of the tree on Thursday, thinking it was a monkey which his dogs had been chasing, police said.

*The trader reported the incident to the police
when he realised his mistake. They classified the
case as murder and detained him.*

"There are three relevant questions:

1. What was someone doing eighteen metres up a tree?
2. Had the dogs been genetically modified?
3. If the hunter thought he saw a monkey rather than a person, does the concept of murder apply?

"Precise answers to these questions may take some time to ascertain. There are, however, already some useful pointers. One dates from August 1990, when Sir Graham Hills, Principal and Vice-Chancellor of Strathclyde University, proposed in a letter to *The Times* that a birth-controlling chemical be added into the food chain. Because of over-population, and because violence against children indicated a large number of unwanted offspring, Sir Graham suggested that 'one essential ingredient of milled cereals should be a heat-resistant contraceptive'. Couples wanting children would follow a special diet. Legislation requiring the sexually active to eat impregnated bread before making love would have to include judicial penalties for non-compliance. A spokesman for the Police Federation dismissed the idea as unworkable at present, but admitted that a feasibility study could be undertaken if police recruitment policy were to be adequately adjusted.

"It is not impossible to imagine genetically interactive substances being similarly passed into the human food chain. It is not certain that policy decisions of this nature would be submitted to public scrutiny.

"Another pointer is discernible in discussions held periodically by food chain activists such as the pro-life Vegans, Nature Over Nurture Vegetarians, organicists, recreationists, and S/PAL (Society for the Protection of All Life). At a recent umbrella conference held in Birmingham delegates were told that a totally synthetic diet, capable of sustaining human life, would be both available and affordable within the next half-century. Complete independence from animal and plant life-forms was obviously desirable, not least because the liberation of the plant kingdom from human consumption was the most neglected issue on the bioethics agenda."

I'm flattered that Ashok shares his preoccupations with me, but it's all too much to take in just now. I've read through these three pages, but there's a whole sheaf of paper still waiting. I can't keep my mind on it. If I read it in stages . . .

Now the phone call comes—Riva, whom I've been expecting and dreading, longing for—whom I'm ready (as well) to repudiate. *Trings*, she says, tomorrow at one. I'm bang on time, but she's early, sitting with her back to the window, looking out for me. I must admit that I gape at her, openly. She wears red feathers and a business suit: pinstripe trousers, flowered waistcoat. In the left side of her nose, between nostril and bridge, sits a single diamond. The air inside is cool—and framing her is the fountain outside in the courtyard, in the background, showering all over her in perpetual motion. A talisman of grace—an infinite rejoinder.

She says (because, as I sit down, I'm still staring), "It's the gender-agenda. What do you expect?" And because she opens her mouth, and pronounces

English words, the other diners (who've also been mute and staring) resume their clatter and chat; and the waiter tends us smooth as silk. The red feathers shine and burn, glow and sputter, alive above the single candle set amid roses and a silver cruet.

"It's a contract," she says, pushing paper towards me, thick paper—tied with pink legal ribbon. "For both our sakes." I do my best to concentrate, but my disorientation is severe, and the feathers are endlessly distracting. Alienation may truly lie in the eye of the beholder, but language, surely, is adaptable and eager to serve. ". . . being agreed (I read) that identity itself is a mere idea and therefore capable of infinite variety. What can't be ceded must be superseded *quod exultate deo*. The parties agree therefore to a fixed term of non-disclosure such term to be no longer than a year and a day from the date of this Agreement hereunder witnessed . . ."

"I'm sorry (I say) but I can't—I mean, what's it about?"

"You know what it's about. Everything's changed."

"You mean Babes?"

"You've involved me. I've been a party to—well (looking around), you know to what. I never imagined you'd . . . How *could* you involve me? How can I go on as if nothing had changed?"

"I thought we were friends," I say sullenly. I hadn't bargained on Riva making all this fuss. "We've discussed it often enough. I can't believe you're surprised."

"That was just *talking*." She's obviously in quite a state. She's left her mussels *au vin blanc garni* cooling in front of her without taking a single bite.

167

She's waved the waiter away, as well, unthinkingly pouring the wine herself.

"You always told me talking was a lifeline for everyone, that words constructed reality. You can't very well turn round now and say talking isn't important."

"You're mad," she sighs. "Plausible, companionable, coherent—but insane."

"I'm no different from how I was a week ago," I respond. "If you think I'm mad now, I must have been mad then." As an afterthought, more to myself than to Riva, I say, "I don't, of course, *feel* mad. But perhaps people don't."

"It's no good trying to deal with this now," she says impatiently, taking the document and putting it away in her briefcase. "Let's finish the meal, and then—"

"Then?" I repeat, intrigued. There's never been any "then" before.

"Then I'd be grateful if you'd come with me to see someone."

"What sort of someone?" I'm suspicious. Does she mean police? Or a psychiatric consultant?

"Just a woman I know. She's been particularly on my mind since—well, since the party."

"Why?"

"Will you just agree to come?" she insists. So I do. Riva's been good to me, and I'm sorry she seems to be so upset. I haven't, anyway, got anything particular to do, apart from getting on with packing and bureaucracy.

After a frustrating hour in the car, we end up in some back part of Cricklewood, where half the street lighting is smashed and a lot of clapped out old cars sit rusting on the kerbsides. "Not quite like Hampstead," I say, sniffing a mix of stale garbage, dog shit, beer cans, and take-away curry cartons, and still trying to humour her out of her grim mood. She doesn't answer; just strides to a back gate, pushes it open, heads for an old iron staircase which zigzags right up the back of a four-storeyed brick terrace.

"There's no front door?" (I try joking.)

"Can't be seen," she snaps, puffing her way up to the top. I follow. Why not?

"Sophie," she says to me, by way of introduction, to the woman who opens at her knock. Sophie has frizzy white hair and seems to be dressed top to bottom in scarves and shawls, though her head and feet are both bare. Evidently she knows my name, since Riva doesn't bother to say who I am. We go into a dark living room and sit down. No one speaks. Not Riva's style at all, I think, looking round. The place is stuffed with Victorian bric-a-brac: tables, vases, silver-framed photographs, candlesticks, brocaded cushions, pastelled engravings in wooden frames suspended from a picture rail, china dogs, brass firetongs, a threadbare Oriental carpet. Sophie sits cross-legged on the carpet and offers us Turkish coffee in tiny glasses held in copper cups. Incongruously, next to red-feathered Riva, is a table with ice-bucket and tongs, crystal decanter and glasses, slices of lemon, and a bowl of pistachio nuts. Maybe it means we'll be here for a while.

The silence is long. We all sip, eyes down. The empty air beats its wings in rapturous freedom. Dimly the daylight falls on the faded colours. I feel strangely contented. Is there something extra in the coffee?

After a long time, Sophie says, "I love only the hidden space at the heart of things, but that I love wholly, with all my breath and bone, with the blood that sings all night in my ears, with the memories behind my eyes. I am wide open. Fear has become a mere idea." (Red-feathered Riva nods and smiles and picks at threads in the carpet. What can beckon better? What can brim bigger with fascination? Is Riva my friend—or my fate?) "Jesus and Jezebel (Sophie stares at me now) are two of a kind, out of one pod, out of one side, or womb, or home, sharing a principle, undivided. Two sides, one coin; and the battle over and done with."

Suddenly she laughs, bends forward, clinks ice into glasses, pours drinks. "Because seeing's believing," says Riva, smiling, relaxed, her mood changed full circle. There's silence again. Then, two drinks gone and safe as houses in the cushioned room, I think of creatures scratching under the eaves: in Europe, birds; in Australia, possums; in North America, squirrels perhaps, or chipmunks after rain. Natural scheme, or human dream—either way, the sounds are a comfort. Grief, when it boils down, is only a function of age, so it's reassuring that the seasons turn through scratching and nesting, scratching and foraging, scratching and dying. Night after night, all over the world, torrents of blood flow on and on as creatures murder and eat each other. Therefore will we not fear, though the earth should move and the mountains be carried into the midst of the sea.

"Seeing's believing (says Sophie, after a long time) and making's mending." She glides across the room to switch on lamps. "I'm working this evening and have to eat now." It seems we're to follow. She covers herself in a brown velvet cape and leads us to the shops nearby. We go into a curry house, sit waiting while she goes out to the back somewhere.

"Who is she?" I press Riva. "Or, more to the point, *what* is she?"

"She'd rule the waves if she could," says Riva, "such a hunger she has for moving the world around. But given the way things are, for all her push and panache, for all her pride and prejudices, she needs an alibi. You'll meet him in a minute. But to answer your question, properly answer it, I need only explain that Sophie is my Babes."

"You never told me. I had no idea that you . . ."

"You never asked," says Riva complacently. "You were so obsessed with explaining."

"But—"

"There are other ways of handling it."

"But—"

"She's a therapy autocrat. She even blackmails people."

"I don't know why—"

"What you need to know quickly, before she comes back with him, is that her alibi is The Man. She always calls him that. It's because, according to her, he has no special distinction of birth or wealth or features or accomplishments or particular neurosis, and because his name was John Brown. 'Meet The Man in my cupboard!' she'll say when she brings him out. And he'll extend his hand and smile crisply and engage us instantly in conversation. He's taller than she is, by about a head, but younger—much younger. It's more suitable, according to Sophie, given her position; and in any case, he leads his own life and travels a lot."

Sure enough, Sophie returns with a tallish young man in tow, who bows expertly and takes a seat as she says, "Meet The Man in my cupboard!" He must have met Riva before, but has such polished manners, such perfect decorum, that I feel as much part of the group as anyone could. A lot of the chat is about people and arguments I know nothing about, but I get my bearings easily enough, given The Man's practised solicitude. Various positions become clear: according to Sophie, for instance (and therefore The Man), it's vulgarly ostentatious to dine alone in public (is this where Riva learned her love of restaurant lunches? I thought it was distinctive, but perhaps all the time it was just another custom agreed within a network I didn't know about.) And, they agree, it's prudent to keep secret one's date and place of birth, and one's antecedents. Further, almost in unison they shudder at the thought of disclosing even the slightest detail of the intimacy they might (or might not?) share. "It's played out," declares Sophie, "all that voyeurism and prurience. Fashion's changing. Mystery's the new exotic: high romance, gothic intimations." I'm unconvinced, but don't want to contest her authority. It's true that fame and fortune dictate their own terms and that the price is already sky-high for whoever discloses what's forbidden. I wonder what my secret would be worth?

Afterwards, Riva drops me home but declines to come in for a drink. "Now that you've met *my* Waterloo," she jokes, "we can get on with the contract. But not tonight."

Next day I see the first obituary. They're late because the press can't have had anything on file. This one's signed by someone called Alwyn Sullivan —must be American, surely—I've never heard of her (him?) and nor has Ria, who's just phoned. It's quite short: printed at the edge of a senior diplomat (male, knighted, two marriages) and partly above a patrician philanthropist (bachelor, Eton and Oxford, various gongs, various directorships). Even the *Guardian* can't avoid getting its priorities right. Maybe "Alwyn Sullivan" is a pseudonym . . . anyway, she (he?) writes: "Veronica Veruschi, born in Somerville, Mass., declined both Vassar and Bryn Mawr, instead heading for UCLA in the radical sixties. There she used her considerable organisational skills to make her mark as an activist in the major civil rights and anti-Vietnam war campaigns. She married Robert A. Shaffner, a junior social sciences professor who later became one of Bell Telephone's executive vice presidents. After divorcing in 1969, she moved to Billings, Montana, where she set up one of the first rape counselling centres in the United States. Following the failure of a second marriage (to country and western singer Jake Dukes), she came to London as a co-ordinator for Experimental Programs, an organisation specialising in short-term and exchange placements for American college students.

Known to everyone, whether friend or foe, as 'Babes', Veronica Veruschi set about establishing the new American feminism in London. This she did almost single-handedly: she set up the first women-only news centre, the first rape phoneline, the first regular women-only cabaret, the first large women's rights march—a spectacular event which moved a phalanx of fifty thousand women from the Embankment to Hyde Park to the accompaniment of dozens of women-only bands, and which initiated passionate exchanges in the national press. For the next two decades, 'Babes' used her charismatic powers on platforms up and down the country, and on every radio and television programme interested in controversy and debate.

All sympathisers of the feminist cause will regret her untimely death and will feel keenly the loss of her brilliant leadership. If ever 'New Wave' feminists are to receive official respect in this country, her name will head the roll of honour."

I have to grin as I file this peculiar piece. It manages to avoid the L word altogether, which of course would alter any ordinary reader's perspective. Dear "Alwyn" wants us to remember Babes as a cross between Joan of Arc and Good Queen Bess. She'd have liked that, of course. She might herself have written just such a piece. It occurs to me that maybe she did write it herself; and someone from her deep American past would be able to decode the pseudonym. Maybe someone found it waiting in her papers and sent it off to the *Guardian*.

When Ria phones, I mention this thought to her, but she brushes it aside. She's angry with me, obviously; much more angry than she's ever been, icily angry, constrained, deliberately diffident. What can I have done? Well, I know what I've *done*, but she doesn't know that. Or, if she does know, how did she work it out? She says we have to meet and talk, but in a bar; she won't visit, or let me visit. No sex, in other words. It's a measure of my fall from grace

—she's not to know, since I haven't told her, that all such desires are beyond my volition.

Sitting in the bar she looks haggard and throws down two whiskys before saying anything apart from hullo-how-are-you. Then, in that same icy tone, she says, "I think someone murdered Babes and I know who."

I'm startled, despite this being half-expected. But I manage to be cautious, say, "Whatever makes you think that?"

"It's Gloriana." Now I'm genuinely astonished, stare at her, while flashing across the back of my mind comes a bottle of green fizz with a bright green label and Gloriana Hardy chirping, "Look what I've got, just for Babes." But Ria doesn't wait for my imaginings—she's letting it out now, all in a rush, a gush, an overflow of torment and speculation.

"She's so strange, ever since. I know she can get obsessed with herself—we all have our weaknesses —I know she can be insensitive and obtuse sometimes —I've known her for years—I know her better than anyone—and she knows that I know her, inside out —what can I do about it? I can't just let it pass—what do you think? She keeps humming all the time— Gloriana *never* hums—it's not her style—and she's been *cooking*. I mean, she never cooks! What does she need to cook for? We always eat out, unless it's for something special. She hasn't been near her workroom since the party—I mean, a day never passes without her doing her stint at her manuscripts, you know that—she's turning into someone I don't know —I mean dramatically—and she's so *pleased* about Babes being dead! She's trying to hide it, but I know!

She's happy, happy, happy—humming and singing —won't call Polly back—and Polly's just frantic—they speak two or three times a day normally—I can't do anything. Polly keeps phoning me about all these deals but what do I know? She hated Babes. No one knew how much, except me."

"Stop," I tell her. "You're getting hysterical and this isn't the place. Let's go home. I won't pester you, I promise. Just come back and be private and let's talk it out. I'm sure you're wrong," (I can be confident about that)—"I'm sure it's just shock or trauma or something."

She glares at me. "Don't patronise me," she enjoins. "Don't bloody patronise me! I'm not an idiot. And whatever you think about Gloriana, she's very impor- tant to me. I really care about her."

"I know, I know," I say, trying to be soothing and patting her hand. It looks bony, helpless, weak against her glass. It never looked like that before.

"And I want to talk *here*," she insists. "If I'd wanted to come over, I'd have said so."

"All right, it's okay," I say, still in soothing mode. I hope it will be all right. Lord knows who's listening.

"It isn't in her character," Ria persists, "to go in for shock and trauma and all that. She doesn't care about people like that. And I tell you, she absolutely hated Babes."

"Why?" I blurt. I can't help it. I'm intrigued. I've always wanted to know what Gloriana Hardy's secret was.

"It doesn't matter now she's dead, I suppose," says Ria. "She was blackmailing Gloriana. That's how she got the collateral for the Databasics loan."

"How? What on earth could threaten Gloriana Hardy?"

"Babes knew that she'd slept with that American publisher to get on that experimental mass market print-run list they were setting up. It was a mega-deal at the time."

"So what?" I'm disappointed. "Gloriana Hardy's slept with all sorts of agents and editors."

"But this one was a man." Ria sighs and sips at her third whisky. I see her point. All Gloriana Hardy's lesbian credentials exploded in one go: out, bang, pop, fizz . . . just another mimsy on the casting couch like all the others—credibility gone, cover blown, a naked empress shivering in the stare and glare of nudge-and-wink cameramen and snide interviewers, not to mention angry howls from mobs of fans, and jibes from lookers-on and also-rans. I quite see why Gloriana Hardy would want the lid kept shut tight on that particular step up the ladder.

"But what could Babes have done? Surely no one would believe it. All Gloriana Hardy had to do was deny it. Babes would be the one to lose face."

"Babes had paperwork," says Ria grimly.

"What?"

"Letters. The bastard sold them to her, ages ago—for a favour. Babes told Gloriana all about it—she had to, to make sure Gloriana would play ball."

"But how—"

"He sought Babes out at the ABA five years ago. Took her for a drink, told her what he wanted, showed her the packet of letters he'd kept."

"So what did he want?"

"Ten per cent."

"Ten per cent of what?"

"Gloriana's royalties. Said it was only fair, that he'd been the one to make it all possible, and so on."

"Why didn't he put the screws on himself? Why involve Babes?"

Ria looks at me with scornful patience. "God, you can be dumb!! If *he'd* tried it, Gloriana could easily have faced him out, said they were forged, accused him back—everyone would have believed her. Men are the enemy, aren't they? Would try anything, wouldn't they? Can't be believed or trusted, can they? If *he'd* tried it, he'd have got nowhere, which he knew. Men might be the enemy, but they're not all fools. Babes, on the other hand—that's a different kettle of fish altogether. Being denounced by a sister! Babes waving letters around—no one would disbelieve Babes! Gloriana wouldn't get away with saying *Babes* had forged them. Why would she? Babes made her mark by saying we all belong together, we must stick together, we're all sisters—"

I interrupt. "But doesn't that mean she'd never do it? How could she keep the faith if she destroyed everyone's favourite hero-writer?"

"She'd find a way," Ria says. That was true. Babes had always found a way to get what she wanted and needed without wrecking her image. I could see how Gloriana Hardy would have felt trapped. She was high on expedience—probably as high as anyone could be—and strong on defiance, aggression, insistence, confrontation, bravado. But relationships were her weak point. The prospect of beavering away in little groups of concerned sisters to woo and flatter and get them on side in some covert power struggle with Babes—no, that wasn't her style, and never could have been. She was too bored by people to take enough trouble. She'd never be able to outmanoeuvre Babes in a war of attrition behind the public battle-lines. Better and easier to pay up. Anyway, she could afford it.

Now, close by, in loud clear peals, I hear the Liberty Bell. Ria has her head back, eyes locked in a fixed stare at the Edwardian décor: intricate panelling, stencilled mirrors, faded etchings of horses and hounds. Does she also hear it? Glad, solemn, deep, entrancing—muffling the sea, drowning out the suck and slap of foam on sand. *Knowledge, beauty, truth, security, power, purity*, it sings. *No connection. No connection.* I can hear everything. Sun to starlight, on and on, round and round, *no connection.* Who can know the depths of desire? The ice in our glasses has long melted. Ria, for the first time, reaches for my hand.

"These letters—who's going to get hold of them now?"

"Gloriana's got them. She told me. She went straight round to Babes' place after collecting sobbing Myrtle from the hospital. It was Myrtle who phoned to say Babes had died, so Gloriana was straightaway into the car and off to rescue Myrtle. She said Jade would deal with all the sensible things so someone should take care of Myrtle. Not like Gloriana to be quite so concerned about a poor creature like Myrtle. I realised afterwards that because Myrtle was camping on Babes' sofa, it meant Gloriana had instant access."

"She must have known where to look."

"Everyone knows Babes files—filed—everything.

Even you and I knew that." She looks at me accusingly.

"And ever since she came back and danced round the kitchen clutching a packet, yelling out, "I've got them, I've got them," she's been doing this awful humming."

"But none of that means she killed anyone," I reason.

"The thing is—there was that bottle of organic something she bought for the party. She told me it was for Babes but I didn't take any notice with all the preparations going on."

"So?"

"So I can't find the bloody thing. I've looked everywhere."

"Flimsy evidence," I say gently. "Pure speculation. You're just upset. And Gloriana Hardy's been winding you up on account of these letters."

Ria sighs. "I knew you wouldn't understand. You're so peculiar lately. We used to see eye to eye about everything."

"I'm trying to be sensible. The police wouldn't take any notice—"

"I'm not interested in the police. Why do you think this has anything to do with the police?"

"What does it matter then?" I ask her. Sincerely. Aren't we all glad Babes is no longer with us?

"God, you're impossible," she says, getting up to leave. I follow her out, say, "What about the post-mortem? That would clarify things."

"They have to do tests or something," she says vaguely. "Jade told me yesterday that they won't release the body for at least another week."

"Unusual, isn't it?"

"Apparently not. Public service cuts and all that. Ask Jade, if you want to know."

"I thought *you* wanted to know!"

"I want to know about Gloriana," she says, angry now. "I thought you'd understand that."

So we part, with no firm plan for next time. I feel both elated and depressed. I didn't bargain on losing Ria altogether, but I think that's inevitable now.

But what if it's true? What if I didn't do it at all?

Sarah is nearly done reorganising the kitchen. Since my room will be free, she's decided to make it into a living room so she can have the present living room for more plants. They've decided to start hydroponic herbs for some difficult things that won't grow thick and fast enough in pots. I like looking at all the glass and water—it's fresh and unreal at the same time. The whole place smells green. Will they stay here for ever? Suddenly I feel very fond of them both. I should pay more attention to what Ashok tells me. I haven't bothered to finish reading what he gave me, let alone writing some comments for him. Not that he seems to mind—he never sulks, is never short-tempered. But he must have feelings, nevertheless. I should be more sensitive.

Upstairs I take out his sheets and start reading again. After everything about the new transgenic creatures, he's pasted an extract from some journal, and then added a note. The newsprint reads, "Estimates are being revised of the amount of energy released when a comet struck the planet Jupiter in late July, 1994. The original estimate of thousands of millions of tonnes of TNT, greater than the impact on earth some sixty-five millions of years ago, which is thought to have ended the reign of the dinosaurs, is now understood to have been extremely conservative.

"As the impact took place on the dark side of the planet, the spectacular conflagration was not visible. It is expected, however, that debris from the massive explosion will form a ring around the planet greater than the Saturnian ring. The number of new moons created may well exceed two hundred. Arthur C. Clarke is reported to have said that the collision will prove to have been the most important event in human history.

"Major changes in the earth's climates are envisaged, including the radical possibility that the climatic zones themselves may shift northwards. Meteorological physicists are currently debating which of their existing models is likely to have most predictive efficiency, given the prevailing disagreements about the 'greenhouse effect'." Ashok's note, added in handwriting, says, "Are transgenic mutations now—as they always were hitherto—simply part of the after-shock effect of cosmological events? Human consciousness has never been demonstrated to be separable from the molecular activities taking place within human brains. How could it, since human brains exist inside the universe and not outside it?"

Does this mean I killed Babes because a comet hit Jupiter? Or does it mean that I only think I killed her? (Meaning, because of changes in the molecular activity inside my brain, really the impact of the comet killed her?) Maybe it could be argued, from this basis, that she really killed herself. On the other hand, back in the inaccurate and illusioning 'real' world, it looks as if I may not have killed Babes anyway. Maybe Gloriana Hardy killed her. What could she have put into the green fizz?

What if it's the case that we *both* killed her? Would that mean we each performed only half a murder?

Sybil still won't say anything, though I know she's sentient. Her eyes are never wide open like that unless she's thinking and processing. And I know she's not working on a dialogue, either. Her eyebrows are always right up when she's busy with that. Nor is she asleep. I won't let her. I won't lie her down until I'm ready to leave. Unless she asks me to, of course. I wouldn't make her sit up with me through all this if she'd talk to me. It's true she's never been terribly interested in Ashok's offerings, given that (from her point of view) she knew all about all those subjects already; more than he knows, she once told me— more than he will ever know. In the beginning, I found it hard to tell when Sybil was just being dismissive and showing off, and when the claims she made were true. Now, though, I'm almost always quite sure about what mood she's in. It doesn't matter all that much if we don't work on the new routines until we get to Australia. We'll have at least four months before the tour starts, given the way the seasons there are different. It's purely personal, I suppose, right now; I'd be easier in my mind if she'd open up now. Not just sit there thinking Lord knows what.

For the next three days nothing much happens; the phone is silent—no Ria, no Riva, no news. I think it isn't wise to draw attention to myself by seeking anyone out. There are four more obits about Babes, and of course a rushed newsletter stuffed with emotional outbursts of loss, regret, sorrow, and so on. The groupies outdo anything a professional writer of panegyric might invent—there's no substitute, in the end, for raw emotion. Then, before we've even had breakfast, AllyPally arrives. She's quite flustered and weighed down with shopping bags. "Glad I caught you in," she pants, saying yes to everything Sarah offers from the kitchen. "Came straight round, except I had to do the supermarket on the way. Bloody Myrtle's had the car non-stop for the last week, going back and forth to Databasics, the hospital, the library, various meetings. I got up early this morning and nicked it before she emerged. She's so caught up in all this business about Babes that she doesn't stop for a minute to wonder how I'm to put food on the table without a car."

"Why don't you let her feed herself?" I ask.

"You must be joking!" barks AllyPally, clearly at the end of her tether. "She's half off her head. You wouldn't believe what it's been like. Weeping and wailing half the night, moping and moaning half the day—I'm absolutely exhausted. I don't know whether I want to sleep for a week or shout for two hours without stopping and then pass out."

"Can't she stay somewhere else?" I ask.

"You don't know what it's like," she responds, calming down now that there's food and coffee. "Anyway, have you heard?"

"What?"

"About the post-mortem."

"What about it?"

"There has to be an inquest. Apparently Babes had

184

all sorts of strange things inside her—Myrtle pestered some junior in the pathology department but didn't understand—of course—what he told her, except that there were things they can't explain properly."

"Really? What things."

"Oh God—I don't know—ask bloody Myrtle. I can't get any sense out of her. She raged round the house last night like a lunatic till three in the morning, and then, when I saw her at breakfast, had done a complete change of personality. I can't work the woman out. All I know is I need a rest from her. She's overwhelming, honestly."

"Why don't you phone in sick today," I suggest. "Stay here. Go to sleep in my bed. I won't tell anyone you're here."

"And Annie and Sal have been cooped up with Portland Jo for the last several days," she rushes on. "Won't answer the doorbell, won't answer the phone. They've had the answer machine on almost ever since the party."

"So?"

"So what's going on? I *hate* not knowing what's going on." I watch her eat and drink, greedily, looking first angry, then thoughtful, then puzzled, then frustrated. It's true. AllyPally's always hated not knowing what was going on. In the end, she acquiesces about staying over. Sarah will take care of her. Since Flo took off suddenly with some vapid youth she met busking, Sarah's seemed a bit lonely, though she never says so. Ashok hasn't yet taken up all the slack left by Flo, having established a library routine to get out from under while they did all the food things. Not that AllyPally will stick around long, of course—unless she realises it might make it easier to get rid of Myrtle.

In the early evening Ria phones. She wants to come round. "AllyPally's here, though," I explain. "She's been asleep all day. Couldn't cope with Myrtle any longer."

"Oh," says Ria. "I don't specially want to talk in front of AllyPally. You know what she's like. And you can't come here."

"Why not?"

"It's Gloriana," she says impatiently. "I told you all that."

"Still humming?" I tease. Unusually, she bangs down the phone. Now I don't know whether she's coming round or not. But it must be about the inquest. AllyPally, wakened by the phone ringing, emerges energised. "We have to call a meeting," she announces. Back to her old self, I notice. Didn't take long. Amazing how a bit of food and coffee and a good sleep moves mountains. "Here," she continues. "With any luck, Myrtle won't hear about it."

"Don't fancy your chances on that score," I say. "I'd rather it wasn't here."

"Don't be difficult, Tessa. It's much better here. Sarah won't mind. I'll ask her, if you don't want to. She likes cooking for a lot of people."

"Do you mean a *party*?" I ask sarcastically.

"You can be very belligerent sometimes," she counters. "I mean snacks and things. Sarah's terrific at all that."

"She is," I sigh. "Go and ask her then." It isn't such a bad idea. I'd quite like to know what Portland Jo and Annie and Sal have been up to. Sarah, as predicted, says she's happy to provide. We give it three days, so we can do a mailout. Should we ask Riva or not? I can't decide.

Peculiarly, as if on cue, the doorbell rings and it's Riva, who's never before crossed my threshhold. "Dinner," she whispers. "I'll wait out here. Don't take too long." Too astonished to argue, I grab jacket and bag and tell Sarah. "Can I join in?" asks AllyPally eagerly. I manage to put her off by asking her to phone Ria for me about the meeting.

Waiting in *Après Paris* are Sophie and The Man. I'm underdressed, flustered, not to mention anxious. "I can't afford . . ." I nudge Riva, but she interrupts. "On me," she says firmly. "I need you." I'm handed a menu without prices and give way to luxury. The others chat, are polite, take little notice of me. The Man and I sit opposite, as do Riva and Sophie. *Hors d'oeuvres* are nibbled, wine is poured—then, looking sideways, I see something extraordinary. She puts her hand on his leg. Riva, smiling, chatting to Sophie, puts her hand carefully, fully, frankly, on his left leg. Her fingertips (I imagine) press down past the faintly furred, subtly woven wool into the lax muscle of the inner thigh. She puts her perfect hand on his iron leg. They share a corner, backs to the wall. In front is a squat-legged rectangular table, empty of diners but fully dressed, tall modern candles dripping, and a pair of flesh-coloured carnations ripe in their vase.

He smokes, between courses, the second half of a miniature cigar. She puts her hand on his leg. From downwind comes the flare of *crêpes suzette*. The waxed waiter folds and smoothes, scoops and lifts, treads on air as he pushes away the noiseless trolley.

Soon he ushers a fresh pair of people to the empty table. The woman is waspwaisted and seems to have diamonds in her hair; the man has a head of silver and is dressed to kill; his studs and tie-pin flash and dazzle. The waiter stands aside, almost clicks his heels. The glasses glow as he pours. To the right are a matching pair, expertly coiffed, swathed in brocade of some kind, extravagantly beringed. Their bosoms rise and fall within an inch of the cutlery. The waiter is respectful, patient, helpful when asked. They've been here before, need to try something different. He clenches his baby bottom from habit.

Riva's hand rests still on his leg. The Man, who is teasing Sophie, asks me about Babes, lifting his eyebrow at the waiter. Quite alone to the left sits a priest, young and small, fingering claret, expecting (I imagine) beef he can see through. He seems to need to think something new, to think things he hasn't yet dreamed of, though he probably thinks of the usual things. His face has the professional vacancy it's been trained for. He needs no waiter—he knows the routine.

She keeps her hand gracefully on his leg, feels through the cloth the beginning of tension, the winding of rope, the pull of the bowstring. Her fingers are slightly splayed. The heel of her hand pushes bluntly against his flank. The waiter comes delicately, seeing the low hand lying. Riva, it's clear now, has been here often, gestures towards Sophie, says to the waiter, "My friend the Ambassador's daughter has changed her name to Sophie so she can meld better," and Sophie—as if all remarks were innocent, and in a voice as well-trimmed as her pale mauve off-the-shoulders huggery—says generally, "Sophia for wisdom, you know." The waiter withdraws bottom first, with the hint of a bow, since she's managed not to look at him at all. "I can't think why you say meld," she says to Riva, "rather than mix. Or blend. Or even fade."

I can't see, of course, whether Sophie has a hand on his other leg. The Man, for an instant, stares at the rise and fall of the bosoms at the table in front of him. I can't see them myself, but I feel what he's looking at, being much-practised. Riva is telling how Sophie used to bring her here, talk about her lovers and her servants, about balls and receptions, about how it was once.

The priest is pleased with his beef. He wants to pick it up in his fingers and wipe each slice across his upper lip, wants to hold each morsel thin on his tongue while the claret passes over it, wants to stand up, display each piece with triumph, slowly, a magician with a scarf plucked now into existence.

She presses his thigh back and forth. Back and forth. Where is the line between need and greed? With her spare hand, she proposes a toast. The waiter finds no one to his taste, thinks of his tips, of the clubs to go on to after. Sophie leans sideways, kisses The Man with wet lips, hard on his earlobe, again on his neck where the pulse must be.

Riva produces her contract over coffee. We must all sign, she announces. We are all witnesses. No one will disclose whatever we've shared, not ever, not to anyone. I sign. I have a lot to lose.

Back in my doorway, as we say goodnight, Riva gives me a folder. Inside, the others are all in bed.

Despite its obvious length, I make Sybil listen while I read out loud what's in the folder. It's headed *Case Study* and is tied with pink legal ribbon:

"1. *Method of Referral.* T. is part of the women's movement network spread through inner North London. We met via shared acquaintances and our sessions have been and remain a socially constructed contract. She is an ongoing client.

2. *Short History.* T. is a 45-year-old lesbian woman estranged from close blood relatives. Her father died some twenty years ago, and her mother five years ago. She was an only child, though a younger boy cousin was brought up in the household, having been abandoned as a baby by T.'s mother's sister. Although he was like a brother to T., she has not maintained contact since leaving the family home in a small village in Oxfordshire to work in London at the age of twenty. T. describes her childhood as happy, but she will only talk about childhood experiences when severely pressed, and never volunteers any material from that time.

Recently T. has felt overwhelmed by a series of problems, including mid-life crisis and ambivalence about her work life. These problems have been exacerbated by feelings of loss and distress caused by conflicts acted out within women's movement circles. She rejects imputations that she might be suffering from stress-related hypertension, and is hostile to alternative treatments such as homeopathy, naturopathy or changes in diet. Two years ago her GP prescribed diazepam to regulate symptoms of high blood pressure.

T. works in the entertainment industry as a ventriloquist and is quite interested in setting up a workshop system for training other women ventriloquists, though she explains that she can't begin this scheme until she has agreement from her partner, S., who is at present reluctant to extend their partnership beyond performing.

T. has a lover, R., who lives separately and who is hostile, like T. herself, to psychotherapeutic models, particularly psychoanalytic theories of all kinds, psychosynthesis, and transpersonal psychology. T. shares her home with Sa., a young female cook and herbalist, and A., an unemployed young male undertaking independent research.

3. Description of Client

a) Physical Appearance and Body Language

T. is of average height and weight, is olive-skinned, and has dark brown hair and eyes. She is indifferent to her appearance, wears dull colours and little jewellery, no make-up, and loose clothing. Her movements, however, are graceful and elegant, and she gives the impression of being well-controlled and systematic. Her gaze is straightforward and her energy appears well-distributed throughout her whole body, though she has obviously consciously developed this effect in order to appear relaxed and engaging on stage. She is able to sit still for long periods, and exhibits many introvert traits, despite the demands of her profession. Her voice is pleasingly low-pitched and unaccented.

b) Psychodynamic Process

T.'s inner psychic world exists very much in the present and is unusually self-referential and anarchic.

She resists any interest in her personal past and is dedicated to 'cleaning' the future. She deals easily with everyday tasks such as housekeeping, personal finances, and so on.

c) Cognitive Process

T. is both a systematic and obsessional thinker. She is neither impulsive nor imperceptive, but relies on conceptual rather than affective patterning to organise her experiences. She has a rich, if abstract, vocabulary and is fluent in conversation. Her written language is annotative rather than descriptive. T.'s sense of humour is more linguistically based than is usual; to the comic social situations of everyday life she responds analytically, almost as an observer; participation is careful and guarded.

4. Initial Presentation

a) Reason for Therapeutic Engagement

T. was suffering from feelings of frustration and inadequacy following news of a friend's suicide by drowning at sea. She was also ambivalent about various feminist orthodoxies. These conflicts coalesced into morbid preoccupations with death: specifically, with different ways of dying. One outcome has been the deconstruction of the super-ego.

b) Underlying Reasons for Engagement: My Interpretation

T. is fending off isolation. She seeks support and a confidante: someone to have lunch with, talk things over with, use as a sanity test. Recognising this, I refrained from answering direct questions wherever possible. T. wants to be in control and suffers from a lack of trust. She needs to feel superior and to have endorsement that she knows best. Her desire to be mothered hardly emerged, since that is acted out in her relationship with R., who offers an indulgent interest in T.'s preoccupations, without delving into any significant detail. R. is in turn mothered by G.H., a successful writer, with whom R. previously had a sexual involvement but who has become a stable protectress. R. does not need, therefore, to be mothered by T., who would be unable, in my view, to respond to the more primitive needs of any intimate.

T. insists on controlling boundaries, so that all our sessions have begun and ended according to her timing rather than mine. Her dominant role is pedagogic. She eschews any attempts I make to draw out her more childish aspects.

5. *The Therapeutic Process*

a) *Interpretations*

I have suggested connections between T.'s preoccupations with death and dying, and her feelings of despair and loss associated with the souring of important relationships. These connections are theoretically demonstrable with respect to incidents and narratives about her childhood experiences: her cousin/'brother' was an intruder, her mother's attention was divided, her father was remote and alienating, her village surroundings were workaday and spiritless. Despite my endeavours to help T. face these long-repressed feelings, she has so far made no substantive connections.

b) *Transference*

I have become T.'s 'alter ego': the fantasy sibling/ companion invented by imaginative lonely children who fail to find satisfactory reinforcement and recognition from the peer group. This is also a countertransference issue for me, given my own preoccupations with the moral energy of revenge. She envies my bank account: I envy her intense argumentativeness. We have, in turn, idealised each other: she has seen me as a cool manipulator, able to rise above the turbulence of naive emotion; I have seen her as a fiery gallant, able to dare everything for the sake of principle. Her admiring comments about my clothes, hairstyle, earrings, and other aspects of my appearance, have been the dominant vehicle for her feelings of warmth and approval, though she has, too, expressed appreciation for my 'trained palate'.

T. has a strong need to transfer onto me feelings of inadequacy and isolation, though there have been no attempts at seduction. A special issue has been "testing for limits" to secure the extent of my commitment.

c) Countertransference

As sessions progressed, I felt increasingly uncomfortable about not disclosing my own morbidity. I realised I had to deal with this issue in order to be properly available for her, particularly following a radical instance of acting out, when T. resolved her conflicts by planning a successful separation from the principal focus of her feelings of frustration. Consequently, I arranged for her to meet So. and T.M., entanglements with both of whom have been the locus of my own conflicts since moving to London. To protect the disclosures we have each now made to the other, I drew up contracts for signing. T. has so far failed to respond to my request for her signature.

She clearly feels harshly treated but has not yet threatened to terminate our sessions. I am anxious to avoid provoking an unsupervised eruption into consciousness of latent paranoia.

I have learned with this client to listen accurately and precisely, which in turn has made me realise how much pressure I have within me to 'get the right answer'. I now know, better than ever before, that there are no 'right answers'. I enjoy the moments of idealisation T. gives me and have become alert to them, so that they do not grow into situations of invasiveness or manipulation.

d) Theory

It seems that T.'s experiences of deprivation must have happened in early infancy (Klein: good and bad breast). She has a bad, internalised mother and an absent internalised father. Paranoid traits are latent: her eyes focus straightforwardly and she has no difficulty in maintaining eye contact. Her posture, however, is rarely relaxed; she remains braced in defence against the enemy. Her need for resolution is intense (Freud: pleasure/pain principles).

I have had to proceed relatively slowly with my interpretations of this client's transference, because although I believe my views to be correct, the client is not always ready to hear and receive them. I have found reading up on similar cases very helpful in this regard.

6. The Outcome

The most important component in my work with T. has been to demonstrate my commitment and reliability, so that she could develop enough trust to enact the resolution of her conflict. This has been very hard for her, because she has had to cope with resistance from her partner S., and with a lack of specificity of interest from her lover R. We have not yet managed to explore the history of her need for control, though I have tried recently to bring that subject within our shared frame of reference. Given the social nature of our sessions this has not been easy, since the timetabling of sessions shares parameters with external reality.

Sometimes I think that the work we have been doing is prototherapeutic in its effects, given the sophistication of T.'s defence system and the high-level capability of her resistance. I am aware of the nature and extent of my collusions, and am genuinely concerned that the quality of her inner life should improve. Her need for an empathetic listener has moved easily into projections of the 'good mother' in the transference relationship.

7. *Form of Completion*

The therapeutic relationship has developed steadily from the beginning and has shown no disruptive patterns. T. is an ongoing client. Working with her is very helpful for me and my own processes; I can often see projective identification taking place and I do not feel threatened in the transference relationship. It has been relatively easy to resist manipulations designed to make me into a responsible and worrying mother, since I know from my own material that I could find my identity solely in looking after others, thus neglecting my own needy inner child. It may be, therefore, that significant re-parenting and reparation has taken place."

Sybil stares. She moves her mouth but I can't hear anything. She's mocking me—she must be. I can hear the hinges of her jaws: clack, clack. I won't let her provoke me, no matter how hard she tries. "Well, what do you think?" I say, taking no notice. She rolls her eyes. She pushes her eyebrows right up under her hairline. She turns her head slowly, from side to side. But I hear no words, not a single one. "I didn't realise (I decide to chatter anyway) that Riva was formalising everything. That sort of profession, I suppose. An obsessional need for self-justification. Or compulsive record-keeping. Or maybe she injects herself with aggrandisement every half year, to keep her spirits up. It must be draining, listening to people's lives all the time. The question is—what am I supposed to do with it? It's not exactly suitable for a CV, though it might count for documentation—you never know—for Australian officialdom. They might want evidence of mental health."

Sybil keeps staring. Then she does something I've never seen her do before. Slowly, deliberately, she pokes out her tongue, and leaves it there, flat and drooping. I feel uneasy, a bit frightened. She looks idiotic.

.   .   .

Myrtle, to everyone's amazement, chairs the meeting without discussion or argument. She's got a sheaf of paper and just takes command. Not a tear in sight, either; she's composed and forthright. The rest of us are subdued; Gloriana Hardy looks distracted and has none of her usual flamboyance, Ria keeps passing cups and plates, AllyPally says she's going to take minutes, Jade sits alone, stern and silent. Portland Jo is most changed: she looks shrunken and stooped and drapes herself alternately across Annie, across Sal. Myrtle doesn't bother with agendas or preliminaries —she starts straight in.

"Like the rest of us (she looks round), I've been trying to make sense of what happened to Babes— trying to process it, absorb it. I've always been blessed —or cursed, in this instance—with a memory for detail, especially the visual detail of people and situations. My feelings, as you're all aware, are much less clear and considerably less reliable. So what I want to tell you is a jigsaw of details, not feelings."

Portland Jo groans and looks as if she might start sobbing, but is hushed by Annie and Sal. Jade flicks impatiently at some speck on the trouserleg of her left knee, says, "What details? What are you talking about? Get on with it." Myrtle straightens her notes, looks reprovingly at Jade, then suddenly smiles, dazzlingly, at AllyPally. For the first time since the party, I feel afraid. None of us has ever seen Myrtle smile—and what a smile! Her whole face lifts and sparkles, offers generosity, wit, warmth, abundance. The atmosphere changes. Everything changes.

"Let me propose (Myrtle woos) a scenario: an imagined possibility, an enacted explanation. And what I'll propose, let's agree, remains in the subjunctive, a personal opinion, a story, a conjecture."

Now we're all audience, relaxed and expectant, hooked on the promise of pleasure, illusion, intrigue, entertainment.

"A party will be held (Myrtle has us now, can play with us any way she likes). There will be noise and confusion, a crowd, and multiple diversions. Suppose, however, that a number of guests—three, let's say—have decided this party will be the perfect occasion for a murder. (No one speaks, or even moves.) Let's suppose, as well, that each of these three women will act independently, not knowing what is planned by either of the others. But in spite of their uniqueness, their individual differences, the method they choose is the same—poison, the woman's weapon, no blood, no fuss.

And suppose, further, that their victim makes the task easy. The victim, that is, has foibles about food, theories about diet, a well-known list of exclusions and rejections. She has set herself up, this victim, for special treatment. In addition, precisely because of this strict régime, this disciplined path, she is vulnerable to pleasure and attentiveness. Poor victim! What could be easier than to tempt her with some specially prepared delicacy, some unusually careful mixture, some thoughtful combination of permitted ingredients. An exotic recipe is almost demanded by such an abstemious victim. Oh yes, thinks each murderous protagonist: she—even she—is not above sensation, is not beyond attention, is not so devoted to denial that she will resist something singular and delicious for the sake of principle. *Take, eat* is all that is necessary; *drink this* is all that's required.

I saw, for example, and can see clearly now, a bottle with a bright green label, unopened, inviting, full of something fresh-looking, bubbling, clear. Think of this bottle. The design on its label is unfamiliar, unique, distinctively designed. The effect, I mean, is midway between commercial and homespun. The label is important: it must not look too hobbyish, too done-on-the-kitchen-table. On the other hand, it cannot look professional, since the victim would refuse anything marketed for mass consumption, given the intricate list of additives she is not permitted. The label, therefore, will neither be hand-written nor bulk-printed, but it will be computer-generated and run off on a laser printer. I can recognise that sort of design, since I use the software myself; and the colours produced by a laser printer are clearer than one is used to.

Remembering the label, I looked for another such bottle in the past few days. I looked in health shops and organic wholesalers. I looked particularly in the places where the victim bought her range of supplies. It's possible, I concede, that a batch of similar bottles with that distinctive label is on sale somewhere—possible, but improbable. Much more probable is that the bottle at the party was the one and only such bottle that ever existed. Naturally it has disappeared. The label lives on only as a memory.

But what does the bottle contain? When it's opened and offered, when just the one glass is poured, fizzing, inviting, in front of the victim's grateful eyes, then handed to her personally, decorously, gallantly, with a friendly grin—what is it that's been secretly concocted? Let's suppose something simple, that needs no arcane equipment, no peculiar processes: something as ordinary as boiling and straining, cooling and pouring, and deftly sealing. Yew, for instance, will do very well. The needles of yew can be stewed and brewed. I looked it up: *taxus baccata,* English yew, hardly unusual, and common in churchyards, whose poison is taxine, definitely fatal. A simple kit can carbonate anything—I've got one myself: bubbles and a twist of lemon make anything feel cool and refreshing in the throat. Yes, bottled yew juice can hardly fail.

What to look for? How long will it take to work? I looked that up too, I looked that up specially. It takes, so the books say, about an hour: a good length of time when a party's going on. Anyone can feel strange after an hour at a party, especially this victim, who suffers poor health on a number of counts and who is almost expected to feel some symptom or other coming on. An hour is a perfect length of time. In an hour the glass and bottle, the label, the rest of the contents—all can disappear without anyone noticing.

But what are the symptoms? Stomach pains? A queasy sensation? Some throwing up, maybe, and diarrhoea? All those, for sure. But some subjective effects, as well? What about giddiness, weakness, vertigo even? Later, there are bound to be convulsions, but they mightn't begin till the victim has been taken away from the party. It's hard to predict exactly how long the passage will take till the final scenes of shock, coma, and death. Best that the last part happens when professionals are there to cope: in a hospital, let's hope, or an ambulance."

Myrtle pauses, but not for effect. We're all spell-bound, not moving, not speaking; we see the bottle, the label, the splendid dark green yews in their dole-ful surroundings, on guard for their broken grave-stones, giving shelter to the rusted lettering, the disfigured statuary, the stained slabs marking the spot where dry bones wait for their resurrection. I never thought of yew; but Myrtle has possibly thought of everything.

"In another room somewhere (Myrtle begins again) a second woman puts together a lethal spread of yoghourt and berry to top some biscuit base the victim's known to like. The yoghourt is easy: the victim tells all her circle who may have to cater for her that fresh goat's yoghourt is the only animal protein she can have. Likewise herbs and spices, flavouring, seasoning —everyone known to the victim knows what's in, what's out, when it comes to dainties. But the berries? Blackcurrant purée I remember was claimed for the fruity purple paste spread through the rest. (There's not the briefest gaze at me: not a look, not the merest glance.) So I set about looking up all things bright and purple. Nothing exotic, remember; just what's easy enough to find and pick, crush and mix. What about *atropa belladonna,* I decided, before even finishing the alphabet of poisonous plants: black nightshade, banewort, naked lady lily—so versatile in the medical alkaloids it yields, so deadly in its natural state.

And will it work straight away? Or take some hours, or even days? My dictionary says six to twelve hours. The blurred vision, loud heartbeats, hallucinations, hot skin, dry mouth, therefore, will perhaps be hidden by the faster-acting taxine already drunk. And the final symptoms—convulsions, coma, and death—are the same. Which of these two poisons, we can ask, did the ultimate work?

Before even asking that, however, there is a third player picking plants. She chooses one of ancient memory, *conium maculatum,* hemlock, whose every part—leaves, roots, fruits and stem—leads straight to oblivion; hemlock, taken by Socrates to prove of equal value the paths of life and death, used by the Borgias, used by village women to remove the countless causes of personal threat. Hemlock leaves, thinks our third woman, will make a delicious salad filling for one of those small Lebanese breads the victim is recently partial to. The toxicity rating is maximum: she won't have to eat more than a couple of bites for success. The eyes are affected, the muscles become paralyzed and the end comes when the lungs won't breathe. And the onset starts, I read, after about half an hour.

I remember the half-hour; how Babes began to sweat and grimace, how she felt unwell, how she said the room was swimming and her legs and arms felt painful and limp. And when I remember, having read what I've read these past few days, I remember the absence of everything mentioned: the halfeaten pitta-style bread, with its thick green filling, the delicate squares of biscuit covered in flecked purple paste, the bottle with its brightly coloured label—gone, all gone, nowhere to be seen or found. Not surprising, you might think, given the artificial mess of a party. Aren't things always cleared away after: rubbish thrown out, bottles removed? But I remember distinctly the rest of the mess—it's that these three items were removed *before* everything else. And they'd have to be, after all. Who of these women would want to be found out afterwards?

We know, those of us who went with Babes to the hospital, that they did all they could: they pumped her stomach, they gave her muscle relaxants, they tried to clean her blood and massage her heart. It was, of course, too late: and how could they know there was more than one poison to deal with? And despite their brisk and conscientious demeanour, I could tell what they thought, what anyone thinks these days: illicit drugs, a mistake or an overdose, a suicide attempt, the wrong pills, or a pill too many. They asked us, I remember, "What is she on?" And looked disbelieving, controlled their impatience, when we said nothing—nothing like that, just herbal remedies, naturopathic extracts, no one could be further from street drugs or abuse of allopathic treatments. The post-mortem, therefore, I have to conclude, was routine stuff. The pathology department wouldn't talk to me: I'm no one official, not a practitioner, not even a relative. I could tell, though, how harassed they were: cuts, they said, understaffed, overwhelmed. 'Could have been anything,' a nurse told me, when I grabbed him in the corridor: 'you know, food poisoning, botulism—she was at a party, wasn't she? Can't trust caterers like you used to—it's all profit these days, isn't it? Cut corners, save costs. You wouldn't believe how many people are brought in after parties. It all gets hushed up, of course. No one sues anyone—too expensive. And all these doctors (he waved at the closed doors around us) are terrified of the insurance companies. I bet it was food poisoning, though; it nearly always is, since I've worked down here.' It got me thinking, then: food poisoning, the poisoning of food—implausible, given the people; unlikely, given the people; but would it make sense of what happened, fit the facts, explain why Babes died? Or, to put it another way, could I prove that it *hadn't* been like that?"

Myrtle stops, right there, and we're taken off guard. Is that the end? Is she not going to name names and make accusations? No one speaks. Eventually, as usual, it's AllyPally who has the least tolerance for silence. "I'll get coffee," she offers, leaping up. "I'll find Sarah. I suppose we'll be here a while, discussing all this."

But Myrtle, too, is on her feet. "Not for me," she announces. "I'm not interested in discussing. I've told you all my scenario—what you do about it is your affair. I just wanted everyone to know what I know."

"But have you told all this to the police?" asks Portland Jo. She looks dreadful: strained, sunken, stricken, her large limbs seeming lifeless and sprawling.

"Of course not," replies Myrtle. "What would they do? What could they do? Babes is dead and buried, the inquest said misadventure, there's no material evidence and no clear motive. And how do you think they'd respond to a tale of not one murder, but three, all planned at the same time, to be perpetrated on the same victim? Too much coincidence, don't you think they'd say? Get real, sister (which makes Portland Jo wince); this is 3-D life we're in, not a police procedural where the plot line is clearly marked. What I've offered you is a scenario. Take it or leave it. It's not for public consumption; for my own sake, I wanted to rest my mind easy. Presumably you all want to do the same. I know I'm not one of you (she says brutally), for which—believe me—I'm extremely thankful; but I'm not as silly as you all think."

"But we don't think you're silly," breathes AllyPally, admiring, flattering, on the brink of adoring.

"We're fascinated. Terribly impressed . . ." But Myrtle is halfway to the door. For the second time she lets out that fabulous smile, full beam, straight at AllyPally, says to her, "I'll see you back at your place later," and lets herself out.

Am I safe? Or not? Now, wherever I get with my own reasoning, there are other people's reasonings to deal with. Other people, that is, even if they know exactly what I know, won't be able to tell whether I did it or not. Even I can't know whether I did it or not. Sarah comes in with coffee and snacks, everyone starts talking at once, but the talk is round and round what Myrtle's said, not focussed, not straight to any point, or anyone's part, not at all, no one wants that, it seems. Though Annie and Sal must have found out already, I can see, about Portland Jo's special salad. She must have broken down and confided, the great slob. And Ria had already rumbled Gloriana Hardy, though without the specifics. I can't see Ria setting off for a library to make notes and lists out of pharmacological textbooks. I didn't even do that myself.

But what about me? Who else, apart from Myrtle, knows about me? Riva, of course; but again, not the specifics. How much does that count? Is part of a story enough? Does only the whole story satisfy? And then? Is anything really changed, or is anyone really different?

I did it for the movement, so the movement will be changed. Even if it wasn't me who did it, the fact that it's been done will change the movement.

"You're very quiet," says Riva, sidling in next to me on the sofa. "I've taken up quietness," I tell her; "haven't you noticed?"

Jade, who's also been very quiet, now pleads for attention and we all listen expectantly. "If what Myrtle's said is true, then someone should own up, surely." The thought reduces me to helpless giggling. How can one "own up", as if to a childish prank? "Have you ever been a school-teacher?" I ask her. Jade glares at me disapprovingly. "Is that relevant?" she counters.

"Babes," Jade says furiously to everyone, "was a wonderful, inspiring, tremendous feminist. She sacrificed everything. Some wicked, deranged women, who might even be sitting right here, murdered her. And you all don't care a fuck."

"Balls," says Ria. "You're new around here. We know what Babes was. Anyway, whatever anyone thinks won't bring her back. And we're not murderers. We're feminists, for god's sake."

"But we can't do nothing." Jade is tormented and passionate.

"Nothing is the only thing we can do," replies Ria complacently. "Myrtle's quite right about the lack of evidence, but apart from that, there's the movement to think of. What would be the point of bringing everyone under suspicion? Think of the credibility we'd lose; think of the scoffing, think what the tabloids would do, think of all the work we've done going right down the drain, think how the men would jeer and leer. Think, dear Jade, of the consequences."

. . .

So nothing's done, as it were. Just another meeting, another issue, another argument, another day, another way. Does it all get left, like everything else, no loose ends tied, no closure from prosecution or defence, no magic mountain or redemptive fire? Only sobbing Myrtle made imperious with contempt? And Ria fretting after Gloriana Hardy's sanity? Is that all?

. . .

Remorse, of course. Remorse, remorse. Where is the remorse that gives some body to the watery dreams of disappearance?

. . .

Sarah's busy planning pre-packed "Food of the Ancients", starting with Greece. She says she'll go door to door for two weeks, if Ashok will give up the library to help carry everything. Since her mother stopped bringing parcels and Flo went off, she's been looking for a new focus. *God is Dead* still brings in enough for her basic requirements, but the prospect of running the house while I'm indefinitely away in Australia has got her thinking about viability and diversifying. Lately she does her accounts in a bound red ledger she bought in a commercial stationer's, rather than on the backs of old letters and other junk mail I keep piled in the kitchen for notes and lists. Ashok got her a *Bookkeeping Made Simple* from the library and opened them a partnership account at the bank. He says he'll get her *Marketing Made Simple* as soon as he can, but the person who's got it out on loan has had three extensions already. I offered to get them a video business pack, but Sarah says it's easier to adapt principles from books. "Texts are abstract," says Sarah airily, "so you can do what you want with them. With telly, you have to take it as it comes."

Ashok says he feels like a short break, having completed his current investigation into human gene patents. At a loose end, with Sarah and Ashok out shopping, and Sybil still refusing to speak, I sit at the kitchen table and dip into Ashok's notes. "The genetic goldrush (it says) of companies staking their claims to parts of human DNA has caught biotechnological marketers on the hop. The question being fiercely contested by philosophers on the one hand and the biotechnology industry on the other, is whether or not biological products are machines.

If the patents currently under consideration are approved, the genes for disorders such as Huntington's chorea (fatal) and diabetes and obesity (chronic and very common) will become the property of multinational pharmaceutical companies. Then people requiring a genetic test will find that their clinics will have to add to the bill royalty costs due to whomever owns the gene.

Recently, the University of Michigan and the Toronto Hospital for Sick Children have billed British researchers for royalty fees in return for permission to investigate the CF (Cystic Fibrosis) gene isolated and located by their researchers in 1989. The British have not so far paid up.

In the early 1990s, the US government's National Institutes of Health applied for patents on more than 2000 genes in the human brain, but international disputes put the application on hold. In Britain, the Medical Research Council retaliated by applying for its own patents on more than 1000 fragments of DNA. Both claims have remained temporarily withdrawn while legal argument and international commercial and scientific diplomacy examine the issues and implications. In France, an inquiry has been set up to determine who owns the DNA fragments from thousands of diabetics held in the database of a private research foundation.

Since many are now arguing that conduct, thought, individual development, and even attitudes, have a base in genetic "triggers", it will become increasingly important to know who owns the rights to genetic materials. Does ownership entail responsibility? Is determinism—complex, as yet unfathomable, but still determinism—the final answer we always suspected was true? But how to reconcile determinism with entropy? Repeating universes? Does Einstein now know whether or not God plays dice?

I don't any longer believe in responsibility: only in decision-making. But it seems probable that I have genetic programming for that belief. History, after all, is merely one component of evolution."

Sarah's recipes from Ancient Greece sit in a neat pile next to Ashok's notes. She's still using a card index system, in spite of Ashok's urging about software possibilities. I suppose all this *embourgeoisement* will end in marriage, as usual.

I think AllyPally's taken a shine to the new Myrtle. Last night Ria saw them together at the club Gloriana Hardy's investing in. Ria said she'd be round today but there's no sign so far. I ought to be filing and sorting, but I'm so restless I can't concentrate properly. I should discusss Australia with her; it isn't fair not to. But what if she says she wants to come with me? How can I invent a new life with the old one by my side?

Riva phones, sounding mysterious; not just lunch at *Cymbeline's*, but please a free afternoon to follow. I can't resist my curiosity, though I shouldn't, given the schedule Sarah's imposing, relinquish so much time. And though everything's quiet on the Myrtle front, I feel uneasy being away from the phone for so many hours at once. On the other hand, given the contract I've signed, Riva is a safe haven and therefore commands some priority.

Cymbeline's is surprising, not at all Riva's usual style: no sparkle, no illusory possibilities, everything functional, efficient, modern. Post-democratic uni-fashion is hard to metamorphose; and the severity of chrome and muzak discourage fantasy of any kind. I wait with some trepidation: this décor and the unexplained afternoon are out of character. And when she arrives, so, too, is Riva: she has cut back her hair almost to the scalp, has made up her face in bold purple, and is clad as a horsewoman: boots, breeches, jacket, stock, and gloves, though instead of a cane pressed firmly between elbow and side, she carries her long red feathers. She hands them to me, says "Change, dear Tessa, is only a symptom of what might have been." No one in the restaurant takes the slightest notice of her appearance, but I say, "A new job? A manifestation? Give me a clue?"

"Tessa," she rebukes, "are you, of all people, questioning the motivation, veracity, integrity, right-to-change, of someone else?"

I park the feathers behind me and settle down to the menu. Her shaved head is distracting and the purple round her eyes makes connection uneven, but we manage, nevertheless, some chat about Myrtle's transformation into forensic pharmacologist and some speculation about the commercial possibilities of Sarah's Food of the Gods and Ancient Greeks.

The point of meeting, though, (we're both aware) is what awaits in the afternoon. She takes me to her car and it's soon clear that we're going to Cricklewood. "Sophie's expecting us?" I ask.

"It's Sophie's things," she replies.

"What things?"

"We'll be there soon. You'll see."

She lets us into the empty flat (I don't know where she got the key and she doesn't say) and heads for what must be the bedroom. I sit in the gloom, still apprehensive, though Sophie's flat, after all, is neither forbidding, exotic, nor uncomfortable. It isn't even unknown.

Riva calls, "In here, in here." So I go. The riding clothes lie neatly stacked on the blue velvet chair under the window. Afternoon sunlight floods on to the large bed, making its brass frame glint and burn, its crisp blue linen shimmer. And at full length, stripped and smooth, arms stretched sideways, breasts spilling sideways, prone and relaxed on top of the luscious blue cover, lies Riva of the purpled eyes and the dark purple lips.

"You've always wondered," she says. "Now is the right time."

I feel helpless, transfixed, say, "No. I have never wondered. Ria . . ." I can't go on. What about Ria? Riva says nothing, moves nothing, glides in the silence. The sunlight rushes in without stopping, the clothes lie quietly on the chair, the bedhead goes on glinting.

"The feathers? I forgot the feathers. I've left them in . . ."

"I know," she soothes. "You must have known that Ria gave me the feathers."

"I didn't know."

"But she told me she'd told you."

"I've been distracted," I mumble. Move towards the bed. I have to. I'm aware, suddenly, of feeling sweaty, constricted. I start on my shirt buttons, but she says, "No. Just come now."

Close to, the eyes themselves turn purple, the lips and tongue are large, strong, fuller than anyone's. She rises over me, allowing the big breasts to swing, swing, and I mouth what I can, where I can, the tips, the arcs, the space in between, no hands allowed, because she is pressing down my hands, palm on palm, wrist to wrist.

I must have what she has, give what she gives, unbutton, undress, undo, abandon, throw, fling, tear, push, leap—oh please—unskin, but she allows nothing, keeps hands pressed down, in perfect symmetry, while she swings her breasts for my mouth. This is (I try to think) for a specified time, a long time, I don't know how long, a timeless time, a time given for this only, only this (let it rest in the mouth, take all of it in, as much as will fit, then tongue at the hard round tip, and then the rest, and suck, and lick) (but the other one all this time is waiting, the other one wants, the other one now) (no talking—don't talk with your mouth full, can't, no need) (but the other one waiting) (swinging this way and that way against each cheek, soft huge round, my tongue out ready for either hard tip, can they grow any harder? my mouth never empty for long) (now the other one waiting) (swinging them on and on, over me, on me, I've caught one, I'm filling my mouth) and at the edge of my resistance, at the end of my tether, at the instant before I have to give way, she sits back, her wet thighs spread across my belly, my hands released, looks down from some spire, some cenotaph, some scaled high scarp; she sits back, this carving—still as a Buddha—this consummate performer, and says—no sign of sighing or panting—and says—this perfectly controlled magician—says,

"You like my tits then?"

Like? Is like a word? What sort of word? I'm clumsy with my buttons and sleeves, fevered, desperate, and she helps not at all, sits insistently astride my legs so I can only shed from the waist up.

"We can reverse the procedure if you wish," she says, cupping my breasts, "but not the position, I think." So that as she strokes and squeezes, as she leans down to lick and suck, her own breasts, bountiful, beautiful, so lately feasted, now grown enormous, go on swaying, swinging, just out of reach.

But her hands, her hands. The skills of the heel of each palm, pushing from underneath upwards, stroking from top to tip, or outwards, or sideways down; the skills of the centre of the palm, pressing in, out, back, forth; the skills of the fingers, the ends of fingers, practised to pace, pull, trace, tease, slide, flick, rub, pinch, play, splay, brush, push. And I, the bearer of breasts so exquisitely attended, prolong, restrain the time, resist with every effort the need, the wish, to pant, to groan—breathe, I instruct myself, just breathe, breathe, it will be the sweeter. And the floodrush from between my thighs is soaking everything.

She rests her palms on my breasts, takes each upright nipple between two fingers, close to the web, says, "Look what I hold in such a gentle vice! I can fashion them either with fingers or tongue," and proceeds, while I breathe, breathe. I dare not speak.

Now that blood and nerves are fully surfaced, the art is to stay, to keep the absolute emerging of nipple to palm and tongue, to keep the mind enacting, over and over, repeating, proceeding, remaining, postponing, extending, to breathe, breathe, to trap this slowed down time and never allow it to gallop beyond its horizon.

The sunlight sprinkles on her swinging breasts and I feel my pelvis jerk and lurch by itself, say fast, "I can't hold out much longer."

"But you can, we can," she replies, stopping the room, the sun, the time we're in, the sensations. Sits, completely still, straightbacked, symmetrically astride. The scent from her fluids comes so suddenly that I forget my resolve and groan.

"We might, in a while, change places," she says, still unmoving. Her eyes, remaining hooded in purple, betray nothing. My pelvis quiets, my heartbeat slows, silence prevails, she stays just sitting, her face like all of her perfectly still. Only the scent remains vigorous, spreading through air and sunlight, lush and lavish.

Let it be, by paradigm, spring, the earth at the equinox, sheathed leaves of bulbs just spearing the soil, and other leaves spreading, uncurling, untwisting, outstretching, rains sudden and frantic, tides risen, everything teeming and profligate; let it be here, this place, Holy England, cleaned and claimed, planned, tamed, immaculate conception, every inch owned and named, known about, groomed. Let her stand on green pasture, at the foot of chalk cliffs, at the edge of any ribbon of river, stream, or overgrown canal, whose soft waves unfurl against her feet. Let her be by profession some singer whose craft makes handsome her jaw, neck, shoulders, bosom, and back; or a brisk wheeler-dealer whose eloquent limbs are as fluid as her chat; or the greatest of tennis queens, so lithe from winning and springing, from training, from wanting and getting. Let her be a seer, brilliant and wise, her mind a jewel, abstracted with theorems and proofs, very spare, very lean, uncluttered, exact, incisive, expensively tuned and refined. Let it be rich, this time taken: let it be opulent, blazing, brooding, beseeching.

Truth is bewitching sings the Liberty Bell so near, so clear; *bewitching, unstitching, bewitching, conditioning, upending, pretending, bewitching, imagining*.

With my own hands I can hold and cup what's mine, push outwards, make firm the cleft for her face, for her mouth to busy and bury, her tongue to trace between. I cannot see her eyes. The skills of the mouth proliferate invention: the transposition from infant to sage, the shift from hunger to pleasure, from need to choice, because there is sucking (or searching) and tonguing (or testing for limits). Thus, in my turn astride, I copy and collude, enact the swaying and handling, the play of mouth on nipple and skin, the splay of fingers and palm. I listen to her breathing; in spite of her sheen of sweat, in spite of her mouth to mine, in spite of her willing display, her breathing is even, perfectly even. I have no notion of who floods more between the thighs, though she lies naked and I'm still covered from the hips down. "I can't . . ." I begin, but she hushes me instantly. "You can, we can," she insists, then takes hold of my hands in her own, moves away, says, "Tea, don't you think? Too early to drink—it's daylight still . . ." and though I protest that nothing is finished, she dresses herself in some of Sophie's things, leaving the riding clothes folded on the chair.

"Don't forget these," she reminds me, waving the long red feathers and heading out to the kitchen. My pelvis quells painfully; I distract myself with buttoning my shirt and instructing myself about not losing face. In any case, tea might be merely an interruption, a prolongation, a managed elegance.

"I have to concede," says Riva, adding milk (as if nothing has happened; as if what has happened is that nothing has happened), "that I may, in the past, when you explored all the pros and cons, have erred on the side of neutral observer. I thought, at the time, it was best; I even thought it might establish a frame for containment."

"But now?" I press.

"Now I wonder whether I misinterpreted; whether my view that everything you were saying had meaning only within utterly personal parameters, was an inadequate reading. I kept disregarding the context."

"And so?"

"I have my own cause to clean."

"You mean Sophie?"

"In her case, the harm is widely documented. Clients, patients—there are dozens of lives she's destroyed; and she goes on doing it, every day. No plans for retiring."

"But . . ." I can't help feeling enormously shocked, but I tell myself that that's natural enough: I know nothing much about Sophie, and even less about therapies, therapists, their networks, or their alliances.

"So I'd better get on with it," says Riva rising, sounding like someone who wants to create the effects of resolution.

"What about us?" I demand, conscious of a different urgency.

"What do you mean?"

"Surely we'll finish what we started—in there," I nod towards the bedroom.

"Things don't get what you call 'finished', Tessa. You of all people must know that by now." She goes on gathering herself, fastening and folding Sophie's clothes about her, running those magic fingers through the short sheen on her head.

"But . . ." Now I'm unaccountably desperate, split, reacting like a spurned lover when up till this morning I had thought of Riva only as a casual companion, a peculiar partaker of formal settings, a skilled twister of sympathetic language. Can things change like this, so utterly, so exactly, simply from falling together on to a bed—simply from feeling the twitch of some volatile nerve-endings? My plans, after all; I shall be in Australia. And my safety: Riva should not be challenged, baited, manoeuvred, constrained in any way. Riva has my future between her extraordinary hands, in her documents, in her assessment of who I am. Don't (I lecture myself)—don't tempt Riva to the least indiscretion. Let Riva come, let her go, let her speak or not speak, let her do what she sets out to do, let her be whoever she thinks she should be, let her prosper (O Heaven! Let her prosper and do well).

"Please understand (she explains matter-of-factly, no hysteria, no insistence, no theatrical lilt, no studied control)—that I had to gear up; I had to make myself ready, find focus, find courage and resolve."

"I do understand," I humour her. "No one could understand better." She smiles. She relaxes the muscles at the edge of her eyes, the hinges of her jaws. The purple has faded—she looks almost familiar.

"That's what I'd thought," she says, with professional satisfaction. Then, as an afterthought, "There are bound to be other times—there always are—for what you call 'finishing'."

Unwilling to stay alone in Sophie's flat, I hurry after Riva, down the zig-zagging steps, on to the pavement, towards the high street where the run-down broken shops huddle hopelessly against the uncaring stream of human need and greed that brushes ceaselessly against them. I know Riva will head for the curry house and that she'll find there both Sophie and The Man. As for me, I can let myself go, just this once; get a taxi, rush off home, bury myself in schedules and plans, in small talk with Sarah, in phoning Ria, and AllyPally, and even Annie and Sal. I can shut the door against Sybil, sleep on the sofa behind the bed, where her wide staring eyes can penetrate nothing. I can take some time over what to note down for Ashok. I can put away, put aside, purple-eyed Riva, Riva who argues, Riva who may always (for all I know) never finish what she starts. There is much I can do. I have to hang on, keep a grip, not give way. The world is my oyster; why not prise open the secret hinge, expose the flesh, discover the pearl?

Alone at night in the garden (perhaps) sits Myrtle the Great, her veins now shot through with a steely substance, in league with our mother, the ice-laden moon. Implacable Myrtle needs only logic to order the world and remove all mysteries. Myrtle-Turtle swimming steadfast through a swirl of eddies, complex currents, has a fully intact antenna, has a mighty sense of direction. Myrtle (for all I know) counts herself now among the blessed, who know what matters, whose faith is neither fractured nor dimmed. Myrtle survives the sins of denial by covering in ice her heart, her devotion, her hopes, her contrition. I imagine her submission as she lowers her eyes (for all I know) to be modest and pleasing to the circling moon.

(And this means, I realise, that for AllyPally, the days of teasing and flocking, of bedding and sharing, of inventing, of endeavouring, are done and gone; and the days of destiny have begun.)

.   .   .

Though the sofa hides me, I can bear no longer the feel of those eyes, the thought of that lolling tongue. The silence flutters at my ears, makes noises of bats and birds, of whirring things. It's the blood in my ears (I say in my head) it's the pulse that must keep beating. Even the dark is unreliable—there are chinks in the curtains, strips of light coming under the door. I have no training for endless solitude; I was not chosen to seek out spirits to calm my soul or instruct me in the paths of heavenly wisdom.

"Sybil! (I command, in the most dreadful voice I can muster), this silence which you think is my revenge or punishment must stop this instant. My survival depends on it."

"You," comes the voice, thin and vacant (and I can't, in the dark, discern her face). "Always you. Believe me, better for you, I mean it, that I hold my peace."

"No, Sybil, whatever I've done, we must stick together, be what we've been to ourselves, each other. Life goes on, after all."

But then, in a high voice, at a pitch I've never heard her use, she sings: *The road to Mandalay turned out to be part-river trade, part swamp, part bywater in imperialist history. Travel the world, travel the past, it is only so much sun and water. Drink or not drink, it makes no difference; burn in the end, burn all the way through. Do you hunger and thirst after righteousness? Is it meat to you, and drink? Do you drink your fill of bywaters, whatever the silt and slime, whatever the small eggs spawning, whatever the slurry and insecticides? Do you have a choice? (Thompson and Bywaters, hanged for adultery, rage, and romanticism, had the public all agawp, not believing such naïveté. Times change. They did, in the end, abolish the axe.)*

Between, let us say, one significance and another, you plot your tax returns and your TV movies, your shall I go here and shall I go there, your I can have this woman, that woman, not this one, not that one, all together children: clap and shout. You dabble in hypochondria. You submit to togetherness, pay your way when you can, acquire little stickers to pay and display in the carpark. You collude, every day, in ten thousand petty tyrannies.

I saw you all those times when you thought I wasn't looking. I saw you cry in the laundrette when the caretaker folded your sheets. She said it was nothing, but you cried anyway. She said it was nothing. Who, all this time, did you think you could be?

(And her eyebrows stay level; she closes her mouth; she stares; she is quiet. The batwings flap invisibly round my ears, their swish and whoosh has a dreadful pattern. Shall I scream?)

"Sybil, no one knows better (I can fight off the batwings, the ice of her eyes; I can fight off anything, anything)—no one but you—never anyone but you—has so exactly been my mirror, been my mentor, arbiter, friend—"

"Cut the crap!" she interrupts rudely, calmly, not singing now. "Get a grip. Go down under the water. Hold your breath, if you must, but open your eyes. *See through the thick green water how everything changes. It was never your element, but you filled your head with mermaids and monsters, tridents and serpents, smugglers, shipwrecks, sirens, odysseys, the Flying Dutchman and the Great White Whale. You read what you liked, imagined you could discover the past, encircle the earth. What do you expect, having allowed yourself such a canvas?"*

"But you never tried to stop me," I plead.

"Whatever you imagine, consider it done," says

Sybil Tormentor, eyeing me up and down, sideways, straight. "Dress me," she commands. "Let's put it to the test."

I do as she bids, knowing without discussion that I should dress myself likewise. It's been a while. The silks are crushed, I fumble the buttons and folds. It's hard, in the dark, to be sure of the right effects, but I think I manage a good result. At least the batwings have gone, and despite my dread, there begins to bubble and lift through me the familiar excitement of performance. Ready, finally, I take Sybil on my knee.

"*Sisters* (she begins immediately) *we know your fears and longings, your labours, your discontents. We know the troubles, the ache, the despair. But we also know your strength. Together we prosper, alone we fail. If we share everything, we can overcome. Are we together?* ("Together," they sigh; "yes, together, together.") *And we share everything, sisters; do we share, do we share?* (And they shuffle and settle, sink back in their chairs, feel collected and comforted. "We share everything," they reply.) *We are the sisterhood, and sisterhood is powerful.* ("Sisterhood is powerful," they echo.) I try to get in the swing, find the right note for the mood, say bravely, "The personal is political!" but the audience is transported, enchanted, fixated—the women hear only Sybil's beguiling voice. I accept my position—it's her show, this time.

From our past wrongs, presently perceived (declares Sybil) *we embody refutations, construct reclamations: incest-survivor groups, rape recovery counselling, anti-harassment procedures, assertiveness training, aspiration building. We do these things despite the passive apathy of men, despite the active enmity of*

*the State. We keep faith with the memory of struggle.
By these methods we intend to survive.*

*But sisters: do we understand the brotherhood of
man?* (The audience mutters; this is difficult—this is
unexpected. "Sisterhood is powerful" shouts a lone
voice; "We are all sisters," shouts another.) *Or, to put
it another way* (Sybil resumes)—*is each sister her
sister's keeper?*

(Now some women are definitely restless. I try
everything I know to distract Sybil from this course,
but she takes no notice, is determined to keep me in
my place. "Get on with it!" demands someone angry
and young.)

*No fight exists that cannot be any time abandoned;
no flight exists that has no honour, at least from one
perspective. So do you all accept that some of you will
pay any cost, go to any lengths, for the sake of us all?
Do you know how powerful sisterhood can be?* ("Sisterhood is powerful" they respond, feeling better.
"Sisterhood is personal and powerful.") *It is part of
the truth, and we must face the fact* (Sybil races for
home, presses forward to the finishing line) *that
occasions arise when a sister must destroy another
sister.* (She raises her voice to quell the protests
beginning.) *I mean destroy: kill, despatch, annihilate,
murder. Not for mean or petty motives; not for personal
satisfaction; but to keep us clean and powerful, committed to change. The question is: who is it who has
made what men call the supreme sacrifice? Is it the
flawed sister slain? Or is it the saviour with blood on
her hands?* (The audience has given up any interest in
medal ceremonies. They rush pell-mell for the exits,
jamming the aisles, pushing to get out. The young

224

group in the front row yell furiously, incoherently—
they feel cheated, they feel assaulted.)

"I hope this isn't a foretaste of what you think
we'll get ready for touring in Australia," I tell Sybil.
"A carry-on like that won't butter our bread. What
were you trying to do?"

"There's no corroboration," says Sybil smugly.
"You've done it all for nothing."

"People have different levels of understanding,"
I say. "I thought you knew that. I never said any of
this would be publicly debated."

"But you've implicated them all," says Sybil. "They
have a right to know."

"Not at all," I counter. "Life isn't perfect. There are
some things it's best not to know about."

"If they can't know, then how can it make a difference? What about responsibility?"

"What do you mean?"

"You've let Riva go off thinking it's all right for her
to remove Sophie."

That definitely shocks me. What has that to do
with me? "I'm not responsible for the whole world,"
I say impatiently.

"But isn't Riva a sister?" persists Sybil.

"Well—she is and she isn't," I reply.

"But you can see where it all leads. No solution,"
she declares.

"No *connection*," I insist.

"But if everyone follows your example? If *anyone*
does? What if the idea catches on?"

"Look, all I want to know is whether or not
you're intending to make that sort of mess all round
Australia."

"Our agreement has always been to tell the truth, hasn't it?" she says.

"So tell it. But not that way."

"What way do you suggest?"

"Make the women feel good, as you always have before. They need hope, faith, security, solidarity—you know that. You know all these things."

"Truth, dear Tessa, is a point of view. I never promised to agree with you. All I ever said was that I'd listen. If the sisters spurn you, it's a price you'll have to pay."

I'm angry, finally, with all this frustration, all this provocation, not to mention the prospect of a failed tour and no alternative income. I never thought Sybil would give me aggravation. She's always been loyal, utterly reliable, imperturbable. "You, Madam," I say brutally, tearing off her silks and flounces, "are going back in your box where you'd better come to your senses. I can get on perfectly well without you, if I have to. I'm not going to be blackmailed, brainwashed, or bullied by you, whatever you think."

"We've never quarrelled before," she says sadly, shivering in her shift.

"You've never made a fool of me before," I counter.

"Wait!" she commands. "Let's try it another way."

"What other way?"

"There was an earthquake (she intones) *and people were buried alive in folds of earth. But after, new forests grew. There was a woman at full term; they slit her open from the navel down, but the child was still-born."*

"Sometimes (I add, getting into the spirit)—you have to do things to save the mother."

"There was a storm at sea and the ship sank, but there was food for everyone that day. There was a forest fire and the settlers died, but the grass came up green and lush next time. There were plagues in Egypt—"

"There was the Ice Age—"

"There was the Great Flood—"

"There were human sacrifices—"

"There were animal gods—"

"There were wars and revolutions—"

"There were laws and administrations—"

"There were liberation movements—"

"There were anarchists—"

"There were individualists—"

"There was the woman at the well—"

"There was the woman behind the throne—"

"There was Marie Curie—"

"There was Edith Cavell—"

"There was Old Mother Hubbard—"

"There was Antigone—"

"There was Pope Joan—"

"Christabel!"

"All those queens!"

"All those poets!"

"All those crowds!"

"All those sisters!"

(By this time we're laughing and shouting, I'm dancing her round the room, despite the dark, despite her thin shift.) "You want to sit up then?" I ask her indulgently.

"No, no," she says fondly, almost sweetly. "I need to sleep. It's been a long time."

In bed, waiting for the dawn, I think of Riva. She

has, I decide, simply sat down as usual in the curry house, talked a lot, felt her way, perhaps, along and round the practised iron leg of Man The Man. What did she really mean, I wonder, about Ria giving her the feathers? Was it permission? Was it handing me over for seduction? Not white, for flight from fight; nor standard white, for purity; not funereal black, nor green for the virgin spring, nor blue for the death of winter—but the red of blood and poppies, lust, life, chivalry, and oblivion.

I dream half-awake, or I drift, half-asleep, in unknown arms. She is sometimes Ria, sometimes Riva, sometimes long-ago Kit, sometimes this one or that one, whose names I forget. In my dream she is Maja. All her skin shines. With words she promises—her words come in fibres, not phrases or sentences. She feeds straight from the sun. She says, *Hasn't the tall girl, the one in your hand, remembered you yet? That you took her by storm, then left?* This Maja sees me, whether she's looking or not; whether I'm looking or not. *This girl in your bed* (she whispers) *is your most recent alibi.*

What girl, what girl? Frantic, my hand feels only pillow and sheet. *Close your eyes, close your ears, close the holes in your mind. In the sea I can tease you, glide under and round, stream over you with words.* But I know, though I race to the sea, so fast, so incredibly quick, she'll be gone, gone. They all go down to the sea, and climb into ships, or grow their hair and their long silver tails. Gone, all gone. I stand beached, whatever the tides, whatever the weather, whatever the satellite predicts, whatever the birdwatchers say, whatever the painters see, whatever the marine biologists find, whatever the camerawomen record, whatever the tourists write on their postcards, whatever the saints pray, or the lovers feel. All the women are gone, all gone, gathered up in the arms of Maja, held to her bosom, under the sea. Even if I roll for hours between the waves, I shall find not one of them, not for me, never again.

The waves, at least, I can feel on my feet, rolling up anyway, sucking at stone. This beach life is secure, supported by microchips and the formalisation of life by statute. Fishermen traipse in and out, empty crabs into crates, scrape rust, smile at boys made eager by fishing rods on promotion. Townsfolk sell from shops or stalls; I buy and consume, make hay through rain and shine. I see, sometimes, this magic Maja, striding the cliffs with seagulls in her hair. She could keel me and I'd still not drown, but she has no intention. I stand, other times, in the supermarket, staring at shelves, taking down anything, caught stock-still with her promises hot on my neck. The tongue will be next, perhaps; or even lips. Her breath is nearly at my ear . . . and yet, and yet, it's only the threat of the batwings again, the whoosh of the dark, the years of regret that lie waiting.

.   .   .

Is this remorse? This hot longing, which can never be satisfied? Should I tell Riva no, stop, it isn't worth it, it fractures the whole world, it dissolves the difference between nightmares and dreams? Should I say, let it be, let her be, nothing changes, no connection?

And if the sisters are all gone, then who am I?

In the morning comes a card from Myrtle the Mountain, Sir Myrtle Faithful, Magnificent Myrtle (how are the lowly raised up! and the least of the sisters empowered!) St Myrtle Magna, you are sent to scourge me; you will perform all the roles of passion and rectitude, with full authority, here in my consciousness —or possibly (is it possible?) on my person. Do I need to fear you, tremble and beg? Do I need to ask you for sympathy and compassion? For the right to be heard? For the space to explain that simple problems may require complex solutions? But no: you have assumed that the dignity of silence must prevail. What, then, is on the card?

"You know, that I know what I know. Be careful, as I am being. I mean, take time to reflect on your position, as I am reflecting on mine. An eye for an eye is a primitive principle and what you would call patriarchal. It is not necessarily apposite. But I'm taking time to consider it, among all the other responses to be considered, so it's only fair that I warn you. It may be that there were mitigations of some kind. If so, I'm willing to listen, if you want to tell me anything. Please be assured that I am discussing this matter and my thoughts about it with no one at all. I am not acting on behalf of anyone. This is not a threat. It's just fair that you know what I'm thinking. Nor have I singled you out—I'm writing this same card to the others who were involved. There is good in everyone, so it's possible that you had your reasons. That is why it's necessary to take some time and to do nothing until things are clearer. I look forward to hearing from you—Myrtle."

So much for sobbing and yearning! This woman has a granite heart and is meditating battle. Shall I humour her, ask her to dinner, try to explain? Or stand aloof?

The phone rings and it's AllyPally, breathless with bliss. "I just have to tell everyone," she pants, but I interrupt her: "I know, I know. You've got it together with Myrtle."

"How on earth did you know?" she asks.

"It was obvious, I'm sorry to tell you. The way you both looked at each other during the meeting."

"But she's so wonderful," AllyPally bursts out, "I had no idea. She's so different underneath."

"Everyone's different underneath," I say brutally. "You can't have lived this long and not known that before."

"But she's really *extraordinary,*" labours AllyPally, desperate to explain what can never be explained: that enthusiasm, that monumental mix of souls on heat. I have to let her tell me; it's a torrent only rage could resist, and AllyPally's never done me any harm.

After I've been unusually patient, even for me, through the long eulogy of stunning attributes, I manage to break in, "So why are you spending all this time telling me when you sound as if you can't wait to be in bed with her?"

"She's had to go out," says the abandoned lover.

"Out? She hasn't got a job, surely?"

"No, no. Not till next term. Did I tell you she's even got a teaching qualification . . ." Hastily, to avoid a sequence of speculation about what a wonder in the classroom this paragon was bound to be, I interrupt again, "So where is she, when she ought to be with you and the phone off the hook?"

"She goes to the library every morning. Has been going there since the party, she says."

"Just like Ashok," I say. "Maybe it's a new trend."

"Some people, Tessa, want to improve themselves," says the teacher.

"Hard to ride off into the sunset if you have to compete with a library every day."

"Tessa, don't you like Myrtle?"

"Not two days ago, my sweet, you didn't like her much yourself. You've forgotten. I'm where you fled to when you couldn't stand another minute."

"That was different. She was buried in all that stuff about Babes."

"You make it sound completely *passé*."

"It is, it is."

"So?"

"So she was upset. People do strange things when they're upset. Myrtle was extremely fond of Babes. She didn't know her the way we all did. I tried to tell her, but it was no use."

"But what did you think of what she said at the meeting?"

"You mean the 'scenario', as she calls it?"

"Yes, the 'scenario'."

"I don't think anything much about it. I think Myrtle was wonderfully clever to think it up—absolutely brilliant—especially looking up all that stuff about plants."

"But you didn't believe it?"

"*Believe* it?" squeaks AllyPally. "Of course not! You don't, do you?"

"Well—" But she doesn't want to know what I think, is riding the wave of her own pent-up incredulity, says, "Couldn't you see how genuinely shocked and upset she's been? I told you how she'd cried all the time, and how she'd rushed around seeing people and looking up things. It was her way of coping. Once she'd finally thought it all out, as if it were a jigsaw, she immediately felt better. Couldn't you see that?"

"Sure," I agree. "But I got the strong impression that she really believes it—not that it was just a kind of therapy."

"She believes it for *now*" says AllyPally illogically. "But it will pass, you'll see. Everything's different now. We've found each other, after all."

"So you think she'll let it drop?"

"Of course she'll let it drop! Tessa, what's the matter with you? People don't go on and on in some fantasy for ever. She left that brute of a husband, didn't she? In the end? I know all of us had very mixed feelings about Babes, but she was kind to Myrtle."

"She was always kind to the new ones," I say. "For a while."

"Can't you remember, Tessa, how overwhelming it was for most of us, that first sweet encounter with real feminists? The commitment, the belonging, the fellow-feeling? We were born again. Even I felt it, in spite of growing up with my mother's planning meetings taking place round the kitchen table. Josie from the women's studies group at the poly was my first real—"

I don't want to hear about Josie from the poly. I want to know whether or not AllyPally can take Myrtle off into the sunset.

"But Myrtle said at the end of the meeting that she

was glad not to be what she called 'one of us'. Don't you remember?"

"That was just emotion. She'd been very upset, as I keep telling you. Of course she's one of us. She'd never abandon what Babes meant to her."

"So you think the 'scenario' was just an unusual sort of leave-taking. Like an obituary, or a panegyric."

"That's right," says AllyPally firmly. "Part of the grieving process. Everyone's different."

Sure enough, I think; but say, "So she'll forget all about it?"

"There are much nicer things to think about now," says AllyPally happily. "Of course she'll forget about it. You'll see."

"Love can be blind," I tease.

"No. This time, Tessa, it's for real. This is it. The real thing. I've finally found what I want, who I want, how I want it to be."

We leave it there. Who can ever understand why anyone chooses anyone? It's hard to imagine flighty AllyPally, full of bubble and gossip, of instant earnest causes and of casual gregarious gatherings, locked fast in the arms of Myrtle the Great, who shows every sign of humourless dedication to every principle in sight. Nor does AllyPally know, it's clear, that Myrtle has not been so borne aloft on the wings of passion that she's neglected her duty towards the miscreants in her scenario. Magic Myrtle, somewhere between bed and breakfast, has taken time to write three warning messages; and further time to deliver each one by hand. It must have been the case that, all this time, despite appearances and despite her upbringing, AllyPally has yearned for second place in a fixed pair.

They might, therefore, for all I know, live happily ever after.

. . .

Because of the space, the silence, the empty house, the neat files almost completed, the face in repose of Sybil (eyes closed, mouth softly shut), the sight of red feathers lying across the back of the desk, the thought of the warning card in fragments in my wastebasket, the strong smell of dozens of herbs from the shining glass in the living room, the pain of Ria far off, back in time, bent on pleasure, moving under the disco lights, gleaming after bathing (oh when? I still haven't told Ria about Australia)—because of Sarah's sandwich board and Ashok's manuscripts, because of the women in Göppingen, who are carrying on as usual according to Annie, because of the groupies who lie in wait for a new queen—because of Gloriana Hardy, condemned from now on to the writing of serious books, whether they sell or not, because of wretched Portland Jo, broken by the coincidence of spite and fate—because nothing changes, because everything changes—I have believed the superstitions of justice, the organic connection between thought and act, analysis and practice, system and systemisation.

No connection, no connection, sings the Liberty Bell, clear, so clear. *Satisfaction is contemplation. Abstract, abstract; truth is perfection, truth is algebra.*

"Everything possible to be believed is an image of truth" I quote out loud, sententiously, with deliberation. Sybil sleeps on; the words fall from the air. What truth is so true that it can only be written in blood?

Enquire within, enquire within, says the Liberty

Bell, softer now. *Enquire within, no connection; enquire within, no connection. The face of truth is a theorem. It has an infinite number of sides. It is not human.*

In which case these schemes and dreams are combinations, permutations, taken from the data banks of dictionaries, themselves constructed and collated by collectors of vernacular renditions. They never broke a butterfly upon a wheel; they merely pinioned it for naming.

"So it's the case, m'Lud, I've come to believe, to understand rather, to contemplate anyway, that the truth is unconnected to bones and blood, is independent of synaptic spaces where the nerve ends meet." But m'Lud is impatient, preoccupied, wearied with translating bones and blood into legal prose and public money. *"You are here,"* says m'Lud sternly, *"to explain yourself. If you can. Which I much doubt."*

"Is there a time limit?" I ask sincerely. I'm not sure whether it's like Parliament or not, where things people don't want discussed are guillotined. The Queen of Tarts said 'Cut off their heads!' so all the documents went meekly to the scaffold and bled to death.

It's hard to tell at this distance, and given the wig and robes, whether m'Lud is a Lord or a Lady. It makes no difference, says the set-up; it's the role that speaks, writes, instructs the jury, passes sentence. It's the role that rules whether the game is fair or not.

"The jury has abdicated," I tell m'Lud. *"The sisters refuse to pronounce. They say the personal is political, not legal."*

"There are plenty of men to take their places," says m'Lud.

"But that would be unjust!" I protest. "The context would be wrong, the meanings would be distorted, the future would be perverted!"

"Calm yourself," says m'Lud. "I will tolerate no outbursts. The point, here, is remorse."

I can think of nothing to say.

"Remorse," says m'Lud. "What is your response?"

Still I can think of nothing to say. M'Lud sighs, and instructs the clerk, "Enter a plea of Not Guilty."

"Does that mean (I ask) that I'm on trial for my life because you are saying I'm Not Guilty of Remorse?"

"My child," says m'Lud indulgently. "We live in a civilised State. We have no capital crimes. All that is necessary is that we understand, so that sentence can be passed. A sentence, you see, must fit the crime as closely as possible."

"But it can't," I argue. "How can remorse change what was done?"

"Life isn't perfect," says m'Lud. "We do what we can."

And so I explain: Babes the Destroyer, the sisters, the need, the future, the cause, corruption, conviction, commitment, change. M'Lud disappears, dissolving under cascading sentences, lakes of concepts, rivers of words. Instead sits Marvellous Myrtle, clad in the bright white of perfect deduction, absolute conclusion, certain commitment. But before she can speak, the phone rings. It's Annie, in some agony of incoherence that takes half a minute to unscramble. I hear, finally, a clear statement, "It's Portland Jo. She's gassed herself. Shut herself in a garage with her bike. Rager, I think. One of those at the party. You know, those bikers. They've got a garage somewhere with their bikes in. She said she was riding somewhere with them but she wasn't. She put herself in there all day. She's dead, Tessa. She's killed herself."

Well, my dainties, I say to the unseen sisters: is this the right solution? Is this remorse? Is this what Mighty Myrtle Magic Turtle can bring off? Poor Annie and Sal. How must they feel?

"She hasn't been herself . . ." I say feebly.

"But all this again," wails Annie. "An inquest, a funeral, all her things, I don't think I can stand it."

"You must be exhausted," I say, feeling sympathetic. "Shall I come over and help?"

"Oh, if you could," says Annie. "I was hoping . . . I didn't know who . . . Sal's coping with the police."

"I'll just leave a note for Sarah and I'll be straight over," I say. Who would have thought that tough farmer's daughter had such soft stuffing at her centre? Who would have thought such a raucous extrovert could breathe quietly those deadly fumes, in and out, in and out, while thinking her closed and secret thoughts till she drifted asleep for ever and ever? Who would have thought Portland Jo could *succumb* to anything? Such a fighter she was, aggressive, insistent, persistent, rough, raw as new rope, muscled and strong. Now a limp bundle, defenceless, oblivious— all that horse's heart just nothing, nothing. The grief there must have been, huge as cities, unable to be withstood by the frail wings of some small fluttering creature that must have dwelt so frightened inside that giant cage. Who would have thought it? Who could have possibly predicted?

I get there just as the police are leaving. Annie explains that Portland Jo left a long scrawled letter. The police have taken it, but Sal had had the foresight to copy it on the fax machine while the police were going through Portland Jo's stuff in the guest-room she'd been staying in since the party. Annie hands it to me:

Dear Everyone,

I'm sorry but I can't go on. Annie and Sal have been great and done their best but it's no good. I can't believe I did what I did. I really loved Babes, more than I ever loved anyone. She loved me too, till Jade turned up. Nothing was ever so good in my life as being with Babes. But after Jade turned up, I hated her as well—Babes, I mean. I hated Babes for dumping me. I couldn't go on seeing her like that, at meetings and everywhere, looking at Jade all the time and going on about her.

Tell the police I did it. I knew about hemlock, where to find it and so on. I was crazy. I wanted to punish her, but after she was dead I couldn't cope. I can't stand the idea that I'll never see her again. Annie and Sal thought I was raving all this time—it isn't their fault. It's just that I can't go on. I'm sorry about everything. Please tell my ma I had cancer or something—it'll make it easier for her. The address is in my address book. She never could cope with me being a dyke and running away to London. It's better if she thinks I was on the way out anyway. As for everyone else, just tell them I'm sorry. I never should have done it. Give my love to anyone who wants it. Goodbye, P.J.

P.S. I'm doing it in the garage where the girls keep their bikes. Rager will tell you where it is.

Annie's in such a state that Sal asks me whether we should get the doctor and ask for sedatives, but I say cognac and a good sleep will be better, if we can persuade her to go to bed. We both promise her to stay right there. After settling her, Sal and I drink coffee in the kitchen and mull over things. She fills me in on what the time's been like for them since the party, which sounds like twenty-four hour nursing to me. Eventually I mention what's most startled me about Portland Jo's letter: "There's nothing in it about Myrtle's 'scenario'. Did you notice?"

"Of course," says Sal. "You can imagine what she was like when we got home after the meeting. Absolutely distraught. She was convinced Myrtle would tell everyone."

"So do you think that's why she—?"

"I don't, no. To start with, she said Myrtle was very clever to have worked out about the hemlock, but that the rest of it was pure invention. She was certain she'd killed Babes—just her. She said no one could survive eating hemlock unless they had their stomach pumped straight away; and that no one else had a reason. She was Babes' lover, after all, she kept saying. No one else would be driven out of their mind the way she was. And she couldn't believe the coincidence anyway. I agreed with her about that, I must admit; so did Annie. We thought Myrtle was acting out some macabre sort of game—bizarre, really —and that she'd got carried away with all the possibilities. She was obsessed with Babes—Myrtle, I mean —anyone could see that. It isn't surprising that she could remember every single thing the woman ate or drank. She probably remembered every word she spoke, as well; and every gesture, every smile, every tilt of the head. She's very intense, don't you think? Myrtle? Very insistent."

"You didn't notice, I suppose, whether a card came for Portland Jo this morning?"

"What sort of card?"

"From Myrtle."

"Why would Myrtle send her a card?"

"To say sorry or something. About the speech. She must have known whoever she had in mind would be upset."

"Nothing came for Portland Jo that I know of. But she would have got to the post first—she always did. Because of not sleeping properly and prowling round the house half the night. She was always up before either of us."

"Nothing on her table or anywhere?" I persist.

"No, nothing. I still can't understand why you think there might have been something."

It's best, I can see, not to continue. Curious, though. Maybe she burnt it or flushed it down the loo. It looks from her letter as if she wanted to take all the blame. The police, anyway, will think it's all very straightforward. But what will Myrtle think?

Towards evening, when Annie wakes up, we sit round again going over everything, talking about jealousy and pain and how different everyone is underneath from how they seem. Neither Annie nor Sal says anything about Myrtle and her scenario. Annie says she'll feel better if she gets on with practical things: writing to Portland Jo's mother, packing up her things, arranging for the funeral. I go home very late, sink into bed, fall into a heavy and dreamless sleep.

Ashok wakens me mid-morning with a tea-tray and another folder, but before I can look at his newest work, the phone rings. Even before I pick it up I know it's Riva.

"Is Sophie okay?" I demand, before she can say why she's phoned. There's a slight hesitation. Then she says, "Sophie's fine. Why wouldn't she be?"

"Because last time I saw you—"

"Last time you saw me," she cuts in, "I was gearing up."

"So?"

"What do you mean—So?"

"So what happened?"

"Nothing happened. They weren't there."

"But you told me they're always there."

"This time I was wrong. They weren't there. What's more, I don't know where they've gone."

"What?"

"They've disappeared, both of them. Disappeared into thin air. Can't find hide nor hair of either of them."

"You're joking!"

"Tessa, would I joke about that? Have I ever joked with you about anything important?" That was true enough. Riva's style has never been what anyone would call comical. What's more, anything she's ever said to or about Sophie has been deadly serious.

"Maybe she—they—sensed what you were planning."

"I wasn't—whatever you think (she says oh-so-loftily)—planning anything. I was going to work through a scenario. You wouldn't understand. It's a technique we use in drama therapy."

"That wasn't the impression I got."

"Look, I didn't phone up to argue."

"Sorry."

"I phoned up to see whether you've got the afternoon free."

"To go to Sophie's place?"

"No. Mine."

Instant lust breaks out all over me in sweat and heat; the memories rush at me, three-dimensional, assault simultaneously all my senses. I'm hypnotised, transfixed; but she, in her well-tempered ordinary voice is saying, "Well? Well? What do you think?"

"I'll have to phone you back," I manage. "Sarah's got some crisis on in the kitchen."

"I'm on my work number until noon," she says crisply. "By the way, have you heard about Portland Jo?"

"I was round there all yesterday," I say, feeling more normal. "Who told you?"

"One of my clients. It's stirring up a lot of anxiety. Which is to be expected, of course. But I'd be interested to know what Myrtle's making of it."

"One down, two to go, I would have thought," I say savagely. The thought of Myrtle pours a whole ocean of freezing water on my fiery fantasies.

"You'll phone me back then."

"I'll phone you back."

Ashok always knows when my need to calm my mind is so desperate that only his speculations will provide sufficient distraction. I go back to bed and read out to Sybil what's waiting in the file:

"The carbon-based molecules of life all have a property called 'chirality', which means they have their atoms arranged in one of two ways. Both ways look like mirror-images of each other, like spiral staircases turning in opposite directions. For life to begin, you need all 'left-handed' or all 'right-handed' molecules. Some theorists now think that the stimulus to achieving this vital balance came from circularly polarised light from outer space. This spinning light could have forced dust to adopt either a left or a right-handed state. Polarised light of this kind could have come from collapsing stars.

Meanwhile, other theorists, called nano-engineers, are creating individual atoms and groups of atoms, known as miniature machines. The dimensions of nano-engineering objects approximate to those of the internal machinery of biological cells. Chemists at Harvard University, for example, have made droplets of water measuring just 10 trillionths of a litre (roughly equivalent to the fluid content of a biological cell). Artificial atoms could be made any size, and could be squashed more easily to see how they react. Research on the creation of pure light remains at present subject to military intelligence controls. It seems clear, however, that algebra said 'let there be light' and there was light, and the light was the light of life, which being interpreted came to mean that the light was the light of the human soul.

Towards the end of the millennium we have seen various signs and portents. In August 1986 a games teacher was tried for battering her lover's lover, a deputy headmistress, with a two pound claw hammer. The victim, who was brain-damaged, paralysed, and confined to a wheelchair, lost her ability to read or write. This orgy of violence, the prosecuting counsel alleged, arose from 'deep hurt, frustration, and jealousy', though counsel went on to speculate about whether or not the jury were able to feel any comprehension or sympathy for 'someone who realised she was lesbian'. On 22 May 1988 the British Home Secretary discussed what he called the 'aimless lust for violence' in the context of research at Bristol Royal Infirmary's casualty department, which found that four out of five serious assaults are never reported to police. In the same year, a nine-year-old called 'Roy' told journalists, 'Mugging is a good job. Stealing and nicking gives you lots of pleasure and money for everything. And it's easy . . . you just get an old lady in your sights and do a 360-degree wheelie on her moustache.' In 1994 a writer called David James Smith, in his account of the James Bulger murder, unearthed case histories of children, both boys and girls, who had murdered younger children. In Manila (reported in the *Straits Times* of Singapore in October 1993), a seven-year-old boy was unable to be charged for murder because of his age, but police were quite sure that he had shot dead the family maid because she switched channels while he was watching the movie *Robocop* on television. The maid had wanted to watch *Young Love, Sweet Love*, according to another servant of the family. The boy apparently used his father's gun for the murder. Stephen Trombley's book *The Execution Protocol* quotes the Baptist chaplain at Missouri State Penitentiary on prisoners awaiting execution, 'I look on the spiritual side of things, as a man who believes there is an eternity, who believes there is a life after death. Our actions and our decisions in this world are going to make a determination as to where our boat is in the next world, and I look at a man such as him, and I see that he is stripped of all spirituality. He is practically a man who has no soul. Of the five executions, my perception has been that they have been hollow: void of spirituality . . . we've had a run of atheists and Muslims.' Trombley details the variety of execution methods and procedures current in the United States and comments at some length on the case of Tiny Mercer, who was four times taken for execution and returned to death row before finally being put to death on the fifth such occasion. During the execution, the prison authorities showed an X-rated movie. And afterwards, as she later explained to Trombley, Mercer's widow Christy had the body dug up so that she could see him again and say goodbye.

We are, let's say, living everybody else's future lives, letting the light spin this way, then that, so long as it spirals, so long as the human soul (inventing algebra) can go on making and breaking the patterns of atoms that go in and out of existence. Time and space are created by light, whose patterns are infinite, if the cast of the die is ever to be believed.

Time was when time was of the essence. Now I know better. Now I know that science can't save what has never been lost, nor ransom what has never been valued. The entire story, told by Lady Light to her Shadow Constant, might be a parable to explain how DNA achieved its release, its dissemination into the whole universe.

End. Millenial MS. © Ashok Rao Vicharkar."

That's that, then, clear enough. They'll get married for sure. It was never an option, anyway, spending a whole life in a library. Whatever it looks like, feels like—wars, and rumours of wars, corruption, pollution, disease, barbarism—this isn't the Middle Ages and no one gets away with dreaming over piles of paper in a monastic setting. This is the age of market forces and even Ashok has to get on with trade or brokerage of one kind or another: profit and loss, budget provision, cashflow projections, product development. They'll make a good team—they do already. In twenty years' time they'll have house and gardener, children at boarding school, time off in the Canaries, in the Alps, on coral islands, on safari adventures. They'll have a thriving network called 'How Herbs Help' or 'Everyday Plants for Healthy Living' or 'Best Friends Are Green Friends'—something like that. Sarah will have her mother for weekends in the country; Ashok will be fêted and spoiled when he goes home for Diwali. They will be a success. One day, or night, at the back of some cupboard, in a loft, or a trunk, Ashok will find his forgotten files, leaf through them, smile fondly for his young lost self, and put all his paper out for the rubbish collection. Sarah, too, will smile with distant memory when she sees on the stack of files the old 'Save Trees' stickers, all browned with purity and age, which once announced brave dreams of recovery and renewal.

But now. And now. I must phone Riva. Declare some intention. Cover my back. (But uncover the rest?) How to decide? Or how to interpret, given that the future is as fixed as the past. Did Sophie know, after all, that Riva's hand was laid on the iron leg of The Man?

. . .

Myrtle's not proud. I can see her in the under-growth, hunting spiders, hedgehogs, things that move. To sweeten her sense of things. Not to hurt, harm, maim, destroy. Possibly to remove. She's a city person, made safe from creeping things. Myrtle Magna is surprised by nature; she finds it interesting and beautiful. How, then, can she absolve what she has taken such pains to absorb?

If Myrtle would disappear I'd be over the moon. I'd be the consort of the moon, reflecting light, calming the tides. I'd be Mistress Faithful, serving the sisters with seamless devotion. I'd take vows. *Never again, never again,* I could offer. I could feel regret for everything.

She might hunt me down before I can leave for Australia. But what might she do with me? Put me in a cage of reclamation, reformation, reparation. "How will you pay?" she'll ask. "Where is renewal?" And though I might sing for my supper, sing for the sisters, sing whatever I feel like, day and night, it will make no difference. Magnificent Myrtle will be implacable. There is no restitution. "If you were sorry," she'll declare, "you wouldn't have done it." And so I'll offer her whatever I have, apart from Sybil.

It's always possible, of course, that they'll persuade her Portland Jo was the sole perpetrator. She might, for convenience, find it was so. It will depend on her new incarnation: will she choose Scourge or Star? (Will she take over where Babes left off, further the work, advance the cause?)

.   .   .

No connection, says the Liberty Bell. *Consider probability. Consider quantum theory.*

248

(If I were sorry, would I know by now?)

.　.　.

What I want is that Marvellous Myrtle should disappear. I want it fervently, patiently, perfectly, piously, ardently, devotedly, wholeheartedly, tremendously, tempestuously. I want it in all my acts of contemplation. I am uplifted by this want, ennobled—given the magnitude of calm required to constrain my longing.

Ah Myrtle: flee into the sunset pursued by hounds; or fly downwards from a steeple in a simple arc, streamlined, unstruggling, your hair flowing outwards; or give yourself, in some exotic place, to a scorpion, spider, snake, or shark; or find yourself caught in an earthquake, hurricane, volcanic eruption, fire, flood, famine, rockfall or iceflow.

I plan no assistance. This is only a wish. I have learnt my lesson, m'Lud. I am not a terrorist. A cause is not worth killing for. A cause, it seems, cannot be cleansed.

.　.　.

(But if Riva claims me? What can I decide?)

.　.　.

"You've just caught me," she says. "I'd decided you weren't going to phone."

"I said I'd phone. I had things to do."

"And so?"

"So it's better not (I hear myself say, though I haven't known what I will say)—considering."

"Meaning?"

"I'm off to Australia, after all. A new life. You can understand that. I need . . . well, I need . . ."

"Have you read about Constance Kent?"

"Why?"

"She went to Australia. You'll be interested if you find out what happened to her there."

"It's not that I don't . . . if you knew how much I want . . . wanted . . . and there's Ria, after all. I haven't been straightforward with Ria. . ."

"Ria's no fool. Ria gave me the feathers, remember?"

"That doesn't make it all right."

"What about our contract?"

"That's perfectly safe."

"But it won't apply in Australia. Things won't be the same there. I'd like to feel settled about everything; close it off properly. I have to deal with Sophie, you know, whenever she turns up again."

"She won't turn up, Riva; we both know that."

"That's not my doing, whatever you've imagined."

"But not because you didn't think of it."

"No harm in thinking, Tessa."

"I don't agree, you see. If I hadn't thought so much about it . . ."

"Today's not important. It can be any day. Just phone me if you change your mind. I won't change mine. I can forgive you, you know—even though you doubt it. Things aren't always one thing or the other. It depends."

"It depends which way the light spirals, that's all. Right-handed or left-handed. One way lies DNA; the other way lies the symmetry of disconnection."

"What are you talking about?"

"Nothing. Just something I read earlier. Some modern fancy footwork covering up the old dualism."

"Still worrying about right and wrong?"

"It's my conditioning, Riva. Who would I be without it?"

"A woman panting in my arms, no doubt," she says, her voice all breath and water, making it hard now, incredibly hard, harder than it's ever been, to stick to no I can't we can't we won't I mustn't shouldn't we can never no it wouldn't work it never could be how it might have been if I hadn't done it—if she hadn't thought of doing it because I'd done it. Between the imagining and the act comes the desire.

"You've gone very quiet," she prods.

"Yes."

"But you might change your mind?"

"All things are possible."

"Till next time, then?"

"Yes. Surely. Take care. Take good care."

. . .

Put Myrtle aside. Calm down. Forget desire. Forget panic. Make lists. Ria should be first. She should have her own list: all things Ria-related to be listed and done. Then Sarah: that's almost completed. Phone, gas, electricity, water, council tax, house insurance—all my exits have become Sarah's entrances. They are only files. Any name will do. They are only bills. Any bank account will do. There are no relationships with the providers of modern survival kits. Sarah has told Her Majesty's Inspector of Taxes about the sandwich board. She wants to regularise her situation, she explains. She wants Ashok to feel secure. "If he feels secure enough," she tells me, chattering happily among her herbs, "he might start talking. I think he will. Everyone stops fighting in the end. Look at me! I let my mother say whatever she likes, these days, poor old thing. And it's all your doing, darling Tessa. You've been such a rock. You're so helpful and reliable."

"The best friend a girl could have," I tease. I wonder what she'd do, if she knew?

Then there's the practical list: what to pack, what papers to take, what letters to write to set things up, what phone calls to make to let people know. And a party. A going-away party: nice music, good food.

Annie phones to say Morag's coming down from Scotland to do the funeral; Portland Jo's mother is flying over; the groupies are writing some sort of tribute; the police say they're keeping the formalities simple; Sal's been a tower of strength as usual; Gloriana Hardy's sent an enormous sheaf of flowers with a condolence card she's actually written herself; the press doesn't seem to have got hold of it, or else isn't interested. I say yes and good and oh and you've-been-terrific, both-of-you, but my mind is split on the rock of purple-eyed Riva of the swinging breasts to whom I've said no without wanting to, without meaning to. At least Annie sounds better. Annie has great recovery powers. But what about me? Shall I ever recover?

Late that evening stands Ria on the doorstep, unexpected, unannounced. Sarah and Ashok are out somewhere. We can have the place to ourselves. Things are half-awkward, half-not, given the mix of familiarity and constraint. We've hardly spoken since Myrtle's scenario.

"We ought to end things reasonably," she starts straight in, "especially given everything that's happened."

While she's sitting there, quiet, soft, sad even, I know, with a wretched surge of instant memories sucking over sandbanks and rockpools, that Ria is not easily dismissed or forgotten. Is this what love does: this wilful, heedless ebb and flow, this wanting and regretting, this here I stand upon this rock (nor can I fail or fall until the final thundercrack)—this raw exposure to my own volitions?

"One can always heal things," I say; "life isn't perfect."

"I'd thought—I thought we both thought—that we'd always be together," she goes on. "That nothing could intrude. That nothing could be stronger or more powerful. I was wrong."

"Love doesn't solve everything," I say. "I have loved you—you know that. I still love you."

"Just words," says Ria. "You've gone your own way."

"Why did you give those feathers to Riva?" I ask her. "I don't understand. You didn't tell me. She told me herself."

"I thought it would be obvious," she says.

"Sex isn't everything," I say defensively.

"No. But it signifies. Both beginning and ending. It's the content that's strange—the middle—what comes between beginning and ending."

"I'm going to Australia," I blurt out. "Touring with Sybil. It's new there, not so difficult, not so many layers."

"It's a myth," says Ria. "There's no such thing as starting again. The sky's the same. You can't start again. You can just go on."

"The context changes things," I reply. "Things can

be different enough to feel new, to be new therefore."

"You'll see," she says. And we fall silent, twist our wineglasses, reach for cigarettes, avoid staring at each other. It's me who breaks down first, finding the silence worse than anything.

"Let's be brave," I tell her. "Nothing lasts for ever. But nothing, either, changes what we had together, who we were, how it was."

"You're wrong," she resists. "Memory changes it."

"Not for me," I insist. "I know how it was, and who we were to each other. It doesn't matter whether you agree or not."

"I'm settling for Gloriana," she says. "She needs me. I'm the one she can lean on. I know her better than anyone."

"In spite of what you say she's done?" I say spitefully. "You're willing and able to forgive and forget?"

"It may be the making of her," Ria says. "She deserves a chance, anyway. Everyone deserves a chance."

"She's already had more chances than half of London gets in a long life," I say, feeling angry and jealous. Why should Gloriana Hardy end up with the solace of Ria's strong arms and sympathetic bosom? Why should rich, cynical, faithless Gloriana Hardy, walking monument to egomania and self-aggrandisement, feast on the uncorrupted flesh of well-tempered Ria, who was made of light? Where can that end, except in a pile of bones picked clean? Ria's bones. Ria's well-springs of integrity all turned dry.

"For art's sake?" I push on. "Is that why? You think you'd better hold hands with Gloriana Hardy so she can imprint her putrid genius on all the forests of the earth? You think that's a cause worth sacrifice and devotion—*your* sacrifice and devotion? You're worth a hundred Gloriana Hardy's—a thousand. Don't feed yourself to something so unworthy."

"You think therapy's a better cause, do you?" she responds nastily.

"There's nothing happening with Riva," I say defiantly. "I told you, I'm going to Australia. I don't know for how long."

"And you've got an agreement, have you, with the Australians, that they'll refuse entry to Riva?" she mocks.

"Riva has no intention of going to Australia," I tell her.

"How do you know?" That provokes another silence. It's never occurred to me. Riva belongs here, to this life. Has her network. Has no reason to be untimely ripped from the poisoned, breathing body of London's women, whom (surely?) she will go on treating with the false, imperfect arts of witchdoctory and superstition. Why on earth would Riva want to go to Australia?

"To the ends of the earth," remarks Ria, half to herself. "Isn't that the romantic dream?"

"I'm not in love with Riva. I've told you that. I love *you,* Ria—but I can't have you any more. Love isn't enough. There are other things."

"Sure," she mocks. "Duty, for example. Fidelity. Or what about justice? You were always keen on justice, as I remember."

"That's all changed," I say wearily. "People aren't born wise. Everyone makes mistakes."

"Riva's been your big mistake," she declares. "You don't seem to have understood that Riva's been in love with you, all this time."

"That's not true, Ria. It looked that way to you because you were jealous; because you never liked her and therefore couldn't understand why I did. She helped me, that's all. She helped me through a bad patch. She understood me."

"And you think I didn't?"

"I didn't say that."

"If you go to Australia," says Ria, "you can be quite sure that one day, not too far distant, you'll find her on your doorstep. You'll see. You must send me a card when it happens. I'm entitled to that."

"It won't happen." I'm equally confident. What can Ria know about what Riva's really like? "I promise you that I'll certainly send you a card, if it does. But it won't. So when you don't ever get a card, you'll know you were wrong."

"I'm happy enough if you promise," she smiles. But I feel desolate. Gloriana Hardy, of all people, of all women, gets the prize.

"I suppose it was obvious, looking back," I say, flooding with pain and self-pity. "I could never have won against someone rich and famous."

"You think I'm a gold-digger, do you Tessa? Or a wife? That's what you think? Because you can't accept that Gloriana needs love, just like anyone? That I need to be needed, just like most women?"

"I never thought it would end this way," I say.

"Nor I," says Ria. "But it has. We don't have to kill ourselves." That, inevitably, provokes discussion about Portland Jo, the party, the end of Babes, the end of everything. "You've decided, have you? that Portland Jo was the killer?" I ask. "All your suspicions about Gloriana Hardy's green bottle you've given up, despite what Myrtle said?" She looks at me strangely, fiercely, her face tight, her eyes brilliant with light. "Myrtle," she says sternly, "said a lot of things about a number of people."

"Did you believe her?"

"I know what I know," she replies. "Portland Jo is dead. There's nothing to be gained by anyone else's life being ruined."

"Particularly darling Gloriana?" I taunt.

"Look to yourself, Tessa," she admonishes. "You can't spend all your life blaming other people for whatever goes wrong."

"Do you think it's helped, though?" I ask. I can't help myself. I have to know. I have to have some indication, at least. "That Babes is gone, I mean. Do you think things can get going properly now."

"The movement you mean?"

"The movement, yes."

"I didn't think you cared. You haven't been to anything since the party. You haven't done anything, Tessa. You've left everyone else to deal with the newsletter, Databasics, the next conference, the Rape Crisis Support Fund, and I don't know what else. You've holed up here just doing your own thing, taking no account of anyone. You didn't do a solitary thing to help with Babes' funeral. Jade's done all the clearing out, all the organising—and she's only been in London for a few weeks. You voted yourself out, Tessa—dumped all of us. Me included."

"I didn't dump you, Ria. I couldn't."

"You could and you did."

"You don't understand. And I can't explain."

"The personal is political, Tessa. Remember?

There'll be another Babes. There always is. It's structural. You can't have politics without leaders."

"Not all leaders are twofaced liars, leeches, hypocrites, fraudsters, powermongering parasites, like Babes. Not all leaders function by destroying the lives of everyone around them. There are good women, after all."

"How naïve you've become! Why would a leader be any different from the rest of us? We're all capable of anything, if pushed to it. Why would a good woman want to be a leader? Good women, as you call them, are absorbed in being good, and doing good. Look at Annie, for example. She's a good woman. Can you imagine Annie running Databasics and taking on the patriarchy? Or Sal? It isn't a matter of skills and accomplishments. It's a matter of will, pure and simple. You can be a good woman, Tessa, or you can be rebellious, make trouble, try to change things, build a politics. You can't have it both ways —I thought you knew that."

"You're infected already," I respond, "by Gloriana Hardy's cynicism. You never used to think like that. We used to agree about things."

"We used to be in love," she says. "That's the only thing that's changed."

.   .   .

Impossible, improbable, inconceivable, immutable, debit outstanding breathes the Liberty Bell. *Refraction, retraction, remission, reversion, permission, perversion, decision, delusion. Recite after me: irreparable, irreducible, indescribable, impermeable, intractable. Insensible, invisible, unattainable, unimaginable, indestructible. Implacable, implausible, impartial. Plain, pure, practised, patterned. Faith, truth, beauty, duty, tutti-frutti, bring the beer on, bring the girls on, bring the house down, knit one purl one, sound the trumpet, ring the changes, crown the winners, burn the losers, world without end amen.*

. . .

Or I can stay silent for ever and a day. I can self-destruct. I was put here, after all, by a noble soul, a sage, a seeing thing, a servant. Sing, she commanded; sing what can be known: everything, anything, whatever can be known. It can't be understood, but sing it anyway. Someone will hear you. It happens. It's the result of history. The residue. The dry bones abandoned when all the feasting is done. And you? I cried, my heart already split and torn, the fish already gobbling, the blood already turning the ocean red. You, oh you? And she replied, I was what I was.

. . .

I can see it all clearly, a long episode, a well-made movie. I look down the telescope, connected these days with invisible wavelengths and algebra, to cables and satellites and mechanised synapses. I see, that is, Queen Myrtle, with AllyPally by her side, a true and faithful consort, busying and burying. Mother Myrtle presides over meetings, organises pensions and housing, heads the Board of the Databasics World-wide Network, oversees the media committees, briefs the mainstream politicians who've been placed where they can influence legislation. The newsletter has become a newspaper, very successful, very populist, its naked page three boys are a hit with a wide range of market segments. Mother Myrtle has an iron grip on any wrong-doing—her spies report faithfully, and the failing sister is taken fast to the bosom of all healing. Failing sisters are given proper succour. They are given what is good for them. They are given whatever they say they want.

Mother Myrtle is a marvel of management. Resources are husbanded. Resources are unlimited, since all that's needed is devotion and invention. Myrtle Victrix believes most ardently, most vigorously, in non-exclusion. All are welcome; all are sisters—even men are sisters. All agendas must be judiciously managed: monogamy, pornography, magnanimity, therapy, fruition debates, community, care and control, fervour and charity. All are survival strategies.

Gentle Myrtle, meek and mindful, hungers neither after power nor righteousness, has no heart for the heat of battle, needs no reassurance, takes no undue credit. Instead she follows her dream of universal love. It's a hard-edged dream, a dream of substance, a dream machine. "Give the women what they want; help them focus their aspirations; design for them the contours of their hidden, secret, inchoate desires, which have lain these many centuries beneath the layers of oppression. Give the women what they want, and what they'll understand they want. That is love. From such fulfilment then can flow the fruits of wealth-creation: top to bottom, in and out, round and round. Oh sisters: work hard, have faith, love one another, so that money may come, and flow, and grow, and thus secure our liberation.

"It's regrettable," sighs Myrtle, "that in this climate of success the earlier works of Gloriana Hardy must make way for fresher voices who can be positive about the future. Let them go quietly," advises Myrtle the Munificent: "let them go quietly out of print. And for her future work, given her deepest desire—which is for peace of mind (says Myrtle)—let Gloriana Hardy write a true and serious account of all the lives around her, omitting no spiritual discovery, however small, however seeming of insignificance. This work, which of necessity will have no ultimate conclusion, will be the labour of her life, undertaken with humility and dedication. She will desire no honour, bounty, thanks, or reputation. She will have what she desires —her peace of mind."

I see it all. I see Ria, faithful to the last, collect, correct, collate these many unread manuscripts. I see her shelve them carefully in the basement (restricted access) of the major new Women's Archive founded by AllyPally and funded by a consortium of blue-chip sponsors.

Women want unity with impunity, and Myrtle delivers; they want equality with immunity, and Myrtle secures; they want peace with prosperity, and Myrtle provides. Who can gainsay such a prodigality of success, such a surfeit of benign managerial genius? Magnificent Myrtle, ever-mindful of all that's requisite, is the Supreme Marketer. Because of Myrtle, all is well, and all will be well; and Babes the harbinger is already long-forgotten.

.   .   .

"Well (I say to Sybil, either here or there, it makes no difference, she is always with me)—didn't Myrtle do well? The women are happy, the money rolls in, the patriarchy foments itself with disillusion and despair."

"It was not what you said you wanted," she points out.

"I was a believer, a campaigner, an idealist, in those days," I say.

"You were a menace," she says, but smiles nonetheless.

"Did you know (I ask her), before it even happened, that I'd never after, never again, be able to break myself open with anyone? Did you know that the fine threads spinning towards spring would always wither ahead of time? That the buds would never peel back or the eggshells crack? Did you know all the time, but not tell me what it would cost?"

"I did tell you. You didn't hear what I said."

"You didn't tell me plainly."

"Truthtelling, dear Tessa, as we always say to the women, is never plain, and is only half-heard at the best of times."

"But you knew? All the time, you knew?"

"Fear no more the heat of the sun, the lakes of fire beneath the cone, the snows that offer eternal sleep, the dark, the rock, the ice wind. There are other stories, there are remedies, there is famine-control and earthquake relief. There is much beyond love and suffering—they are only the first things, the unfocussed shapes an infant sees when the eyelids first flutter apart and the light rushes in."

"But the performance we have to plan?" I press.

"We can start now," she says.

I am the uncoverer, the discoverer, the voyager, the true other (Sybil intones). Her voice is changed: her voice is thrilling, commanding, mesmeric—it is a miracle of music, perfectly timed, even more irresistible than the Sirens who sing down the funnel of five thousand years. *I was troubled by the paths I trod, the skills I misused, the flaws in my soul which I hid from sight. I was human, and therefore for a large part I lived in error. But I loved whom I loved as well as I could; I was capable of shame; I felt, sometimes, the pain of regret. I had my needs and vanities and they proved, on the whole, overwhelming.*

There's a pause. Because the beauty of her voice is so enthralling, the pain of its loss is instantly unbearable. I see, nevertheless, what I've never before seen. From Sybil's eyes fall tears.

Because of my sins (she continues now) *you denied me what you permit to yourself. You took from me my own patterning, the chances and choices that were mine to make, to take, to refine, to refuse. You removed from me all you take for yourself: air, earth, water, fire, the light of desire, the blaze of the mind, the hope of renewal. Your own sins you have put aside, found them unworthy compared with mine. You have stopped up my mouth, destroyed my heart, for ever and for ever.*

As Sybil stares, her face begins to shift and adjust, the mouth retracts, the eyes grow smaller, the cheekbones lift up and outwards, creaselines appear on the narrowing forehead. Here, after all that's passed, after all this time, after everything sorted, courted, acted, rescinded, is the face of the vanquished Babes.

The music that's held me holds me still—I can't look away, get up, change my mood or my mind.

At the end (says Sybil, says Babes)—*and I knew it was the end—I had no breath to scream or fight, no words to frame the revolution in my flesh. I was abandoned to the torments of a thousand blades, a thousand fires, before I could lie senseless in the vacant dark. You forced me to this mystery; but not till now have you imagined how I felt, or what I had to feel.*

"Sybil, Sybil, come back, I need you," I sob and cry, a torrent of panic ascending and falling.

I'm here. I shall never leave you (comes the entrancing voice, the rich, low, spendid resonant ring and chime). *You could have walked away, left me silent, left me to my own devices and desires. But you have throned me where your own recourse to pity and wisdom once ruled, and so I stay where you have wanted me to stay, to be your friend, lover, guide, devoted colleague, constant companion. I am your only other now, till death unmasks us and you make your own way into the dark.*

"But your face, your face," I cry out.

Let it be (replies Sybil). *I have suffered enough.*